DANGEROUS HUNGER

A SCOTT HUNTER MYSTERY

DANGEROUS HUNGER

A SCOTT HUNTER MYSTERY

MYRON BEARD

SUNSTONE
PRESS
SANTA FE

Sunstone books may be purchased for educational, business, or sales promotional use.
For information please write: Special Markets Department, Sunstone Press,
P.O. Box 2321, Santa Fe, New Mexico 87504-2321.
Printed on acid-free paper
∞
eBook: 978-1-61139-759-8

Library of Congress Cataloging-in-Publication Data

Names: Beard, Myron, 1947- author.
Title: Dangerous hunger / Myron Beard.
Description: Santa Fe : Sunstone Press, 2024. | Series: A Scott Hunter
    Mystery | Summary: "Psychologist Scott Hunter receives a mysterious note
    from an unknown person fearful of being harmed, leading Scott to
    eventually investigate her murder and the hidden world of the Santa Fe
    culinary food scene"-- Provided by publisher.
Identifiers: LCCN 2024046360 | ISBN 9781632937360 (paperback) | ISBN
    9781611397598 (epub)
Subjects: LCSH: Hunter, Scott (Fictitious character) |
    Murder--Investigation--Fiction. | Santa Fe (N.M.)--Fiction. | LCGFT:
    Detective and mystery fiction. | Novels.
Classification: LCC PS3602.E2515 D36 2024 | DDC 813.6--dc23/eng/20241004
LC record available at https://lccn.loc.gov/2024046360

WWW.SUNSTONEPRESS.COM
SUNSTONE PRESS / POST OFFICE BOX 2321 / SANTA FE, NM 87504-2321 /USA
(505) 988-4418

DEDICATION

To Ann, my wonderful wife who believes in me and encourages me to follow my dreams.

ACKNOWLEDGEMENTS

I am deeply grateful for the support and endless encouragement of my loving wife, Ann. From the conceptualization of the book to her careful editing of every page in every chapter, more than once, she has helped me become a better writer.

I am also very appreciative of the help of my son, Matthew Beard, who is the kind of writer that I aspire to be. Along the way, he gently made suggestions that taught me to be clearer and more focused in my writing.

Likewise, I am grateful for the careful final editing of Brooke Culbertson. She has a terrific eye for identifying ways the manuscript can flow more easily and hold the reader's interest.

I am particularly indebted to Chef David Lazarus. In discussing the plot with him, he was kind enough to guide me through some of the highlights of his journey to becoming an esteemed chef. His experience and perspective helped me better understand the nuances of working in an elite culinary environment.

I am extremely thankful to my publisher, Sunstone Press, and to both Carl Condit and Jim Smith for their willingness to back my work and guide me through the publication of my third in the Scott Hunter mystery series.

Finally, I am most appreciative, and humbled, by all the support and encouragement of those who have read my previous books, sent emails, and posted their experiences and reviews on Amazon, Goodreads, Facebook and other social media. Their interest and comments make all the difference.

PREFACE

Santa Fe is a well-known destination for foodies-those people who have developed a finer appreciation for its unique and delectable dishes. This recognition has been accompanied by several James Beard Awards Finalists and Semifinalists for chefs and restaurants, including a food truck; Wine Spectator Award of Excellence designees; and multiple *Conde Naste* endorsements.

Traditionally, Santa Fe cuisine has been known for its use of locally sourced foods found in its Northern New Mexico dishes with recipes passed down from generation to generation. The most notable of these is the use of both red and green chile, grown in the Rio Grande Valley and made famous in Hatch, New Mexico. Favorite dishes include enchiladas, tamales, pozole (or posole), burritos, chalupas, and huevos rancheros. They are usually topped off with a freshly made sopaipilla and honey for dessert. These were the dishes of my youth, still favorites of mine today.

What is less recognized is the contribution chefs from different cultures and countries have made to the success of the Santa Fe culinary scene. In fact, recent James Beard Award Finalists have been chefs who have relocated to Santa Fe from Slovakia, Kenya, Mexico (two), and Los Angeles in the USA.

Having grown up in Santa Fe, many of my friends and colleagues were first- or second-generation immigrants. I often had the occasion to hear their stories and the many trials their families faced in pursuing a better life. I admire anyone who has *both* street smarts and the ability to learn new and complex work skills to succeed in an unfamiliar environment. I thought it would be interesting to write about a newcomer to New Mexico who, like many of my friends and their families, was successful in spite of enduring a challenging background. Being in the food industry in Santa Fe seemed like a natural background for this mystery. Such was the genesis of the central character, Sofia Lopez, aka Julia Gomez.

I thought that with the introduction of an enigmatic and beautiful stranger in the unique setting of Santa Fe, combined with its rich culinary history, I had the perfect recipe for an intriguing mystery. Adding in some spices in the form or jealousy, revenge, and envy, the ingredients for danger would be complete. It is with this blend of conditions that *Dangerous Hunger* was conceived.

Even though I am a psychologist, I am regularly surprised by the motivations that drive people both for good and, unfortunately, for evil. In our culture, we often mistakenly measure our value by our financial worth, our position or status in life, or the degree to which we believe we are admired and esteemed. As a result, we often fall prey to comparing ourselves to others, which is an activity that often leads to downward spiral. The "green eyed monster of jealousy" has the unfortunate result of feeling perpetually dissatisfied with who we are, what we have, and where we are going. Such is the foundation for *Dangerous Hunger*.

As you read this book, you may see the motivations of the characters in yourself or someone you know. I hope the storyline provokes your thinking about just how good you are *as* you are.

PROLOGUE

The walk was very dark and very quiet from where I parked my car to the alley in back of the building. Even though it was only a few blocks from the Plaza, it seemed vacant and lonely. It was a stark contrast from just a few hours ago when the streets were filled with people, locals, and tourists alike, talking, laughing, and admiring the uniqueness of Santa Fe. But I had an appointment that I had to keep. I was filled with both curiosity and a heightened sense of apprehension.

I reached the corner of the building where there was a small one-way thoroughfare, rising on the hillside and just big enough for delivery trucks during the day. I followed the path to the alley where I had been told I would find an unlocked door into the building. I noticed that the light above the door was broken, and no lights were on in the building.

Puzzled, I checked my watch to make certain that I was arriving at the right time. Yes, it was eleven, just on time. My eyes barely adjusted to the dark, but I could make out the three steps leading down from the alley to the door. I felt uneasy and looked both up and down the alley before descending down the steps.

As I arrived at the door, it was slightly ajar. I knocked asking, "Is anybody here?"

Not receiving a response, I entered the dark room and felt my way along the wall. I called out again, "Hello, it's Scott, is anybody here?"

Still no answer, I walked slowly into the main room, the kitchen. The light from my iPhone provided very little coverage. The room was soundless. I could almost hear my heart beating.

Suddenly, my progress was halted by a loud noise. It sounded like a metal object, like a pan, falling from a shelf. I stopped in my tracks.

"Is anyone here?" I asked tentatively.

Just then my foot touched something soft but unmoving. I stopped, my heart in my throat. What could this be? Kneeling with the light of my iPhone to guide me, I saw the white of an apron. As I followed the contour of the apron, I could see I had stumbled onto a body, with empty eyes staring up at me. As I pointed the light to the face, I recognized who it was and was sure that this person was dead.

1

We basked in the afterglow of being together as nighttime blanketed us with its warmth. Not only was my feeling one of great contentment, but also of great appreciation and gratitude. The time I had spent with Maria had given me a second chance in life, one that I often doubted would ever exist after my very public and humiliating divorce. The words of an old mentor stuck in my mind, "The worse things are never the last things." Little did I know how relevant they were for me. Lying beside me was the partner I had longed for but never believed existed. To my delight, Maria moved in with me at my new home on East Alameda just blocks from the iconic Santa Fe Plaza.

Maria was a member of the storied Montoya family, well-known in the community for business, philanthropy, commerce, and politics. We had connected shortly after my reappearance in town a couple of years ago. The relationship with her had grown from being colleagues, to dating, to never wanting to be without each other. It had been an amazing development and one for which we were both thankful. And now here we were, delighted to be sharing a home.

Initially, our relationship centered around a nefarious businessman and gallery owner trying to exploit Maria's father, Roberto, and his well-known restaurant the Guadalupe. I was working "under the radar" as a consulting psychologist with Chief Detective Miguel Montez of the Santa Fe Police Department. He was in charge of the case involving the murder of my ex-wife's husband, who had also been the one who tried to exploit, and cheat, the Montoya family. Since that time, I had worked with Miguel and the SFPD on several other cases, all in my role as a consulting psychologist.

As Marie and I basked in the reverie of our intimacy, on the verge of nodding off, I was stirred by a slight noise that seemed to be coming from somewhere below the second-floor bedroom. It was not uncommon to hear noises outside in the evening, but it was now two and a bit late for road traffic. I could not tell if the noise was from within the house or from outside. As I gathered my thoughts, Maria also woke up. I got up and looked cautiously out of the upstairs window to see an individual slinking away into the dark. Neither the individual's face nor gender could be seen, but the person appeared to be dressed in jeans, tennis shoes, and a dark colored hoodie covering the head. This person was of medium height and slight of build, had a brisk pace, and quickly descended into the night.

I slipped on my robe and slippers, grabbed the flashlight out of my bedside table, and quietly descended the stairs to the first floor. I soundlessly looked around the first floor, focusing my light first in the kitchen at the back of the house, next in my study at the far side, and finally in the dining and living areas in front of the kitchen. I checked the back door going out to the patio. Locked. Next the door going to the garage. Also locked. I was relieved, yet perplexed, that nothing seemed to be out of the ordinary. What was the individual doing near our house at this hour in the night? A teenage prank? A homeless person looking for a place to rest? I could not imagine why anyone would be looking around our home.

I was about to make my way back up the stairs after checking the lock on the front door, when I noticed an envelope on the floor that had been slid under the door. On the outside of the envelope was written: "Señor Doctor Scott Hunter, Private"

2

Not yet wanting to turn on the lights and not being sure if another interloper might be outside, I began making my way back up the stairs, envelope in hand. I returned to the dimly lit bedroom to find Maria, wide-eyed and standing by the bed, breathing shallowly, and shaking.

"My god, Scott, what is it?

I took one more glance back at the street to ensure there was no one else in the yard. The yard looked empty. The light cast by the streetlamp had no one in its glow. Now comfortable that there was no one in view, I closed both the blinds and the shades. Only then did I dare go over to the bedside table, turn on the lamp, and invite Maria to sit beside me as I carefully opened the envelope.

Answering Maria, and showing her the envelope, I said, "This was slipped under the front door."

Inside the envelope, there was a neatly folded sheet of unlined paper with a cryptic message, all written in block letters:

SEÑOR DOCTOR HUNTER,
I NEED TO SEE YOU EN SECRETO. ESTOY EN PELIGRO AND I NEED YOU TO HELP ME. ENCUÉNTRAME A LA FARMER'S MARKET IN LA RAIL YARD DESPUÉS DE QUE CIRRE TOMORROW NIGHT AT TEN. ESTARE SOLO AND LA PUERTA TRASERA ESTARÁ ABIERTA. VEN SOLO Y AND DO NOT TELL NADIE, ESPECIALMENTE LA POLICIA. NECESITO TU AYUDA.
I PRAY THAT YOU COME. POR FAVOR!
SL

Maria and I read and reread the note wondering what it could mean and who the heck SL was. While my speaking and understanding of Spanish was passable, I needed Maria's translation to fully understand the message. The writer believed themselves to be in trouble and was imploring me to meet them at the Farmer's Market that very evening at ten and to tell no one, especially the police. I was confused that the message had been written in both Spanish and English.

In Santa Fe, residents who are of Hispanic descent often speak both Spanish and English. Often, Spanish is the preferred language at their homes, with their families, or in the company of others who speak predominantly Spanish. However, in the school system, classes are taught mostly in English. Locals who have been in Santa Fe for generations are often fluent in both languages. The mixture of Spanish and English in the note implied that the writer was not as fluent in English, or the note would have been written without Spanish words. The thought occurred to me that the writer may actually not be fluent in English, or it was written that way to throw me off track. At any rate, it was perplexing.

The late-night visit no longer seemed like a prank. The note left for me did give the appearance of someone really in trouble.

With the message still soaking in, Maria asks, "Shouldn't we tell Miguel?"

Maria was referring to Miguel Montez, my good friend and colleague, and Chief Detective of the Santa Fe Police Department.

"Normally, I would agree with you," I answered. "But I think I will hold back in this case. First, Miguel is out of the country on a vacation and will not return for several days."

"Secondly," I continued, "I do not have the same relationship with others in the SFPD as I do with Miguel.

"And finally, the note explicitly asks me *not* to include the police. At this time, we do not know if there is a crime or even the potential of a crime. I think calling the police would be jumping the gun."

Maria reluctantly agreed and we decided to keep the note and the initials of the writer between us, but there was something bothering me.

"Why the Farmer's Market?" I asked.

Maria replied, "The Farmer's Market is only open in the evening to restaurants wanting to get fruits and vegetables for the next day. It is not open to the general public. It also shuts down at about nine so it would be vacant after that until early the next day. I think SL must be connected to the restaurant business. Let me check out my network tomorrow to see if I can determine if there is anyone with the initials SL that rings a bell with folks."

Maria had deep roots in the Santa Fe culinary scene. Her family founded, and has owned and operated, the Guadalupe restaurant in Santa Fe for generations. Her grandfather established it over forty years ago, following a vision he had while praying at the Cathedral Basilica of Saint Francis of Assisi. Since then, it has become a gathering place for both locals and tourists, including many of Santa Fe's prominent business owners, celebrities, and politicians. Maria's father, Roberto, had been a state senator and, as a result, the Guadalupe had become a gathering place where politicians often assemble after hours to discuss and debate policy. Many a deal had been cut over margaritas in the conference room of the Guadalupe.

"I think that is a great idea," I replied, "but only with the condition that you proceed very cautiously and be careful not to discuss the note nor the author's initials with anyone, including Roberto."

Smiling, Maria agreed, and our sleuthing partnership began.

"Now," Maria said, "let's try to get some sleep. Daylight will come much too soon."

With that, we shut off the lamp and fell back into each other's arms for a brief slumber.

3

Six in the morning came too soon. Having had a hard time getting to sleep following our eventful evening, I was both tired and, paradoxically, revved-up. My adrenaline was pumping.

Maria was having a bite to eat before leaving the house to begin her investigating. We kissed, vowing to see each other back home for dinner, and I went for my morning run. My house was across the street from the Santa Fe River. The river is an intermittent stream fed by two large reservoirs east of the city. It meanders for several miles and provides about forty percent of the city's water supply. The path beside the river is shady and lined on both sides with tall hardwood trees that create a canopy over the river's edge. It is a beautiful and popular place to run. The morning air is usually cool and crisp, and I always looked forward to my morning routine.

Afterwards, I made my way to my favorite coffee shop, Java Joe's on Rodeo Road, to reflect on the recent events and get some breakfast. Java Joe's is one of those unique places where locals hang out. It is a short drive from my house and far enough away from the Santa Fe Plaza that tourists have not discovered it. Dave, the owner, always has local artwork for sale hanging from the walls. It feels more like someone's living room than a coffee shop and it had become one of my regular hangouts. I could always find a quiet corner there when I needed to focus my thoughts while having coffee and a homemade New Mexican pastry.

Carmen, the barista, was well known to me now having been introduced by Miguel. She always greeted me with a big smile and a hug.

"Scott," she began, "so good to see you. With Miguel on vacation, I do not get to see my favorite regulars as much. Would you like your usual?"

"Hi Carmen," I replied. "It is always great to see you, too. Yes, I will have my usual and will sit over at my regular spot in the corner booth."

In a very short time, Carmen brought me my usual-a large Mexican Mocha coffee and a green chile and cheese croissant. After thanking her, I got down to work.

Taking the suspicious note out of my pocket, I noticed something in the light of day that I had not detected the night before. It was a slight smudge in the lower right-hand corner of the paper. Looking more closely, I noticed that it looked like some kind of food residue. I smelled the smudge and could detect the faint odor of cinnamon within a darker stain. "Chocolate?" I wondered. "Why," I wondered, "would anyone be writing a note while eating or cooking?" It was another clue, but what did it mean? I wished that Miguel was in town; it would be great to be able to brainstorm with him.

As I continued looking at the note, I noticed that I was referred to as "Señor Doctor Hunter." This told me that I was probably *not* acquainted with SL, or they would have referred to me as "Scott." The fact that they knew I was a doctor indicated that SL must have known that I was a psychologist, or maybe thought I was a psychiatrist. Where did the writer get that information?

Another thought jumped out at me. The writer had addressed me as "Señor" before Doctor. The "Señor Doctor Hunter" formality also suggested that this was not a highly sophisticated individual, but one who acted deferentially to authority. This often happens in relationships of servility, like a maid or landscaper referring to their boss as "Mister John" or "Miss Ann" rather than either Mister Smith or Miss Pacheco. This kind of reference in either conversation or writing was not common in Santa Fe. Was this a person who was an immigrant in a service industry?

I wondered what he or she wanted. Typically, when people felt threatened, they would go to the police, but not this person. I was both intrigued and feeling cautious. Going alone at night to any building was scary, but more so to the Farmer's Market.

Now noting the time, I knew I needed to get to my office. I had scheduled several Zoom calls with clients that I needed to make. I waved to Carmen and left Java Joe's with more questions than answers about the note. I looked forward to following up with Maria over dinner.

4

Maria left the house, just after Scott went for his run, and thought to herself, "SL, who the heck is SL?" She ran through her mental rolodex of people in the Santa Fe food industry, but no SL came to mind. There are over two hundred restaurants in Santa Fe, each with a staff of from one to ten executive chefs, sous chefs, etc. "Where should I begin?" she wondered. Fortunately, because Maria had grown up in the business and her family owned the Guadalupe restaurant she already had a high number of restaurant personnel whom she knew. These acquaintances included restaurant owners, managers, and kitchen staff. However, she was also mindful that she had promised Scott that she would proceed cautiously.

Santa Fe has an amazing assortment of cafes and restaurants. Multiple places are regularly recognized with the coveted James Beard Foundation award and there are many chefs who are semi-finalists for the Best in the Southwest honor. Maria knew them all. She decided that the best strategy was to begin with those whom she knew the best, Anna Pacheco, part owner of the La Fonda hotel; William Ratliff, head chef at the Inn of the Anasazi; and George Maez, manager of the Staab House restaurant in La Posada hotel.

Maria decided that face-to-face conversations worked best. Santa Fe is unusual in that, while high-end restaurants compete with one another for business, the owners, chefs, and managers are supportive of each other, knowing how challenging the hospitality industry can be. They were what had been referred to as "frenemies," being both friends and competitors.

Maria began her queries with Anna Pacheco at La Fonda, known as "The Inn at the end of the Santa Fe Trail." The site of La Fonda, on the southeast corner of the Santa Fe Plaza had been the site of a hotel for over four hundred years. It was the best known of all of Santa Fe's hotels, regularly featured in travel magazines and blogs. Its colored history included being one of the Harvey House hotels initially catering to train passengers.

The Harvey House hotel chain was noted for its high standards, fine dining, and exceptional waitresses known as "Harvey Girls." It had subsequently changed hands, but the high standards remained, maintaining its popularity as a venue for locals and tourists alike. Over the years, La Fonda catered to well-known celebrities and leaders and the guest list included actor John Wayne; existential author Simone de Beauvoir; and the thirty-fifth President John F. Kennedy.

Anna Pacheco was a part owner and the managing executive of La Fonda. The Montoya and Pacheco families had long been friends and significant donors to Santa Fe's philanthropic activities. Maria and Anna met for late morning tea at the Bell Tower Bar on the fifth floor of the hotel. Typically opened in the late afternoon and evening, it is situated above the city and has a bird's eye view of the Cathedral Basilica and the breathtaking picturesque mountains. They were able to be alone and have a free ranging conversation with Maria learning that Anna could not account for an "SL" on her staff.

Maria had the same experience with both William Ratliff at the Inn of the Anasazi and George Maez at La Posada. It was great to catch up, but nothing came up to shine more light on who "SL" may be.

Being careful not to create too much suspicion, Maria also researched the local restaurant guide for names. There are over one thousand restaurant workers in Santa Fe listed in the guide. She could eliminate the three restaurants that she had become more familiar with, plus the Guadalupe, but she still had a way to go. At least she now knew there were no "SLs" at the top of the restaurant hierarchy.

"Needle in a haystack," Maria thought to herself. "I was hoping to find out who SL was, but no luck. Frustrating." After following up on all of her leads, she had reached a dead end. There were plenty of "Ss" for first names and several last names beginning with "L" but there were no names with both S as the beginning of the first name and L as the beginning of the last name.

It was getting close to the time when she and Scott had agreed to meet for dinner, so she stopped her musing and left for home.

5

I was waiting for Maria and had already prepared some chile stew and heated flour tortillas. Her favorite Malbec had been poured and the table was set.

Hanging up her jacket and throwing her keys in her purse, Maria saw the table was set and exclaimed in a flirty tone, "I thought you had a date at the Farmer's Market tonight, were you hoping for some pre-meeting motivation?"

Smiling back, I said, "I know we do not have much time to catch up before my rendezvous, so I thought I would give us a head start."

Over dinner, Maria reviewed what she had learned through her meetings and research on who "SL" may be and expressed disappointment that she had hit a dead end.

I summarized my thoughts about the note writer being in a service role and feeling subservient to authority. I also concluded that the individual's native tongue was Spanish. Based on his or her mixture of Spanish and English, this person had probably not been in the United States very long or the note was a ploy to throw me off.

Placing the edge of the writer's envelope in front of Maria, I queried her on the food stain on it. Maria confirmed that it appeared to be traces of cinnamon in a chocolate smudge. Like an expert sommelier, Maria looked at the smudge more intently and smelled it.

Looking perplexed, Maria said, "Hmm. This is not your typical chocolate. I can smell cumin, onion, and garlic. It smells more like a mole sauce than simply chocolate. You typically have these types of ingredients in high end restaurants. Let me do some additional research with the smudge and see if there are any other clues there."

With ten o'clock drawing closer, and any romantic liaisons being unlikely, I suggested we organize a plan for me to meet SL at the Farmer's Market.

Santa Fe Farmer's Market is less than one mile southwest of the Santa Fe Plaza in an area known as the Santa Fe Railyard. The Santa Fe Railyard has a history that dates back to eighteen-eighty when the Atchison, Topeka, and Santa Fe Railway Company pulled its first train into Santa Fe. The entire area was originally where trains would bring provisions and shipments of building materials to the area and drop them off at Santa Fe Builders Supply, known locally as Sanbusco.

The Railyard flourished with tourists, new residents, and materials being brought into Santa Fe. For almost one hundred years, the Railyard became the center of many activities for commerce and tourism. However, like Railyards in other urban areas, rail service became eclipsed by the Interstate Highway system in the nineteen fifties. By nineteen eighty-seven, the Railyard was declared a blighted area. It took several years, and a strong community effort to resurrect and redevelop the Railyard. Today, it is once again a center of community activity with shops, galleries, museums, restaurants, new residential offerings, and a robust Farmer's Market.

Active during the day, the Railyard becomes quiet and vacated in the evenings except for a couple of restaurants. It takes on a very dark and eerie feeling once restaurants, shops, and galleries close and there is virtually no traffic in the area. Going to the Farmer's Market alone at ten was not my idea of how to spend an evening in Santa Fe.

In spite of my protest, and because of the location and being in the depths of night, Maria insisted on accompanying me. Even though Maria and I had discussed coming up with a plan, nothing seemed to be feasible short of having a police escort. We agreed to each take separate cars in the event that SL would want me to take her somewhere. Maria agreed that she would stay in her car in the parking lot on Chili Line Lane, a short distance from, and in sight of, the large Farmer's Market building. The plan was for me not to lose contact with Maria, so I called her, kept my phone in my jacket pocket on mute, and she would be able to hear everything I was encountering. At least she could hear me if I was being assaulted.

We arrived in separate cars a few minutes before ten o'clock. I elected to park on Callejon street, a couple of blocks away from Farmer's Market. It felt like a very odd place to meet, and not entirely safe. The Farmer's Market was just ahead as I exited my car. As expected, the Railyard was deserted this time of night. Only dimly lit, I walked near the remaining railroad tracks, a closed gallery, and across the street to The Farmer's Market. The only light was a streetlight a block away. It felt eerie. I was diligently watching for anyone else who might be in the vicinity but saw no one. The night was very dark, the air cool, and the walk silent. Because of the cobblestone street, I could not walk quickly. I double-checked to ensure Maria could hear me, checked that the phone was on mute, and put it into the side pocket of my jacket.

The back door of the Farmer's Market was just ahead.

OAXACA

6

Sofia was standing at the stove cooking for the family's evening meal as she did most nights. She had just turned sixteen but had the responsibilities of an adult. Since Pablo Ramirez had moved in with her mother, Sofia had been responsible for doing all of the cooking, cleaning, and caring for her siblings and step-siblings. Her step-father's alcoholic rages left her and her mother fearful and cowering. Her mother spent most of her days depressed and asleep in her room.

Sofia's father died when she was only six, an innocent casualty of Mexican gang wars, leaving three young children for Sofia's mother to raise. Coming from a very small family, Sofia's mother had only her grandmother, whom she called abuela, to whom she and her children could turn for a place to stay upon her father's death. They lived in a small adobe home with four rooms and a tin roof. They were able to survive on Sofia's mother's day jobs as a maid and selling her grandmother's dishes to local workers.

They were poor but the few years that she spent with her grandmother had been happy ones for Sofia. She had learned to cook at her grandmother's side. Her abuela was patient and thorough, always taking time to teach Sofia new dishes. Sofia learned to cook empanadas, tlayudas, carne asada and, of course, mole for which the region is famous. Sofia and her grandmother would venture out to construction sites with their buckets filled with these wrapped delicacies and sell them to workers during their lunch breaks. The workers were also poor, but always generous. Between what her mother could bring in as a maid and the proceeds from the workers for her grandmother's food, they were able to make ends meet. Then it all ended suddenly when her grandmother suffered a fatal stroke. Sofia's mother had nowhere to turn.

Despairing and needy, her mother began entertaining a series of men in and out of the small run-down structure they called home. At the end of her rope and desperate, her mother got the attention of a monster of a man named Pablo Ramírez. He traded a semblance of financial security, such as it was, in exchange for her mother raising his two children-a son, Raul, and a daughter, Fatima, both younger than Sofia. Pablo's wife had fled to whereabouts unknown, probably leaving for the same reason Sofia was leaving now.

Living with Pablo and his children was an arrangement made in hell. As Pablo's drunken abuse worsened, Sofia's mother became passive and depressed, leaving the housework, cooking, and minding her siblings up to Sofia.

On that night, as Sofia stood at the stove frying tortillas, she could smell the alcohol on his breath before she felt her stepfather's hand wrap around her waist as he whispered in her ear, "Mi querida, te deseo." Little did he know that he had abused her for the last time.

Now Pablo lay on the kitchen floor where Sofia had doused him with hot cooking grease followed by a solid hit to the head with the frying pan. Sofia realized that she needed to act fast. She knew that she could not save her mother or younger siblings Ana and Inez, but she could save herself, and now was the time.

Without confiding in anyone, Sofia had prepared for this moment. She had hidden an oversize canvas purse under her bed, filled with all of the personal belongings she could fit into it, including a couple days' worth of clothing, a few pesos, and her most prized possession, a tablet with her grandmother's handwritten recipes. The house was in turmoil with all of the children screaming at the site of Pablo on the kitchen floor, blood oozing from his head. Sofia grabbed her hysterical mother and hugged her hard letting her know that she would not see her again.

As Sofia was about to leave, she heard the slurred speech of her stepfather exclaiming, "No matter where you go you little puta, I will find you. When I do, I will have my way with you and then I will kill you."

She ran into the dark, tears welling up in her eyes, knowing that it would be the last time she would see her mother or siblings.

7

Oaxaca de Juárez, typically just called Oaxaca, is the capital city of the state of Oaxaca in southwestern Mexico and is surrounded by mountains at an elevation of over five thousand feet. The state is known for its beautiful setting, moderate temperature, brightly colored buildings lining the streets, and many indigenous groups. The result is a very rich mixture of both dialects and cultures that extends to arts, local festivals, and cuisine. It was here in Oaxaca, one hundred thirty miles from her hometown of Tuxtepec, that Sofia went to begin her new life.

Oaxaca is built on a grid pattern that is very walkable. It was founded in fifteen hundred twenty-nine and originally occupied by a group of Zapotec Indians. The middle of the city continues to be the center of economic, political, social, religious, and cultural activities. El Zócola is the main plaza in the heart of the city. Anchored by the Cathedral de Nuestra Señora de la Asunción, dating back to the fifteen hundreds, the plaza bustles with street vendors, performers, food carts, and concerts. The streets are lined with colorful buildings and warm, engaging people.

The food scene in Oaxaca is robust, fueled by tourists coming to enjoy its architecture, museums, galleries, and rich history. It has world-class gastronomy and is well-known for its popular markets and traditional street foods. Sofia had heard about Oaxaca from her abuela, and this seemed like the best place for her to escape and put her life back together.

It did not take Sofia long to find a local food stall in need of a cook. With the culinary guidance Sofia had received from her grandmother, she was able to establish herself quickly. The kitchen in the food stall seemed glorious compared to the pitiful space in the hovel she had called home. She found that her dishes were a match for those of any of the other food stalls. She quickly regained her confidence and began experimenting with her grandmother's recipes.

Both tourists and locals alike raved about her version of tlayuda. It is a simple, but delicious, serving of a crispy corn tortilla topped with refried beans, Oaxaca cheese, strips of meat, and spices, then baked until the cheese melts. The twist that Sofia had on the dish was what here grandmother called her secret, hojas de hierbas, a variety of seasoning and herbs she used to make it unique. In addition to her tlayudas, Sofia began experimenting with other recipes, including new versions of moles, chapulines, and beverages like mezcal and tejate.

Sofia's capabilities with moles were particularly notable. Made with ingredients such as dried chiles, peanuts, sesame seeds, chocolate, cinnamon, and anise, the mole sauce brings interest, complexity, and unique flavors to life in main courses like chicken, pork, lamb, and tacos. By incorporating her knowledge of herbs and spices learned from her abuela, her dishes became even more distinctive than those of other local cooks. She learned quickly and, within a surprisingly short time, had more than mastered even complex dishes.

Daytimes were glorious and Sofia quickly became part of the street food sorority, meeting new friends, learning new ways of cooking, and receiving praise from patrons and staff alike. The street stalls generally stayed open from mid-morning until crowds diminished in the late evening. Even though the days were long, Sofia was up to the task. What she had already experienced, the loss of her father and grandmother, having to leave her mother and siblings, and the abuse of her stepfather made here wise beyond her years, resilient, and scrappy.

Whenever she was presented with free time, Sofia would wander around El Zócola Plaza and taste the offerings of other food vendors. She particularly enjoyed experiencing the nearby Benito Juárez Market where she was exposed to many herbs, spices, and vegetables that were new to her. Sofia was always looking to for ways to improve her mastery of Oaxacan cuisine.

Nighttime's were a different story, at least initially. Even though Sofia was tough and strong, certainly for her age, sleeping on the street was a harrowing experience. Most of her co-workers had homes to which they returned after work, but not Sofia. Initially, she would sleep on the sidewalk near the food stall where she worked. It was cold, but by sleeping on flattened cardboard boxes that she unpacked during the day, and covering herself with a makeshift blanket, she stayed warm enough. She always slept holding a knife in her hand. She was determined that she would never be abused again.

While Sofia had numerous acquaintances and was readily accepted by those in the street food world, she resisted getting too close to anyone. While she longed for the kind of intimacy she had experienced with her abuela, parents, and siblings, the abuse at the hands of her step-father created a hardness and a suspiciousness in her. While she had many offers to join men in their homes, she resisted, preferring the streets to the potential danger of a controlling and abusive relationship. However, it was not long before the female owner of the food stall in which she was working presented her with the option of sleeping in the food stall at night, ostensibly for security reasons. Sofia gladly accepted this offer.

Street food vendors in Oaxaca are many and varied. They include food carts, food trucks, markets, and stalls. The stall in which Sofia worked was a small unit in the side of a building with a cement floor and a metal door facing the street that rolled down and locked to secure the stall at night. Inside the stall, there was a small refrigerator, a sink, a preparation table, some cabinets for condiments and spices, and a two-burner stove. Above the stove were hooks for hanging skillets and pots. In a corner was a small gas fired heater, typically used on cold days, but sufficient to keep the stall warm during cold nights. The stall was small, but sufficient. Compared to sleeping on the streets, it was heaven. But this arrangement did not last long.

8

Restauranteurs in Oaxaca periodically wander through the city center sampling the fare at various vendors looking for new recipes and, at times, even new talent. Usually, these forays result in nothing more than having filled up on the street foods, often for free. On occasion, they would find a hidden recipe or talent that intrigues them.

Having now been in Oaxaca for over a year, it was Sofia's good fortune to have her food stall visited by the executive chef at Los Danzantes restaurant. Los Danzantes is a well-known and highly regarded restaurant in Oaxaca. Locals and tourists alike venture into the restaurant to enjoy their authentic and locally sourced foods. Not knowing who the executive chef was, Sofia recommended her pork strips covered with mole sauce and served on a bed of seasoned and shredded cabbage. He paid for the plate and left, just like any other patron.

The next afternoon, he returned to the food stall and offered Sofia a job at Los Danzantes on the spot. She would be working as a Line Cook and reporting to the Sauce Chef, or the Saucier. He offered her steady pay and, to top it off, there was dormitory-style housing for the staff just a bus ride away from the restaurant.

Sad to leave the food stall and appreciative for the opportunity she had been given, Sofia was also excited about the new opportunity. She gave her employer two weeks' notice to find a replacement. Then she was off to Los Danzantes.

Now approaching her eighteenth birthday, but appearing and acting much older, Sofia began to learn both the culinary and business sides of a restaurant. It did not take long for her to move up the ranks in the restaurant. Within a year, the Sauce Chef resigned, and Sofia was appointed to be the new *Saucier*.

Los Danzantes proved to provide an education that was far beyond anything Sofia could have received in the Oaxacan street scene. The experience broadened her understanding of the possibilities for her in the culinary world and ignited her motivation. The culture of the restaurant was one that was encouraging and often referred to by the executive chef as his familia. The staff, numbering about twenty, was always supportive and created an atmosphere of mixing play with work. They celebrated birthdays and holidays together and Sofia felt like this was like the family she had never had.

She was like a sponge, always learning and experimenting with new recipes and preparations. Los Danzantes was also part of the Slow Food movement, focusing on zero waste and locally sourced foods. Sofia was being immersed in a world she had never known, one that was expanding her awareness by the day. She was beginning to imagine her future much differently than she had when she arrived in Oaxaca. She had gone from surviving to thriving and now had visions of having her own restaurant someday.

Then, quite unexpectedly, her world was once again turned upside down.

Walking through the Mercado Benito Juárez early one morning, selecting vegetables and meats for the restaurant's evening menu, a young lady came up to her saying, "Excuse me. Are you Sofia Lopez from Tuxtepec?"

Startled, Sofia looked at her and studied her before recognizing her primary school classmate, Adelina Cruz. Sofia instantly replied, "Adelina, is that you?"

With Adelina nodding, they embraced, tears filling Sofia's eyes. It was in that moment that Sofia suddenly felt an old, but familiar, sense of dread. She had told no one that she was leaving Tuxtepec. How had Adelina found her? What did she want? Did anyone else know?

"What are you doing here, Adelina?" Sofia asked.

"I moved here to Oaxaca after I graduated from high school last year. Tuxtepec was too small for me. I have been working in a clothing store not far from here. But what about you, Sofia? You just vanished and no one knew where you had gone. There had been rumors that your stepfather, that drunken Pablo Ramírez, had killed you," Adelina responded.

Still stunned, Sofia was cautious with what she said, and offered, "I wanted to learn more about cooking like mi abuela taught me, so I ran away down here to Oaxaca. I have not been back to Tuxtepec since I left."

Upon hearing that from Sofia, Adelina was quiet, hung her head, and took a deep breath without replying.

"What is it, Adelina. What aren't you telling me?" Sofia probed.

Slowly looking up, Adelina replied softly, "So, mi amiga, you have not heard?"

"Heard what?" Sofia responded, a sense of urgency in her voice.

Haltingly, Adelina told her, "Your mother died over a year ago, and your brother and sister had to go live in a residential care home until they are eighteen. We thought you were dead, or I would have tried to find you."

Breathing shallowly and feeling like she was going to faint, Sofia leaned on Adelina.

Grabbing her arm and guiding her to a nearby chair, Adelina said, "Let me take you over here to sit down and we can talk."

Sofia thought to herself that her sense of dread when she and Adelina hugged was warranted. Something bad had happened. Now that Adelina knew Sofia was in Oaxaca, in spite of Sofia's attempts to stay anonymous, Sofia needed to know about the family she had left behind.

Now sitting, Sofia said, "Please, Adelina, tell me what happened."

Adelina told Sofia what had happened as she understood it. Sofia's mother died in suspicious circumstances. She was found deceased and cold on a back street in Tuxtepec, her body bruised and beaten. The police questioned Pablo Ramírez, but his children offered an alibi for him. Having no leads, and because her mother was poor and of little note, the police quickly moved on to other matters. Because Sofia's siblings were not Pablo's children, they were sent into the residential care system, and were safe as far as Adelina knew. Pablo's siblings stayed with him. Adelina also mentioned that there had been rumors that Pablo himself was possibly going to relocate to Oaxaca.

Shattered by all of this news, Sofia felt simultaneously guilty, angry, and afraid. She felt guilty that she had not been there for her mother and her siblings, in spite of her youth. She was angry at all of the destruction Pablo had brought to their lives. Most of all, she was even more fearful, remembering the last words of Pablo, "No matter where you go you little puta, I will find you. When I do, I will have my way with you and then I will kill you."

Learning that Pablo might move to Oaxaca brought terror to Sofia.

She decided then and there that she was not long for Oaxaca, but wondered where she could go to feel safe. That was the question.

Trying to compose herself, Sofia looked at her old friend and said, "Adelina, it has been a very unexpected surprise to see you. In spite of the bad news you have given me, it is so good to see you and reconnect. I have to get back to work now, but let's keep in touch."

Sofia stood, embraced Adelina, and left Mercado Benito Juárez carrying a bag with the whole day's provisions for the restaurant, her mind as heavy as the bag of provisions. She needed to do some planning for her next move, and fast.

SANTA FE

9

The closer I got to the back door of the Farmer's Market the more anxious I became. I was usually calm under pressure, but this was the first time I had been requested to meet with anyone alone, late at night and in an unusual location. I would have felt much more comfortable if we were meeting in a more public place like a bar or restaurant.

I knew I had to get better control of my racing thoughts. I know that in times of stress, the human mind often takes journeys to fearful and crazy places. These thoughts are almost always negative and rarely accurate. Being a psychologist, I knew these intrusive thoughts could disrupt how I normally assess a situation. However, knowing this did not make me immune to having these irrational thoughts on occasion. "Get a grip," I told myself.

The back door was now within reach. There was no light over the door, so I took a deep breath and slowly pushed down on the doorknob. It moved easily and I was able to push the door open effortlessly.

If I thought it was dark outside the building, the inside was like being deep in a cave with no light at all. I could not see a foot in front of me. On one side, the building had several garage doors that made it accessible to trucks at night. Once closed, these doors were sealed tightly to make sure that unwelcome small creatures would not have access.

On the pedestrian mall side of the building, there was a single garage door giving the public access during the day and early evening. Like the other garage doors, this was also sealed tightly. The result was that I was faced with a pitch-black space, one that would be very hard to navigate. There was not a sound coming from anywhere.

"Great," I thought to myself, "I can't see, and I can't hear." I could feel my heart racing and considered retreating. What if this was some kind of ghastly trap? Was I about to get kneecapped by some unknown nefarious stranger? I decided to forge ahead nervously.

I had hoped that there would be some light to guide me to where SL was but there was nothing. I quietly closed the back door behind me and hoped my eyes would adjust to the dark. In what seemed like ten minutes, but was only a moment, I saw a faint light waving across the building. It looked like the light from a mobile phone. "This must be SL," I thought to myself.

Being careful not to disconnect Maria who was still in her car listening to my every move, I cautiously pulled my iPhone out of my pocket touched the light icon on my iPhone and waved back. Without hearing a word, I could see the light wave back to me seeming to instruct me to keep walking in that direction. Still wary, I slowly moved toward the light, noting anywhere around me that could serve as a hiding place for a potential surprise attacker, under tables, behind hanging sheets or even overhead.

Even though I kept my iPhone light on, I bumped into one of the stainless-steel tables used to display a farmer's goods during the day. My bump did not make any noise, but it hurt my thigh like hell. Continuing to wave our lights back and forth to each other, I slowly made my way in that direction. It was only when I was within about five feet of the light that I could distinguish a person. She was sitting in a corner huddled on a chair and draped with a dark colored shawl.

Whispering, I heard a woman's voice with a heavy Mexican accent saying, "Doctor Hunter, is that you?"

Replying quietly back, I replied, "Yes. Is that you, SL?"

I could hear her let out a big sigh as she said, "Yes, it is me. Please sit down."

Turning off my iPhone light and placing my phone back into my shirt pocket, I noticed a chair three feet opposite SL. Following her instructions, I sat down. I knew from the note I had received from her that she was likely fearful and suspicious. I knew that the absolute best approach in a situation like this is to simply follow her lead.

With my eyes having adjusted to the dark, I could see that I was across from a woman who had a tense posture, seating on the edge of her seat. She was shivering, even with the shawl draped over her. She held herself with both arms clenched across her chest. Her eyes were darting, as if looking to see whether or not I had brought an accomplice. She was breathing quickly and shallowly, and she clearly seemed to be anxious. There was something about her that seemed familiar, but I could not place her. I decided to let her initiate the conversation.

After some time of silence, and after she had assured herself that I was alone, she started to breathe more evenly and slumped back into her chair. SL began, "Thank you for coming, Doctor Hunter. I know this must seem unusual, but I need your help."

After another silent pause, I probed saying, "You are right, this does seem unusual. I debated whether or not to come at all. When I walked into a pitch black very quiet space, I wanted to turn around and leave, but my curiosity got the best of me. Why are we meeting here and why all of the secrecy? There are any number of other places we could have met. The Farmer's Market late at night seems very odd to me."

SL responded sorrowfully, "I am sorry for asking you to meet me here. I am afraid to be seen with anyone in public who may make people suspicious of me. I am worried that I am in danger. Please forgive me."

Believing her to be both sincere and fearful, I replied "Okay, we are here now. Can we start by getting on a first name basis? Please call me Scott. What is your name?"

Hesitating and biting her lower lip while looking at the floor, she replied, "My given name is Sofia Lopez, but I changed it when I came to this country and now, I am Julia Gomez. Please call me Julia."

10

I thought it was notable and a bit unusual that Sofia had changed her name, but now was not the time to pursue this line of questioning.

"Julia," I began, "I need to know something about you before I commit to helping you. I don't know you. Tell me about yourself."

With that ultimatum, while looking around anxiously, Julia gave me highlights of her life. She told me about growing up in Mexico, running away from a horrible stepfather, and working in Oaxaca. With some satisfaction, she talked about her capabilities as a cook and discussed the training she had received at her grandmother's side. She mentioned how her grandmother's cooking acumen had served her well with unique Oaxacan recipes. She was particularly appreciative for working at Los Danzantes and learning at the feet of the executive chef there.

She reported how she finally made her way to the United States and became a legal immigrant. She chronicled her moves from restaurant to restaurant first in El Paso, then in Lubbock, and finally in Santa Fe. Prior to coming to Santa Fe, her life had been a difficult hand-to-mouth existence. Her luck changed in Santa Fe.

"Of all of the places you could have lived, why did you choose Santa Fe?" I asked.

Julia then told me about a fluke weekend trip from Lubbock to Albuquerque and a last-minute decision to visit Santa Fe. Her presentation became softer as she quietly talked about how much Santa Fe felt like Oaxaca. The Santa Fe Plaza, the Farmer's Market, and the Cathedral Basilica of Saint Francis of Assisi, or just "the Cathedral" as Santa Feans called it, all felt like her home in Mexico. She said that she always lit candles in the Cathedral in memory of her mother and grandmother. Periodically, she would offer prayers of thanks reflecting on how she had come from scraping together a meager living in her abuela's house with her mother and siblings to now being financially independent. She knew her mother and grandmother would be proud of her.

"Was it hard to get a job here?" I asked.

She then told me about getting a job with Larry Ulibarri as a cook in his Rolling Burrito food truck. She proudly acknowledged that, because she was able to combine her Oaxacan recipes with the traditional New Mexican dishes, the volume of customers at the Rolling Burrito had increased.

"Are you still with Mister Ulibarri at the Rolling Burrito?" I asked.

"No," she responded. "I have been working at El Farolito restaurant for a couple of years.

"Why did you change your name from Sofia Lopez to Julia Gomez?" I asked.

Thinking about the best way to answer, Julia replied, "When I left Oaxaca, I was afraid that my stepfather, Pablo Ramirez, would find me. He had already killed my mother, and I was afraid he would come after me. That is why I left Oaxaca in the first place. Mi abuela's middle name was Julia. The executive chef at Los Danzantes last name was Gomez, so I combined the two. I thought it might bring me good luck.

Now satisfied that Julia wasn't a crank and that she may have legitimate concerns, I decided to dig into the reason for our meeting.

"Good. Julia, now tell me where you got my name and why do you think I can help you?" I asked.

Julia answered still shakily, "Scott, I have seen your name in the *Santa Fe New Mexican* on a couple of occasions. The articles mentioned that you are a psychologist and have helped the police solve a couple of cases, but that you are not a member of the police force yourself. Is that correct?"

I was impressed that she had researched information about me from the newspaper. She was partially correct. I had previously assisted Chief Detective Miguel Montez in solving some high-profile cases. I had consulted with the Santa Fe Police Department and was put on a retainer. However, I am not officially on the force.

"You are correct," I responded. "I am a psychologist and have worked with the police, but I am not an employee of the police department." I then questioned, "But why me? Why not go directly to the police?"

Answering warily, she said, "In Mexico, where I grew up, you cannot trust the policia. Sometimes the policia are the ones you need to be afraid of. From a young age, I was taught that if you had a problem, you needed to solve it yourself. The policia were often the most corrupt."

Thinking about recent, and very public, stories about the police violating the public's trust, especially in relation to people of color, I understood Julia's skepticism. In fact, even here in Santa Fe, my colleague Miguel Montez had been instrumental in uncovering police corruption that had led to the dismissal of a police chief and the early retirement of two of his cronies. However, I also believed that now the Santa Fe Police Department was highly ethical and committed to the safety and welfare of all in the community.

I replied, "I understand your concern, Julia. But the police here in Santa Fe can be trusted."

Looking at me more directly now, she said, "That may be so, but I needed to know I could trust someone. I have heard that there is such a thing as client confidentiality that you psychologists have to practice, and that you cannot repeat anything I tell you to anyone else. Is that right?"

Again, she was partially correct. Psychologists have limited patient-client privileges. There are two exceptions to the rule. The first being the Tarasoff Duty to Warn, based on California case law. If patients reveal that they are either a danger to themselves or to others, psychologists have a "Duty To Warn" appropriate legal entities or people who may be in danger.

The second exception occurs when the records of a psychologist have been subpoenaed, in which case the psychologist is legally bound to turn over notes and diagnostic material and may even be required to testify. This is true primarily in divorce cases in which the custody of children is involved. Otherwise, psychologists do maintain client-patient confidentiality.

I explained these exceptions to Julia so that she would know the limits of confidentiality.

After hearing my explanation, Julia said, "That is what I needed to hear."

With that, she reached into her pocket and handed me a folded twenty-dollar bill, saying, "I want to hire you to be my psychologist."

11

Maria, sitting in her car in a lot one block from where Scott parked, had her phone on mute while she listened to the conversation between Julia and Scott. She knew that Scott had his phone in his shirt pocket, so the sound was somewhat muffled. She strained to hear the conversation.

When "SL" identified herself as Julia Gomez, Maria sat up abruptly, almost dropping the phone from her hand, shocked that SL was in fact Julia Gomez.

"Well, I'll be damned. She is the Julia Gomez, the sous chef at El Farolito." Maria thought to herself. This could explain the smudge on the envelope slipped under the door at Scott's house. Maria had identified the smudge as some kind of mole sauce with chocolate and odors of cumin, onion, and garlic. It made perfect sense now.

Maria remembered that El Farolito has struggled through several ups and downs over the years. It has a great location just a few blocks off of the plaza but has received mixed reviews from patrons and other restaurant proprietors. The owner, Fernando Romero, is someone who always wanted to be at the top of the Santa Fe social scene, admired for his status in the community as a successful restauranteur. Instead, he had developed a reputation for trying to get what he wants by "skating around the rules." As a result, the admiration he has sought had eluded him.

After having failed to win the popularity, he had pursued through less than gracious means, he began changing his strategy about six years ago. At that time, he was able to lure a chef from New York City, Michele Ronaldi, to come to be his head chef. Michele had been a sous chef at some fine restaurants in New York city and rumor had it that Fernando had offered her a handsome raise and an executive chef position. Since then, Michele was able to make the restaurant more reputable, the food more consistently good, and Fernando the owner had improved interior ambience. While it was still not considered "upscale," El Farolito had, at least, become a respectable restaurant.

Even with Chef Michele, El Farolito had not reached the level of status or success that Fernando, and his ego, had envisioned. He wanted his establishment to be among the top in Santa Fe. In that pursuit, two years ago Fernando was able to bring Julia Gomez on as sous chef. He discovered Julia cooking at one of the popular food trucks in Santa Fe, the Rolling Burrito. She was a refugee from Oaxaca who was nothing less than a culinary magician. The combination of Michele and Julia had begun to make El Farolito a serious player in the Santa Fe culinary scene.

In fact, Maria mused, El Farolito had become a competitor to her own family's restaurant, the Guadalupe. Like the fabled Phoenix, the Guadalupe had reinvented itself, literally rising from the ashes. The restaurant had been the target of an arsonist who had completely destroyed the original building in a fit of revenge over a business deal gone bad. Roberto designed the new restaurant to be both expensively appointed and, also, very comfortable. It appealed to multiple types of guests including tourists, locals, politicians, and attendees at elaborate events. The fire had actually allowed Roberto to modernize the kitchen. He had also been able to create a luxurious conference room suitable for business lunches. The changes to the restaurant made it more popular with waiting lists for reservations becoming the norm.

Maria's father, Roberto, had wanted to recruit Julia to come and work at their restaurant. Roberto had heard about this amazing cook from Oaxaca when she was cooking at a local food truck. He went there on a couple of occasions and, like many others, found the food she served to be unique, complex, and delicious. On his third visit to the food truck, Roberto went to speak to Julia with an offer to come work at the Guadalupe as their sous chef. What he found instead was that Julia was no longer there, having taken the sous chef position at El Farolito. Roberto wasn't sure what bothered him most, not having tried to hire Julia soon enough or losing out to Fernando Romero.

Knowing that Scott was talking to Julia Gomez heightened Maria's curiosity. She wondered what danger could possibly be threatening Julia. Was it work related? Could there be a problem with Fernando? She was anxious to learn more.

12

Julia asking me to be her psychologist startled me. While I was a licensed psychologist in the state of New Mexico, I had limited my practice to working with businesses on leadership and strategy development and working with Miguel Montez in the police department. I had not had a clinical practice seeing patients for psychotherapy in over fifteen years. I felt uncomfortable entering into this kind of relationship with Julia, or anyone else for that matter.

The practice of psychotherapy is one in which practitioners typically have an ongoing caseload of individuals, couples, and families. They are seeing their patients regularly and most psychologists continually upgrade their skills to become even better therapists. I no longer considered myself a therapist, but a business or organizational psychologist and consultant. Any skills I may have had as a therapist had become very rusty.

I knew that I might lose any connection with Julia if I declined, but I could not in good faith act as her psychologist or therapist. I returned her twenty dollars and said, "Julia, I would be happy to discuss your situation with you informally and be of any help I can. I promise you that I will keep what you tell me private unless I perceive you to be in danger or violating any laws. However, I cannot accept your money as a down payment on a counseling relationship. I know longer do that kind of work."

Having said this to Julia, I knew that by means of Maria hearing the conversation, I was already sharing information. However, I wasn't willing to let Julia know that Maria was listening, originally for my safety. I considered myself to be sticking to the principle of the agreement rather than the "letter of the law."

With her face a bit drawn and her eyes down cast, she raised her gaze and replied with disappointment, "I do not have anyone else I can trust, so this will have to do. I need your help as long as I know that you will not involve the police."

I responded, "Julia, you have a deal. Now, tell me why you slipped the note under my door."

Julia reached between her blouse and shawl and pulled out an envelope with the words "Chef Julia Gomez" written on the outside. Reaching out to me she said plaintively, "This was left for me on a table at the restaurant this week. It was a very busy night, and I was not able to determine who may have left it. I knew that the table on which the note was found had last been occupied by two elderly ladies, both regulars. I knew they would not have left it. It was probably dropped there by someone else upon leaving the restaurant. Look at it and you will see why I got in touch with you."

As I continued to listen to Julia, I still had some reservations about the situation. Before I accepted the assignment or looked at the envelope carrying the note, I needed to know more. I needed to know that I was not being set up or drawn into anything criminal. I needed to know more about Julia. I understood that, once I opened the envelope and read the note, I was going to be fully involved without any chance of going back.

Knowing that she might decide to bolt, but needing assurance that I was not being set up, I said, "Julia, I take working with people very seriously. It is a sacred trust when I am taken into their confidence. I know nothing about you. Before I look at this note, I need you to tell me more about yourself, your background, and what led up to this point."

Clearly irritated and impatient, she took a deep breath, blowing out through her mouth while puffing her cheeks, looking skyward, and rolling her eyes. She paused before answering. Her response was a clue, though not a definitive one. Often the clients that are the most demanding and in the greatest rush to have you help them are also the least reliable and, many times, the least committed to a process. I wasn't sure this was true with Julia, but it was data.

Finally, she responded, saying, "Okay, what do you need to know?"

Julia quietly, but quickly, provided an overview of her past several years-her escape from her birth city of Tuxtepec to Oaxaca, her abusive stepfather, her relationship with her grandmother who taught her to cook, and her grandmother's subsequent death. She talked about working at Oaxaca street food vendors and then at *Los Danzantes,* her trek from Oaxaca to El Paso then on to Lubbock, ending up in Santa Fe and, eventually, being hired at El Farolito.

Her most shocking revelation was bumping into her childhood friend in Oaxaca who revealed that her mother was murdered, her siblings had been placed in residential care, and her stepfather was thinking of moving to Oaxaca and was looking for her. Julia had never forgotten his threats to do her harm. I was beginning to understand why she felt endangered.

In the meantime, it was clear that Julia's cooking ability had served her well, maybe even saved her. I wondered if her grandmother knew that by introducing Julia, then known as Sofia, to cooking at an early age she would in some respects be carving out a path for Julia's life. A mentor of mine once suggested that serendipity plays a larger role in life than planning. It was certainly true in Julia's life.

As Julia told her story, I could see how the events of her life had shaped her character. She was strong, resilient, and adaptable. She was also driven and ambitious, not letting barriers stand in the way of improving her life. She was adventuresome with strong determination. Like many immigrants, she had overcome significant obstacles and challenges to make a better life for herself. I marveled at her hardiness.

Knowing that her father died at an early age, and that the devastation of his loss had rendered her mother helpless and needy, I guessed that Julia had to grow up quickly. Also, the loss of her grandmother and the abuse at the hands of her stepfather, would have made her suspicious and untrusting. I suspected that beneath her veneer of self-sufficiency she had a lot of anger. In fact, I hypothesized, it may have been the anger that had driven her.

We had only been together for a short time, but it seemed much longer. Her history was both fascinating and helpful, but I needed to know more about the present and her time in Santa Fe. Afterall, it was here that she was experiencing some sort of trauma. Before I looked at the note she had given me, I *still* needed to have more context.

When she paused, I said, "Thank you for giving me your background, Julia. This is very helpful. Now, let's talk about your time here in Santa Fe."

Taking a deep breath and letting it out, Julia replied, "When I came to Santa Fe, I worked with Señor Ulibarri at the Rolling Burrito food truck. I was grateful to have the job and he allowed me to use some of the recipes I had brought with me from Oaxaca. It seemed that our customers liked the food I cooked, and we became very busy.

"One night just before closing, Señor Fernando Romero came to the food truck. I had seen him before as a customer, but I did not know who he was, or what he did. It was strange for anyone to come so late at night, and I was a little anxious. Then, he introduced himself, said that he liked my cooking, and asked me to work for him at El Farolito. He said he would double what I was making at the Rolling Burrito.

"I knew about El Farolito, but I had never been there. The thought of working for a restaurant was exciting and I believed it would give me more stability than the food truck. It was hard to decide to take the offer because Señor Ulibarri had been so good to me, but I knew I had to go. I remembered my very good experience at Los Danzantes in Oaxaca and thought that working at El Farolito would be similar. I began there about a week later. I have now been there for four years."

Not having yet looked at the note that Julia gave me, but knowing it had to have been threatening, I asked, "Tell me, Julia, during this time at El Farolito, has there been anyone who may not like you, is jealous of you, or is someone you may have offended? Why would anyone have left a threatening note for you?"

It had now been over an hour since Julia and I first met. Julia had given me ample information about her history. However, instead of relaxing as time went on, Julia became more agitated, squirming, hyper-vigilant, was scanning the dark warehouse, and became highly reactive to slight sounds. Both her anxiety and paranoia were beginning to surface more intensely. I sensed that she was about to bolt. I had to decide now if I was going to read the note in my hand or give it back to her and leave her on her own. Julia needed an answer to whether or not I was going to help her.

Believing that Julia had no other options, and still wondering if this could be more of a "tempest in a teapot" than a real threat, I relented. Taking the envelope in my hand, I said, "Julia, I believe that you think there is a real threat to you, and I will help you, even without having read your note."

With tears in her eyes, Julia crossed herself and took my hand in hers saying, "Oh, bendita madre de dios, Señor Scott. I am so relieved. Muchas gracias."

At that moment, a loud clamor came from the opposite corner of the warehouse. It sounded like a small metal container falling from a shelf. We were both startled. Julia whispered, "I need to leave this place. Please take the note and read it. Can you come to the restaurant tomorrow night about eleven after we close? I will be there alone. Come to the back entrance off the alley."

Without giving me a chance to answer, like a ghost wrapped in her shawl, Julia was gone, leaving from a side door. I was astonished by her rapid disappearance. Now, sitting alone, envelope in hand, I made my way to the door from which I had entered.

13

Still listening intently, Maria was able to piece some aspects of Julia's story together with her work at El Farolito. There had been reports over the years that working for Fernando Romero was a hard gig. In fact, he periodically hired people of dubious character to work for him. He had also regularly broken the unwritten agreement among Santa Fe restaurants of not poaching some of their chefs and even waitstaff.

However, Fernando also had some respectable people working for him. His head chef, Michele Ronaldi had been trained at the prestigious Culinary Institute of America in New York and worked in the New York City restaurant scene prior to coming to Santa Fe. In fact, rumor had it that Fernando had dined at the restaurant in New York where she had been the sous chef. Fernando made her an offer she could not refuse, promising her an opportunity to have equity in a Santa Fe restaurant.

In fact, Maria recalled, the story told about the incident was that Fernando had left a note in an envelope on the table with Michele's name on it. He asked the waitstaff to make sure she received it. Hmm, this is the same thing that happened to Julia.

With her extensive training and background, Michele had been able to raise El Farolito's caliber, but it was still not considered one of Santa Fe's elite restaurants. Her cooking seemed to cater more to the New York crowd than that of Santa Fe. Rather than trying to adapt and become more creative, Michele doubled down on the Manhattan style of cuisine.

Northern New Mexicans take great pride in the uniqueness of their food, almost a snobbishness. The Santa Fe food scene rivals that of New Orleans, New York, or San Francisco, but on a much smaller scale. The food is characterized by vegetables and spices resident in the region, and often fused with more traditional recipes, creating a truly distinctive tasting experience. Maria knew that Julia had brought some of her Oaxacan spices and moles to El Farolito. The partnership of Julia Gomez and Michele Ronaldi was beginning to raise the standard of El Farolito to those in the area well-known for upscale cuisine.

Over the past couple of years, El Farolito was being talked about with the same esteem as Maria's father Roberto's restaurant, the Guadalupe. It had caused Roberto some concern that some of his regular diners were now frequenting El Farolito. In fact, El Farolito was beginning to be judged to be at the same level as other fine Santa Fe restaurants. As Maria thought more about the recent success of El Farolito, she was perplexed about what could possibly have gone wrong for Julia.

Through Scott's iPhone, Maria was able to hear the clatter of something suddenly falling in the building. She heard Julia quickly implore Scott to meet her the following evening at El Farolito. It was at that moment that she sensed that Julia was leaving. Listening to Julia's quick departure, and surprised by the quick turn of events, Maria sat up behind her steering wheel about to depart from the scene.

As she became upright, she saw a figure bolt from a side door of the building, not the same door that Scott entered but on the other side. While not completely visible, Maria could make out that the person, dressed in a hoodie and sneakers, ran toward the far end of the parking lot away from the building and down a side street. He, or she, did not look toward Maria in her car.

The person quickly entered a small, dark colored, sedan, started the engine, and took off quickly with the lights of the car turned off. Maria watched the car's taillights until it was out of sight. She wondered if she should try to catch up to the car and follow it, or just let Scott know. She decided it was more prudent to note the direction the car was pursuing and tell Scott.

Forgetting that my phone was still on a call to Maria, I was startled when I heard Maria's voice coming from my pocket. "Hey baby, I just saw someone leave out of the side door. Are you okay?"

I retrieved my phone from of my pocket and replied, "Yes, I am fine. We heard a noise coming from the back of the building and a door open, but we didn't see anyone. Julia got spooked and left from yet another door. I am about to leave the building now. We have a lot to talk about."

"I am freezing in the car. I will see you at home," Maria said in a shaky voice.

I said, "I'll be home in ten minutes."

14

The clanging of something falling and the sound of a door slamming open had spooked Julia. This confirmed that someone was after her to the point that they had followed her to the Farmer's Market, probably not knowing she would be meeting Scott there. Julia's heart was racing as she bolted out the side door of the building. While she was relieved that Scott Hunter was going to help her, she still felt very nervous and frightened. She wondered to herself about what might have happened if Scott had not been there.

As she left the building, she cautiously made her way to Guadalupe street, the main street going into the Rail Yard. She had about a mile to go in the cold dark. Julia cautiously but quickly made her way from one streetlight to the next. She had never bought a car and usually relied on friends whenever she needed to travel any distance.

Her walk home seemed much longer to her than it felt in daylight. She was scared, but she knew that the street smarts she had developed when she was homeless on the streets of Oaxaca would serve her well anywhere. There had been more than one night in Oaxaca when she found herself fighting off a man who wanted either money or sex. She had learned to be careful and crafty. Besides, under that shawl, she carried an eight-inch hollow edge chef knife carefully placed in a leather sheath. "Scared but prepared," she thought to herself.

She let her mind drift momentarily and reflected on the meeting with Scott Hunter. She knew that her options were limited, and he seemed genuinely concerned, showing la empatia. She also appreciated both the seriousness with which he took her concerns and described his ethics. Even though she would have preferred that he take her money, she was equally impressed that he hadn't. She was impatient for them to have their next meeting tomorrow night. She needed to know what to do.

The sound of a twig breaking behind her brought out of her brief musing. She quickened her pace as she neared her house just ahead. Still holding onto the knife, Julia fumbled for the keys in her small purse as she approached her porch. She could hear the sound of footsteps on the sidewalk near her as she put the key in the door lock, quickly opened it, and stepped inside. Just as she closed the door, she caught a glimpse of what appeared to be an elderly gentleman continuing to walk on the sidewalk, past her small apartment and further down the street. Was this someone who had been following her, or just a coincidence. She wasn't sure, but as she locked herself in, she felt a sense of relief, at least for the moment.

Julia pulled the shades over the windows facing the street and collapsed onto her couch with her heart still beating rapidly. Taking a few breaths to calm herself, she thought to herself, "When will it ever end? Just when it seemed like my life was getting better, I get this threatening note. What have I done to deserve this?"

Her thoughts took her back to growing up in Tuxtepec when things were better. Oh, how she missed her madre, her abuela, and her hermanos. For the first time in a long time, Julia felt both lonely and alone. Holding her head in her hands, she allowed herself to have a long and deep cry. Her only hope was that Scott Hunter could help her.

After giving herself time to grieve and then pulling herself together, she reflected on her time at El Farolito. She was the sous chef at a very upscale restaurant. She had to admit to herself that El Farolito was even better than Los Danzantes in Oaxaca. Julia thought to herself, now able to smile, "Mi abuela would be so pleased. And I did it by out-working, out-thinking, and out-maneuvering all of the others. Head Chef, watch out!"

Her ambition and strong work ethic had been noted by the owner, Fernando Romero and Head Chef, Michele Ronaldi. Julia was always the first to arrive and the last to leave. She had taken over the responsibility for selecting produce at the Farmer's Market and was developing a reputation for her fine cooking.

In fact, it was just last week that a gushing review of the restaurant by food critic William Maestro appeared in the Maestro's Musing column the *Santa Fe New Mexican*. In his review, he cited the extraordinary fusion of traditional foods made with locally sourced produce, paired with unique Oaxacan herbs and sauces that had elevated the quality of the food. He particularly identified their fine sous chef, Julia Gomez, as the person most responsible for the sudden rise of El Farolito.

Reviewer Maestro, enthusiastically endorsed the Oaxacan Pork entrée, marinated in mole negro, a complex, slightly sweet sauce, containing ingredients such as chili peppers, cloves, cinnamon, chocolate, and nuts. His review included the Mezcal cocktails that Julia created for pairing with some of her unique dishes. With the Santa Fe food culture being so competitive, high-end restaurants are always looking for ways to differentiate themselves from the competition, and Julia's Oaxacan-fusion cookery was a game changer.

However, not everyone saw Julia in such a favorable light as William Maestro. Some staff in the kitchen saw Julia as manipulative, self-serving, demanding, and, at times, undermining their work. There even appeared to be some friction between Julia and head chef Michele. Many saw that as petty jealousy. Julia brought into her management style the toughness she had learned in the streets of Oaxaca. She knew the importance of her role, and even though she was still the sous chef, she commanded respect.

El Farolito could not have paid for better advertising than the review by William Maestro had provided, and it had all been free. The evening following the review was a night to remember for El Farolito. The restaurant was at capacity all evening. The praise of customers was glowing and enthusiastic. Julia's presence was requested several times for customers to show their appreciation for her wonderful cooking.

The night had been magical...until it wasn't.

When closing hour approached and the wait-staff were completing the final clearing of the dining room, a waitress noticed a sealed envelope left on one of the tables and hand addressed to "Chef Julia Gomez." Thinking the note might carry with it a large tip or, at least, a note of appreciation, she quickly took it to Julia in the kitchen. Julia was admonishing the crew to not only clean up but also to prepare a few items in advance for the next day, which was expected to be very busy.

Being too distracted to open the note just then, Julia put it in her pocket and resumed her preparation activities. It was not until she got home, both tired and elated from the evening, that she remembered the envelope still in her pocket. She opened the note and quickly fell to her knees. How could this be happening?

It was the note that had frightened her and caused her to hand it over to Scott Hunter and ask him for help.

15

Maria took a shorter route back to the house from the Farmer's Market parking lot and graciously had a Scotch on the rocks waiting for me. Maria had helped me expand my drinking repertoire from mostly beer and wine to some of the finer offerings served at her family's restaurant, the Guadalupe. I now counted Scotch, Manhattans, and martinis among those drinks I enjoyed.

Hanging my jacket on the clothes tree in the entryway, Maria and I looked at each other with a mixture of shock and disbelief at the events of the evening. Before I had a chance to enjoy the first swallow of my Scotch, Maria let me know that, in addition to hearing the entire exchange between Julia and me, she witnessed a person quickly leave the building and then get away in a small dark colored car. While it was still fresh, I wanted Maria to review any details she had noticed about the person leaving the building.

Maria noted the person had on a hoodie and sneakers. After thinking a little more, she said slowly and thoughtfully, "You know, now that I think about it, the person had a strange gait. It wasn't exactly a limp, but more like excessive movement from side to side. It was strange. It almost looked like a balance problem, but I'm not sure."

I thought about gait abnormalities and their possible causes. This could be a good clue to at least identify who may have been at the Farmer's Market when Julia and I were there.

Anxious to now open the envelope given to me by Julia, Maria exclaimed, "Scott, let's see what the note says in the envelope. Maybe it will help us understand what Julia is going through."

Not having Maria's knowledge of the food industry in Santa Fe, I needed more information to put whatever we were about to read in context. I replied, "I want to look at it too, but first and for perspective, what can you tell me about Julia Gomez and El Farolito?"

Maria detailed her knowledge of both the owner, Fernando Romero, and the restaurant. She noted that Romero had a mixed reputation in town from other restaurant owners. She cited how he tended to "skirt" unspoken, but generally agreed upon, guidelines regarding "poaching" both staff and chefs. She also believed that his driving ambition had been to be in the company of those influential business leaders in Santa Fe who were seen as being instrumental in both the economy of the city and its future direction.

She had heard from the restaurant grapevine that, when Romero did not get his way, he could become angry and even lash out at his detractors. Maria also observed that, when he had been able to bring head chef Michele Ronaldi to Santa Fe from New York, some of his over-the-top and unseemly behavior had calmed down. The addition of Julia Gomez had not only strengthened El Farolito's reputation but began making it competitive with other top tier restaurants in Santa Fe.

"Honestly," Maria concluded, "I was shocked to learn that the person who slipped the note under your door and who met you tonight was Julia Gomez. She has brought some real creativity and uniqueness to the Santa Fe food scene. She would be a clear choice to become the head chef at any number of other restaurants in town. She has been at El Farolito about three years, I think. Even my father, Roberto, wanted Julia to work at the Guadalupe. She is a real catch."

We then reviewed the meeting with Julia and began wondering about the cause of her fearfulness. We were both impressed and intrigued by Julia's story. Maria noted that Julia's journey was similar to that of her family. Maria's grandfather, Luis Montoya, had been in New Mexico when the state had been granted statehood in nineteen hundred and twelve. He had migrated from Chihuahua, Mexico to the New Mexico Territory with his parents in the later part of the nineteenth century. In fact, Maria still had some distant cousins in Chihuahua. Stories her grandfather had told her gave her insight into the difficulty of being where migrants didn't always feel welcome.

Maria finished her review of El Farolito and Fernando Romero by asking, "What do you think, Scott?"

It was still too soon after my meeting with Julia for me to have much perspective. However, one thing I have learned about self-revelation is that the more specificity a person has, the more likely their story is true. Julia's story was full of precise and unique details which made it believable.

The warm Scotch began to calm my nerves. We sat down at the kitchen table and put the envelope on the table. I wanted to examine the outside of it for any tell-tale signs before opening it. After briefly inspecting it, we unsealed it.

The envelope was heavyweight material, four by six inches, and made of expensive paper. Neither the envelope nor the paper inside were the kind you would buy in a general retail store. If this was purchased in Santa Fe, there were only a couple of fine stationery stores that would carry this kind of stock.

The writing of Julia's name was thick with bold block lettering, typically more representative of a man's writing than that of a woman. Knowing that the envelope would already have both Julia's and my fingerprints, I didn't want to further contaminate any possible fingerprints from the writer. Using latex gloves, I handled it carefully.

The envelope was only lightly sealed, so getting the note out was not a problem. The note was written on heavy-duty card paper with a double border of outer gold and inner maroon. It looked very professional as if someone had wanted to make a strong impression.

Written on the note in thicker, cursive handwriting as on the envelope, it read:

Julia,
After all we have been through, it is too late to back away now.
We have plans that are special for both of us. Did you think
you could ignore me? Do not try to ruin everything! Besides,
I know too much. We need to meet soon. I will meet you at
the regular place. But this is our secret, so keep your mouth shut!
R

At first reading, it had the feel of a desperate lover trying to hold on to a relationship that was on the brink. Suitors being dumped often resort to bribes or threats in order to keep a relationship alive. They rarely work. But this assumption didn't seem to sync with Julia's description of her love life. In the brief time we had spent together, Julia had not indicated anyone special in her life.

There was a lot to unpack with this note and there was also a sense of urgency needed to get to the bottom of it.

What was the meaning of the message? The "been through" note suggested that Julia and the writer had a history. What did "back away" mean? Back away from what? What were the "special plans?" What did the writer mean by "I know too much?" Why was it delivered in the restaurant? Why was it on such fine stationery? Why was the envelope addressed in block lettering, but the note written in cursive? Most importantly, who was R?

The last sentence about keeping her mouth shut clearly suggested a threat to evoke fear. It was clear that Julia needed to interpret all this if we were going to understand it. Maria and I were exhausted. We decided to get some sleep and plan our next move in the morning.

16

Six years earlier, Fernando Romero had been distraught. Nothing had worked to increase the popularity of his restaurant La Cocina, now renamed El Farolito. He had tried every gimmick he knew from offering a low-cost menu and shifting to a more fast-food approach to promoting free margarita night. With each innovation, there was a burst of new activity followed by a return to the same paltry customer volumes he had experienced in the past. Even though the restaurant was just blocks from the Santa Fe Plaza, restaurant expenses were beginning to exceed revenues.

He was even more upset because, once again, La Cocina had not been invited to participate in the Best of Santa Fe voting which was a real slap in the face. He was also not invited to attend the annual gala announcing the winner of the Best of Santa Fe awards. While he believed that most of those included were jerks, or had probably bought their way into the event, it still irked him. It had been his driving desire to be recognized at the top of the business heap in Santa Fe. He knew he had to do something very different.

It was on a trip to New York City with his cousins, his primos, that an idea came to him. Fernando and his cousins took an annual long-weekend trip of debauchery to different cities, leaving their wives back in Santa Fe. They called these trips their annual "business meetings." Over the past few years, they had been to Las Vegas, Los Angeles, Miami, and New Orleans. The cities were different, but the same themes always played out.

They would eat and drink excessively, go to local shows, gamble when they could, and always look for women who would entertain them, for a price. Nothing good ever came out of these trips and they often had to pay a price with their spouses upon their return. They would joke that they hoped the airport had a great gift shop so they would not return to their wives' empty handed.

This year's trip found Fernando much more anxious and distracted than usual, behaviors not lost on his cousins. He was feeling desperate. He was out of ideas for reviving La Cocina, and even considered selling his space to another restaurateur. Because the space had been handed down to him from his family, his legacy would be destroyed by his financial priority to sell. Then, like a dove descending from the heavens, it happened.

While dining at one of New York City's fine restaurants, Fernando marveled at how there was a line of patrons outside wanting to indulge in the restaurant's cuisine. What did they have that his restaurant didn't. The maître d' was pleasant and the waitstaff were competent, but nothing seemed extraordinary in any way. The dining room was like any number of other dining rooms he had visited with square tables covered by white lined tablecloths, a setting for four, and basic chairs. What did they have that attracted so many patrons?

It was only when his plate was presented to him that the answer became obvious. He had ordered a hand-chopped grass-fed steak accompanied by whipped potatoes, grilled marinated mushrooms, and garlic and grilled polenta. The plate itself looked like a work of art with food delicately placed on the plate in an artistic fashion. The beauty of the presentation was matched by the amazing flavors igniting all of his senses. Never had he tasted such wonderfully prepared food. He was perplexed by how such incredible tastes could come from these relatively simple ingredients. Why, he wondered, couldn't he offer this kind of food at La Cocina?

He visited the restaurant three times while in New York, twice by himself. Each time he ordered something that could be prepared back at La Cocina, nothing too out of the ordinary. On his second visit, he ordered a pork chop and seasoned rice topped with a rich poblano sauce. Divine. It was at the end of this second meal that he requested to meet the chef. He needed to know who was behind this magic? He was told that the executive chef was on vacation and that the meal had been prepared under the direction of the most senior sous chef, Michele Ronaldi and the waiter would arrange for her to meet him.

Michele, a young woman in her early forties with blue eyes, blonde hair, and a shapely figure, appeared at the table in her chef's coat. They introduced themselves. She came across as confident and competent, but with a slight attitude, often found with chefs and artists. She declined to sit with him, but allowed Fernando to lavish her with praise as he quizzed her about how she was able to turn such humble foods into the cuisine of gods.

He also confided that he was from Santa Fe and owned a restaurant himself. The conversation only lasted a short time, but Fernando was hooked, and the wheels of his mind began turning.

On his final evening in New York, he was able, again, to secure a reservation through his new acquaintance with the maître d' and a one-hundred-dollar incentive. Staying with foods that could potentially be served at La Cocina, he ordered the roasted buttermilk chicken with pan roasted broccoli and cauliflower and boiled baby potatoes with parsley and butter. Again, his surprise and delight were renewed. He could not stop being amazed at how the simple ingredients, advertised as farm-to-table, could be so delicious.

Once again, Fernando requested the presence of Michele to thank her for her culinary wizardry. However, this time was slightly different.

When Michele arrived, having met Fernando the night before, she had a bit less attitude and seemed warmer. She was more accessible. After a brief discussion, Fernando changed the nature of the conversation.

"Michele," he began, "I have a proposition for you."

Surprised but curious, Michele replied, "A proposition? What do you mean?"

Fernando was ready. "I have experienced your amazing food and how you regularly transform the ordinary into the extraordinary. This is exactly what my restaurant in Santa Fe needs. I know from our previous discussion that you are aware that Santa Fe is well-respected in the culinary world. I would like you to come to Santa Fe and work for me at my restaurant. You would be our executive chef and I would double what you are making now. What do you think?"

Now Michele sat down. "Well, Mister Romero, I was not expecting this. This is a complete surprise. I will have to give this some thought."

"Of course," Fernando said handing her an envelope. "I have taken the liberty of putting my offer in writing. Please review it and let me know your thoughts. I will be leaving New York tomorrow, so you can feel free to call me before I leave or in a day or two. Take your time. Just know that I would give you complete creative control of the back end of the restaurant."

After a few more moments of lighter discussion, Fernando left with Michele still sitting at the table.

Within two weeks, Michele had accepted his offer, tendered her resignation, packed, and was off to Santa Fe.

17

Michele Ronaldi, now the head chef at El Farolito, was preparing the menu for the day when Julia arrived for work. It was highly unusual for anyone, much less diva Michele, to get to work earlier than Julia. Given the events the night before, and the meltdown Julia had experienced as a result of the mysterious note, her eyes were red, and she looked tired and drawn. It was eight, and the restaurant would not be receiving lunch guests until eleven-thirty. Some of the kitchen staff had arrived but most of them did not begin work until ten.

"Well, look what the cat dragged in. You look like you've been rode hard and put away wet," exclaimed Michele, chuckling to herself. "Don't think for a second that, just because you kissed Maestro's ass to get a good review, you can stop working. Get your damned apron on, we've got work to do."

While Julia was tough and had street smarts, it had not been in Julia's nature to challenge authority. She demanded respect from the rest of the staff, but she hadn't ever crossed either Michele or Fernando. Taking a deep breath, Julia went to her locker and exchanged her coat and purse for her white chef's apron. In spite of Michele's tirade and Julia's fatigue, Julia enjoyed a certain satisfaction in knowing that, with Maestro's column and the accolades she had received from customers, she had publicly bested Michele.

Michele continued in her ugly tone, "The produce you got yesterday from the Farmer's Market is crap. Some of the squash is beginning to spoil and the tomatoes are too ripe. Take a look at those avocados, hard as rocks. What were you thinking? Julia, you are going to have to up your game and not let your head get too big. Now get your ass to work!"

Julia began to wonder if Michele had written the note the night before. Their relationship had been frosty since Julia began working at the restaurant. Julia had kept her head down. Julia was also aware that Michele had exchanged some of the recipes Julia had brought to the restaurant for ones that were more familiar to Michele, which she could then claim as her own. Michele did not have Julia's creativity or drive. Julia was always looking for her chance to advance-and maybe it would come sooner rather than later.

Fernando arrived at the tail end of this interaction but heard enough that he knew he had to separate them. "Shit," he thought to himself. The last thing he and the restaurant needed was a cat fight between its two top chefs.

Pulling Michele aside, Fernando reminded her that the most recent very positive review by the local food critic in the *Santa Fe New Mexican* focused almost exclusively on the Oaxacan recipes brought to El Farolito by Julia. He told Michele that he needed both of them, and that Michele needed to continue to mentor Julia and not degrade her.

Michele listened briefly to Fernando's plea. Then, getting more frustrated by the second, she pulled off her chef's apron and threw it to the floor exclaiming, "This is bullshit! I have forgotten more than she will ever know. If you think she's so damn good, you don't need me," slamming the door into the alley as she left the kitchen.

Clearly frustrated, Fernando turned back to Julia and said, "Please prepare both the lunch and dinner menu for today. I will be back." He thought to himself, "As if I don't already have enough to deal with." Then, he quickly followed Michele out the back door and into the alley.

Fernando knew he was walking a tightrope with his head chef, Michele. She was an outstanding chef but, like many artists, she had a fragile ego. Any comments made about her dishes was taken as a criticism of her competence. The daily tone of the culinary staff, from dishwasher to waitstaff to preparers, was dictated by Michele's mood on any given day. Times of civility and calmness were few and far between, giving way to a tense and fearful environment.

The situation had only gotten worse after hiring Julia Gomez as sous chef. It was quite a paradox that at the height of the popularity of El Farolito, with high praise from patrons and professionals alike, internally the dysfunction was at its peak. Something was going to have to change, or the entire enterprise would implode. Fernando knew he was at yet another crossroads and he did not like his options.

Additionally, Fernando's recent rise in the community had been dependent on having Michele and Julia working together. He had paid a heavy price to get both of them, and the prospect of losing either of them could be devastating. He was also starting to feel uncomfortable that the success of the restaurant was being associated with Julia's culinary wizardry and not to his management acumen.

Still reeling from the events of the previous two days, Julia was too shaken to revel in Michele's departure. Michele had never warmly welcomed Julia as the sous chef, and she made her seniority known to Julia often and unequivocally. Michele's anger was mainly because of Fernando's insistence that the menus began including some of Julia's recipes on them. The divide between Michele and Julia only widened when patrons began asking for the Oaxacan-fusion dishes. The recent food critic's gushing review of Julia's dishes had strained the relationship to its breaking point.

"I hope that no one ever finds out what I had to go through to get that review," Julia thought to herself wondering momentarily if the note had come from William Maestro. Then she suddenly came out of her musing and began barking orders to the staff. They had to get ready for the lunch crowd.

Without Michele's presence, the mood of the entire kitchen staff lifted. There was a difference between Julia's demanding and forcefulness and Michele's moodiness and meanness. Julia always had quality, efficiency, and customer service at the center of her focus. However, with Michele you never knew if you had a target on your back. You might be the next person she would attack, and you might not even know why. She would regularly, and publicly, shame the staff for even the smallest mistakes-and sometimes for no mistakes at all.

Then there was the relationship she had with Josef. Josef Castellano was the maître d' and controlled where guests sat and who got to serve them. This had huge implications for the kind of tips wait staff received or how much they would have to work if the customer was challenging. You did not want to get on his bad side or talk poorly about Michele to him. The staff would snicker behind Josef's back that he had become her whipping boy. They were a match made in hell with human implications.

The dining room at El Farolito had the feel of a high-end Santa Fe home. The restaurant was divided into four smaller rooms with three to four tables in each room, each with a freshly ironed white tablecloth. The ceiling was low and covered with latillas, hand-peeled wood poles placed between vigas in a herringbone pattern. The walls had rounded corners and were covered with white stucco, giving the interior an adobe feel. Each wall had either New Mexican art or *nicho* boxes holding small statues or Native American pottery. Lighting came through wall sconces decorated in a southwest motif. Each room had a corner fireplace that was lit at night, providing a feeling of warmth and coziness.

Even though Michele and Fernando had left the restaurant together, each in some state of consternation, that did not seem to have a negative effect on Josef's behavior. He greeted customers with a smile and the same charm as always. If he was irritated, he kept it to himself.

The lunch and dinner crowds were busier than usual. Cooking and service were executed seamlessly. Patron comments, by way of waitstaff, were very favorable and the returns were few. Michele's absence did not seem to have been noticed. Julia was very busy and focused on ensuring that customers' demands were met.

In spite of the demands of the kitchen, Julia was still very uneasy from the note she had received. She found herself to be extremely vigilant and a little cautious with the staff, looking for any signs that she may have angered them. Strangely, her tentativeness was interpreted by the team as her stepping back and having more confidence in their abilities. In turn, they performed better than ever. As Julia watched the cadence and choreography of her team, she thought to herself, "This is where I belong. Gracias Dios y gracias mi abuela."

She then remembered that she was going to be meeting Scott later that night at the restaurant. Maybe it was fortuitous that Michele was gone.

18

Bill Dirschauser, aka William Maestro, sat at his desk and smiled to himself as he reflected on the many conquests he had experienced in Santa Fe. What a difference it was from working at that dirtbag paper in Des Moines.

Dirschauser had worked for small newspapers in various positions for several years after college. He was a journeyman reporter whose ego far surpassed his talent. His career, such as it was, had taken him from small town newspaper to small town newspaper. His average length of stay was typically about two years, just enough for the job to exceed his competency or work ethic. If it wasn't his incompetence that got him fired, it was his philandering and bravado.

"Big Willy" as he liked to be called for obvious reasons, fancied himself to be ahead of his time in that he never discriminated when it came to his conquests. His libido knew no boundaries-single, married, black, white, young, old, Hispanic, Asian, rich, or poor. However, he did draw the line at sexual preference; he was a full-throttled heterosexual. It was no wonder that he had never married. He thought to himself, chuckling, "Why buy the cow when the milk is free?"

Dirschauser was clever in that he knew the power of creating "obligation vacuum." He identified something his potential victim wanted and would provide it in exchange for sexual indulgences. He always made certain that the exchange of "favors" carried with it a certain guarantee of secrecy. In effect, it was a form of extortion. It had served him well in other places and he believed that it would serve him well in Santa Fe.

With the onslaught of local newspapers closing and giving way to national brands like *USA Today*, it was becoming more difficult to find jobs in local newspapers, especially given Dirschauser's track record. The jobs that were available tended to be lower paying and required the writers to assume second jobs to sustain themselves. Nevertheless, seeing his name in print on a regular basis gave him a sense of importance, mostly a false sense.

Having been fired most recently from the newspaper in Des Moines, Dirschauser reached out to an old college fraternity buddy, George Mayfield. Mayfield, a legitimate journalist, and entrepreneur had become the managing editor of the *Santa Fe New Mexican*. Dirschauser's timing had been perfect because the newspaper had unexpectedly lost Martha Hays, its long-time beloved food editor, to a massive heart attack. Mayfield had not had time yet to find her successor. Dirschauser had held a similar position in Des Moines.

Mayfield offered Dirschauser the job reluctantly because of the tight labor market. Dirschauser had now been the food editor for the *Santa Fe New Mexican* for the past three years. He was in his late forties, paunchy, and had an air of superiority about him. He convinced Mayfield to allow him to write his weekly column under the penname "William Maestro," and suggested that "Maestro's Musings" would give the column a certain pizzazz. Reluctantly, Mayfield agreed.

Following Martha Hays as food editor had been no easy task. She had been a long time Santa Fe resident and was admired by all who knew her. In addition, she had always been considered even-handed and fair in her restaurant reviews. She left big shoes to fill.

Because of both the longevity and the notoriety of Martha Hay's restaurant and culinary reviews, the power of the position of food editor was disproportionate given the size of the city. Restaurant owners and chefs alike assumed that whoever was hired to follow Hays would have the same honest, down-to-earth, and even-handed approach that she had. They could not have been more wrong. Regardless of their disappointment, the job suited Dirschauser just fine and he basked in the influence he had garnered.

As Dirschauser had so many times before, he began using his position of power and influence to gain "personal favors." In return, most recently he had been able to wield this power successfully over Julia Gomez, sous chef at El Farolito. He was now ready to cash in. Julia was a particular prize with her dark brown eyes, jet-black hair, gorgeous facial features, and shapely figure. After he had given her and the restaurant an extraordinary review, he could only imagine his reward. He had created his signature "obligation vacuum" with Julia and, in spite of an earlier derailed attempt, he believed that she would acquiesce. The fact that she had previously rebuffed his advances would only make his reward that much sweeter.

19

Morning broke too early. It had been a short night. It had felt even shorter because I had difficulty in falling asleep as I kept mulling over the events of the previous night, the talk with Julia, the mysterious person in the shadows of the Farmer's Market, and the contents of the note to Julia that she had passed onto me.

Despite Julia's fears, the conversation with her and the contents of the note did not seem to me to cross, or even approach, the threshold of a crime. If the individual in the Farmer's Market was a threat to her, that could pose a problem. However, there was no threat that was obvious to me at this point and nothing illegal had been implied. Until I could uncover more information, I simply needed to treat the situation as one that may be serious but not illegal. The police didn't need to be involved, at least not yet.

Because of Maria's position in the restaurant industry, I knew that she would be of great assistance in sorting out the mystery. Having promised to meet Julia after hours in *El Farolito* tonight, I wanted to get as much information as I could before our meeting. Maria and I began developing a plan to discover as much as we could prior to that meeting.

Maria was going to look at Julia's situation from the perspective of a sous chef. I was going to look at the possible personal issues implied as well as what little we knew about the mystery person leaving the building.

We kissed goodbye and I began the short walk to my office. I walked down Alameda street parallel to the Santa Fe River. The Santa Fe River is an intermittent stream beginning in the Sangre de Cristo mountain range and flowing through the city emptying into the Rio Grande. It provides about forty percent of the city's water supply.

I enjoyed a lovely walk past a few tall trees, mostly cottonwoods and poplar, lining the river and past the park benches providing a respite for visitors. Of particular interest are the many life-size statutes carved out of the stumps of diseased and dead trees. It makes for a fascinating jaunt. This morning the air was cool and crisp, and the walk was quiet. My course took me past the iconic La Fonda hotel across from the plaza.

I knew I couldn't get too far into my research without some breakfast and coffee. One of Santa Fe's best breakfast restaurants, Tia Sophia's, is located just two blocks from the plaza and three blocks from my office. It was one of my regular places for breakfast. I quickened my pace in anticipation.

Tia Sophia's specializes in Northern New Mexico food that is simple, authentic, and delicious. This morning, I selected the Huevos Rancheros, two eggs on blue corn tortillas with chile and cheese served with beans and a flour tortilla. I chose red and green chile, known locally as Christmas, and added a side of pozole and black coffee. This is as close to heaven as a native Santa Fean can get.

As I waited for my order to arrive, I thought back on what I knew about Julia Gomez and what I still needed to know. In particular, I was interested in Julia's, or Sofia's, background. Was there anything in her background that would suggest a threat? Had she been in trouble either in Santa Fe or prior to coming here, including in Mexico? Were there any obvious individuals or situations that would have warranted Julia being threatened? Was this all a hoax? Was I being played? If so, why?

The waitress brought my meal and, for the time being, I was distracted by what was right in front of me. I was impatient to get to work, but I wanted to savor every bite of my Huevos Rancheros. Researching could wait.

My office is in Sena Plaza on the northeast corner of the Santa Fe Plaza. Sena Plaza is the site of a house built by Don Juan Sena for his bride in eighteen hundred and thirty-one. It is now the site of three smaller plazas with added on sections of the large two-story house wrapped around each plaza. The various rooms of the house are now shops, boutiques, and restaurants, with a few professional offices on the second floor. I was fortunate to have been able to secure one of the small offices.

I arrived at my office and began an internet search on both Sofia Lopez and Julia Gomez. I wanted to understand if she had made any obvious enemies. Because of my affiliation with the Santa Fe Police Department, I had access to a few specialized data bases, including both criminal records and immigration applications.

I was able to confirm Julia's legal immigration status and the legal change of her name from Sofia Lopez to Julia Gomez. There had been no criminal activities in which Sofia Lopez been mentioned as a victim or a witness to a crime in the states. However, there had been an arrest warrant for her in Tuxtepec, Mexico in connection with an assault of Pablo Ramírez. It had later been abandoned based on insufficient evidence. Having overheard Julia's accounting of the abuse at the hands of her stepfather, I thought that I wouldn't have blamed her if she had killed the bastard. I had to wonder if he could have been the one threatening her.

As for Julia, it was a different story...

By searching multiple national criminal data bases, I was able to identify some interesting activities of Julia's since her arrival in the United States. Of particular note was a single reference to credit card fraud having taken place in El Paso. The information on the National Crime Information database identified several unspecified charges on a credit card in the name of James Gonzales of Las Cruces, New Mexico.

According to the file, Gonzales claimed to have lost his credit card on a trip back from Juarez to El Paso. He indicated that he had been in the company of a Julia Gomez and fell asleep inebriated in a Motel Six. After waking up, he claimed that his wallet, along with about fifty dollars, a credit card, and a debit card were missing.

The credit card charges added up to about two hundred dollars and were at unusual locations like the Dollar Store and Good Will, mostly for clothing. There were no CCTVs at these stores, only signed receipts. Gonzales subsequently refused to press charges and no further action was taken because the total amount did not reach the credit card threshold for fraud conviction.

While Julia was not completely free of past legal difficulties, she did not have an arrest record. Except for James Gonzales, I was unable to identify anyone with reason to have written the note that Julia received. I was looking forward to seeing her at the restaurant later tonight to better understand the note she had received.

My phone pinged indicating I had received a text. It was Maria requesting that I come to the Guadalupe restaurant to commiserate about what they had collectively discovered. I quickly texted back, "Be there in fifteen minutes." I was curious about what she may have found out about Julia.

20

Getting kicked out of the university had been the last straw for Jackson Wyman, and he was now making his final offer to his ne'er-do-well son, Randolph. Jackson Wyman was the CEO of Security Insurance, a national insurance company headquartered in Boston. It had been founded by his great-grand father during the great depression in nineteen thirty-one because his great-grandfather saw the depression as an opportunity to be exploited. When people were losing their homes and livelihood, he believed that they would be keen to purchase insurance to help secure their futures.

He began selling life insurance, convincing men and women with children that it was the best way to provide for their families should either parent pass away. The industry was unregulated, and he was able to grow the company through acquiring other similar insurance organizations. He soon had a significantly large number of subscribers. Being wilier than most, while other insurance companies were closing or being shut down because of fraud and deception, Security Insurance was thriving. His timing had been perfect in that it was prior to the Social Security Act of nineteen thirty-five.

The reigns of the company had been handed down from generation to generation. Jackson was now the fourth CEO, preceded by his father and grandfathers. It had been Jackson's hope to pass on the leadership of the company to his eldest son, Randolph. However, his plans were derailed as Randolph's behavior never conformed to that of a responsible Security Insurance CEO.

Being the son of a very successful and wealthy father can certainly be an advantage, as in the Kennedy family of Massachusetts. It can also serve as a noose around the neck when the son has been given all of the opportunities afforded to him without having developed a sufficient work ethic. Randolph fell in this category.

People would often joke that Randolph was born on third base and always thought he hit a triple. He attended the finest schools, went to elite summer camps, and traveled extensively with friends. He was able to act the part, but this façade was always short-lived. Contrary to how his father had succeeded in all his endeavors, Randolph was always "just this close" to being kicked out of school, ostracized from the social clubs to which the family belonged, and even arrested for any number of grievances. Trying to be a good father protecting his family reputation, Jackson would always rescue Randolph, give him a stern warning, and expect his behavior to change.

Au contraire, because Randolph was always able to sidestep the rules and he began to believe he was invincible. He became arrogant and antagonistic. Any problems he had were always explained by pointing the finger of blame at others, his family included. Randolph did ultimately get kicked out of one of the finest small colleges in the northeast. His egregious behavior of flaunting the rules, exploiting women, and using drugs were beyond the ability of his wealthy family to abolish. Jackson had long ago given up the hope that Randolph would be his successor and had now began grooming his daughter, Felicity, to be the next CEO.

After consulting with the family attorney, financial advisors, and Randolph's psychologist, to whom he had gone only four times, Jackson was advised to "cut the cord" with Randolph. To Jackson and his wife, Alastair, this counsel served as both a relief and also a deep sadness at Randolph's fate. They always questioned how they could have parented him better.

Jackson set up a trust for Randolph with funds available to him at five-year intervals until he was forty. Sitting down with Randolph, Jackson told him that he was no longer welcome at the family home, gave him a check, and wished him the best. There was no hug, no handshake, just Randolph grabbing the check indignantly and storming out of the house.

For the next several years, Randolph traveled first in Europe, then across the United States, but never put down roots. Anywhere he went, he was initially able to develop a network by mostly buying relationships. However, without fail, once the full force of his arrogance and exploitive behaviors were felt, one-by-one his network dissolved. Then he was off to the next place.

Aware that the final payment from his trust fund was approaching and not having a plan to sustain himself or his lifestyle, he found himself getting drunk in a bar in Santa Fe. He had just recently arrived and overheard an exchange about the closing of a restaurant just a few blocks from the Santa Fe Plaza. The conversation centered around what a shame the closing had been, confusion about why there had been a revolving door of owners and, given the location, opinions as to why it had not have been successful.

It was then that a lightbulb went off in Randolph's head. Buying the restaurant would be the perfect solution to sustain his lifestyle once dad's money ran out. After all, how hard could running a restaurant be? You hired a chef, cooked food, advertised, got people through the door and it would then become his own cash machine.

Randolph's arrogance and grandiosity took control as he thought to himself that, this time, it would be different. He would show his father that he could be just as successful as his father had been and he would have done it on his own. He didn't need to be the CEO of Security Insurance. He would be the CEO of his own company, a chain of restaurants starting in Santa Fe and expanding all over the United States. What a plan. He would show them all.

Within a week, Randolph met with a commercial realtor and submitted a down payment on the vacant restaurant. Within six weeks, he was able to reopen the restaurant with a new name, Rojas. Now all he had to do was to sit back and let the money roll in.

21

It had been about one year ago that Randolph Wyman had asked to meet with Roberto Montoya. In addition to owning the Guadalupe restaurant, Roberto has an office four blocks west of the Santa Fe Plaza on the corner of Sandoval street and Water street. It is an office away from the restaurant where Roberto could have private business meetings. Roberto suggested they meet there.

Roberto Montoya, Maria's father, was a big deal in Santa Fe. The Montoya family had deep roots in New Mexico, going back several hundred years. In fact, the Montoya name was one of the most recognizable and influential names in politics, commerce, and philanthropy throughout New Mexico. Having at one time been a state senator, Roberto's connections were both deep and wide. If you wanted to know something about almost anyone of note, Roberto would know. It was no wonder that Randolph would want to meet with Roberto.

Roberto had not met Randolph but knew that he had only recently moved to Santa Fe and had purchased the vacated restaurant adjacent to the Saint Julian Hotel, renaming it Rojas. Wyman, in his early forties, was viewed as somewhat peculiar. He came from the east coast and appeared to have a lot of money. Many speculated it was "daddy's money," and that he was a trust fund baby. He had an air of superiority about him that shouted, "expensive private boarding school."

Santa Feans have a love-hate relationship with outsiders coming to town flashing, but also spending, their money. Because tourism is such a large part of the Santa Fe economy, it is seen as necessary for Santa Fe to thrive. However, locals often feel slighted and treated in a condescending manner by some wealthy outsiders taking their large egos wherever they go. With their recently purchased cowboy hats, boots, native jackets, and bolo ties these "urban cowboys" are viewed more comically than taken seriously. They are seen as more exploitive than really adding value.

As a result, these relationships are much more transactional than authentic or meaningful. As one person put it, these ostentatious tourists "pop in, pop off, and pop out," with no real commitment to the community. At the very least, locals are suspicious of them and, at worst, despise their public displays of self-importance. Wyman was viewed through this lens and had not yet "passed the sniff test" of being in Santa Fe to truly be a part of the community.

Just as in the housing market, the location of a restaurant can make or break it. The location of Rojas was only four blocks from the Santa Fe Plaza. It seemed to be the exception that proves the rule in that several previous owners had not been able to make the restaurant a success. In fact, many in town speculated that the restaurant had been part of some kind of a money laundering scheme for its owners, maybe even the mafia. But in all of the years of openings and closings, nothing had risen to the level of an investigation. Roberto was very curious about what Wyman may have wanted.

Wyman presented himself at the meeting about ten minutes late. "Curious," thought Roberto. Here is a person wanting to speak to me and showing up late?

Dressed like many outsiders having relocated to Santa Fe, Wyman appeared in pressed jeans, a white shirt with a bolo tie around his neck, a tan suede jacket and cowboy boots. Topping his costume, Wyman had a cowboy hat with a feather sticking up from the brim. He fit the tourist profile to a tee, much more than a person who had assimilated into the community. His long hair, visible on the sides of his cowboy hat, was the final touch.

If Roberto had any reservations prior to meeting Wyman, those suspicions were on red alert now.

Roberto graciously invited Wyman into his office and asked him to take a chair at the small circular table where Roberto joined him.

After a brief introductory conversation, Roberto began graciously with "Please, Randolph, what brings you here to my office, and how can I be of assistance?"

That question began an hour-long meeting during which time Wyman talked at length about his famous wealthy father, his privileged upbringing, and his quest to make his own fortune independent of his father. He spoke about his travels, travails, venturing out west and, finally, ending up in Santa Fe.

Having had no prior restaurant experience, nor much significant business or work experience as far as Roberto could discern, Wyman decided to purchase the restaurant adjacent to the Saint Julian hotel. Wyman used the last trust fund check from his father to purchase the vacated space, renamed the restaurant Rojas and, eventually, opened its doors to the public. By all accounts, the grand opening had been underwhelming but not according to Wyman who described how the opening of Rojas as one of the biggest social events of the year in Santa Fe.

As Roberto heard Wyman's story, he was initially in disbelief followed by a sense of contempt. Roberto reflected on his own strong work ethic instilled by his father and grandfather. They believed that hard work built character and was a precondition for success. Here was Wyman whose cockiness and self-assurance were only matched by his sense of entitlement. Wyman's values were at the opposite end of those Roberto held firmly and had instilled in his children.

As Wyman's monologue droned on, Roberto found himself becoming impatient, wanting the conversation to end. But, before it ended, he was in for a big surprise.

As Wyman appeared to be coming to the end of his lengthy narrative, he said to Roberto, "I have come prepared to make deal with you."

Roberto knew that there was no kind of deal in which he would agree to partner with Wyman. Nevertheless, he was curious.

"Oh," Roberto replied, "what exactly do you have in mind?"

Wyman indicated that he was wanting to "partner" with Roberto to make the Guadalupe and Rojas become "sister restaurants." As Wyman phrased it, the partnership could be a "win-win" situation for both of them, being able to refer customers back and forth, creating greater financial leverage with vendors and sharing staff in the tight Santa Fe job market. He had it all laid out, at least in his mind.

Wyman cited how successfully the Shed, an iconic Santa Fe restaurant, had a second location on the southside named La Choza. He also noted the more recent expansion of the Plaza Café to an additional location called Plaza Café Southside. Plaza Café is a celebrated restaurant on the Santa Fe Plaza dating to nineteen hundred five. He had it all figured out. The only difference was that both the Plaza Café and the Shed had been very successful *prior* to branching out. From what Roberto knew,

Rojas had not been. In fact, Roberto saw this as a ploy to bring in the Guadalupe expertise, and probably funds to help salvage Rojas, rather than any possible mutual value.

The final challenge from Wyman was that he had also spoken with Fernando Romero about partnering with El Farolito but wanted to give Roberto "the right of first refusal." If Roberto had any thoughts at all about partnering with Wyman, which he didn't, that statement firmly put an end to them.

Roberto quickly declined Wyman's offer, escorted him to the door, shook his hand, and wished him the best of luck.

As Wyman left Roberto's offices, Roberto could only wonder about the mess that Wyman had gotten himself into.

22

Maria was waiting for me after having spent the morning talking to her father, Roberto. Maria had been certain that talking to her father was a good place to begin learning about Julia, and she wasn't disappointed.

Maria had taken the liberty of ordering lunch and the two of us were secluded in the conference room of the Guadalupe. Once together, Maria began. "What I learned from *mi padre* and a couple of other calls may surprise you," she began. And it did.

Previously, Roberto had unsuccessfully tried to hire Julia for his restaurant the Guadalupe. Maria knew that he would have done his homework prior to seeking her out. If there was something to understand about Julia, Roberto was the best source of information and, Oh, what Roberto knew.

Roberto reported that Julia's food truck experience, prior to being employed at El Farolito, had been more tumultuous than he had had known at the time. He had followed up with Larry Ulibarri, owner of the Rolling Burrito after Julia left for El Farolito. Larry revealed that, while Julia had some unique and amazing culinary skills even for Santa Fe, her relationships with some of the staff were characterized as turbulent. Julia vacillated between being accommodating and sympathetic to being quite demanding and harsh. She had made a lot of food truck enemies while there.

Larry noted that he had only learned of her behavior after she left. Anytime Larry was present, Julia's behavior was totally appropriate. Also, Larry revealed that her interaction with customers often bordered on the flirtatious. He said that he thought her coquettish behavior encouraged customers to return and had been an asset to the business. After her departure, the remaining staff suspected that Julia might have been subsidizing her food truck income with "after hours" activities with clientele. However, no solid evidence was found to support this allegation, only rumor and innuendo.

Larry further conceded that following Julia's departure to El Farolito, business at the Rolling Burrito had declined significantly. Customers loved her Oaxacan version of Northern New Mexican food, and, without it, customers went to other venues to satisfy their appetites. Larry acknowledged that Fernando Romero had given him a large sum of money in exchange for being able to hire Julia away from the Rolling Burrito. "Worst business decision I ever made," Larry lamented.

The decline of the Rolling Burrito's business was additional confirmation to Roberto that Julia did indeed have a special talent. He was somewhat surprised to hear about Julia's relationship with other staff, but this was not unusual in the food industry. Culinary masters often see themselves as artists with a special understanding of unique recipes, herbs, spices, rubs, marinades, and food combinations that evade the average chef. Their work is an extension of who they are, and the more notoriety they receive, the more particular they become. Chefs commanding their kitchen crews, barking orders and, occasionally, having outbursts is common. You cannot have a fragile ego and work for one of these divas.

Roberto had a unique way of dealing with elite chefs. He was able to manage them in a way that was respectful, clear, and kind. His culinary staff all saw Roberto as the father they wish they would have had. He would have loved to have Julia in his kitchen. He believed that he could have helped her further refine her culinary skills and develop relationally as a person as well. For now, he was thinking that "delayed is not denied."

Wanting to let Maria know what I had discovered, I began, "On my database searches..."

Maria interrupted, "Wait Scott, first I need to tell you I conducted some research of my own."

Yielding to Maria, I said, "Tell me, please."

Maria reported that she had determined it would be a good idea to check out Michele Ronaldi. Being the head chef for El Farolito and having no Santa Fe roots, Maria wanted to find out more about her.

She began, "I have been keeping my ear to the ground and I got in touch with a culinary contact in New York City, Belinda Brennan. I met Belinda when she and her partner came to Santa Fe several years ago on vacation. Belinda has worked in several restaurants in New York City, and we have kept in touch."

"Well," I replied expectantly, "tell me what she said."

Maria replied enthusiastically, "When I asked Belinda if the name 'Michele Ronaldi' was familiar to her, she snickered and said, 'That's a blast from the past. Please, don't tell me you have hired her at your father's restaurant.'

"She told me that Michele Ronaldi was well-known on the New York City restaurant scene as both talented and unscrupulous. In fact, she had been fired from several top restaurants because of her inability to control her ego and anger. At one of the restaurants, she had threatened the executive chef and even accused him of being sexually inappropriate with her. A subsequent investigation found the accusation to be fallacious and she was terminated.

"In fact, Belinda reported that it had been rumored Michele was just days away from getting fired yet again when she left the City. This was several years ago, and Belinda had not kept up with her."

"According to Belinda, time and again, the problem stemmed from Michele's volatile temper when threatened and her seeming inability to manage her behavior. She had a pattern of being hired because of her considerable culinary talent, making a strong initial showing, and impressing the restaurant owner or manager. This pattern was followed by significant tumultuous interactions with the executive chef, demanding more recognition and, in some cases, demanding to replace the executive chef altogether. When this did not work, her behavior typically escalated to the point of giving the restaurant owner no choice but to terminate her."

"Wow," I exclaimed. "The plot thickens. Now I will have more information for when I talk with Julia later. Great work."

I reported the information I had researched online regarding both Sofia Lopez and Julia Gomez. Combined, our investigation painted a picture of a person whose background had given her great resilience and fortitude along with an ability to manipulate situations for her benefit. The pattern fit closely to members of street gangs in any inner city. The difference was that members of street gangs rarely rise above their plight in life, often ending up either dead or imprisoned. Julia had been able to use her unique capabilities for cooking and her strong desire to escape her upbringing in order to move out of her traumatic and impoverished upbringing.

However, all things considered, what we had discovered did not explain someone wanting to scare Julia as was indicated in the note she had received. It is one thing to offend and piss people off, but it is quite another thing for them to go to the trouble of being a real threat. Julia certainly seemed to have her rough edges and she might even be manipulative, but these survival skills that she had honed on the streets of Oaxaca did not appear to make her a real threat to others. It was clear that there was more to her situation than met the eye. The information we uncovered posed more questions than answers. I was looking forward to getting some clarifying answers from Julia to the serious questions I would be asking when we met later.

Maria and I finished our lunch and parted until dinner. I wanted to conduct further investigation prior to meeting with Julia so I returned to my office to continue my research.

23

It was now late afternoon, and I still had several hours before meeting Julia. I decided that it was unnecessary for Maria to serve as a "lookout" this time during the meeting with Julia. Because Julia and I would be meeting at El Farolito, there seemed to be little need for any extra security. I took time to review the note from Julia again and identify the questions to be asked.

The walk from the Guadalupe restaurant to my office takes about fifteen minutes and I always stroll through the plaza, even though it adds time. Even now, after nearly four hundred years, the plaza is still the heart of downtown Santa Fe. It is a National Historic Landmark in the style of traditional Spanish-American colonial cities.

The plaza consists of a central park with grass, trees, and benches. It is surrounded on all four sides by art galleries, restaurants, retail stores, and museums. At different times of the year, it is the host to the Indian and Spanish Markets, concerts, special events, and community gatherings. The most notable building is the Palace of the Governors, on the north side of the plaza built in the Territorial Style of Pueblo architecture. It is the oldest public building in the United States and served as the seat of government for New Mexico for centuries. until nineteen hundred and one.

In the warm months of the year, you will find local Native Americans selling their wares on blankets under the portal of the Palace of the Governors. Around the central park, people sit on benches with their coffee either marveling at the lovely surroundings or solving the world's problems. Being here brings back great nostalgia from my youth, and memories of strolling in the plaza with my family and friends, eating a Frito Pie, and listening to music in the plaza's bandstand.

I arrived at my office eager to take another look at the note Julia had thrust into my hands before her sudden departure the night before. The note was vague to me, but I suspected clearer to her. I wondered who "R" could be. Was it the initial of someone's first or last name? Was it the initial of a nickname? If Julia knew this "R," why wouldn't she have just talked to him, or her, upon receiving the note?

The first line, "After all we have been through..." indicated that "R" and Julia had a personal relationship and that they had worked through problems of some sort. Was this a boyfriend? A former lover? A sibling? So many possibilities. It did not suggest a new or a casual relationship.

The note referred to "special plans." What could they have been? Did the author of the note believe that they were getting married? Could the writer have been a stalker? Had Julia been romantically involved with someone?

Then the threats, "...did you think you could ignore me?" and "...do not ruin everything!" suggest a relationship gone bad. Then the admonition to "keep your mouth shut" added more complexity. If this was a relationship gone bad, why would Julia have to keep it a secret?

It was obvious from Julia's seeking me out and her fearfulness that she was very much afraid of whoever "R" is.

As I read through the note, I began jotting down the questions I wanted to ask Julia. I had to determine if what I was reading was actually a serious threat, or just indicated a romance that had gone astray.

I reviewed again the information on Julia that I had downloaded from the national databases to try and make sense of the note. I was hoping that I could find some small clue that might tell me about the identity of "R." That was to no avail. There was nothing that furthered my understanding of Julia, the threatening note, or "R."

In addition to working part-time with the Santa Fe Police Department, I have a business conferring with corporate leaders on a host of issues related to leadership and strategy. Since becoming involved with Julia, I had let my professional work as a consulting psychologist take a back seat. Consequently, I had several emails that required my attention and a couple of phone calls to return.

The rest of the afternoon was spent with these calls and emails, and it was getting close to dinner time. I realized that I needed to get my mind off my upcoming meeting with Julia, if only briefly. I texted Maria and suggested that she meet me at the rooftop terrace at the Drury Plaza Hotel before my late-night sojourn. We could discuss my approach to Julia over a glass of wine and some hors d'oeuvres. To my delight, she quickly texted back in the affirmative.

The short walk from my office to the Drury Plaza Hotel took me by several Sena Plaza shops, the Institute of American Indian Arts, and the beautiful Cathedral Basilica of Saint Francis of Assisi. It is truly a walk-through history with cobblestone streets, adobe buildings, wooden plank walkways, and historic buildings on both sides. This part of Santa Fe has a feeling unlike anywhere else in the states, with architecture that is part Native American, part Hispanic, and part Anglo. It is one of the many reasons people are drawn to this special location and center of blended cultures.

The Drury Plaza Hotel resides in the repurposed and remodeled Saint Vincent's Hospital. The hospital was the oldest in the state of New Mexico, founded in eighteen hundred sixty-five. When vacated, the building had undergone several iterations until it was purchased by Drury Hotels. The hotel enterprise has been careful to preserve the history and original architecture of the building and is now home to artwork that is native to the area and serves to maintain the Santa Fe ambience.

My own history was interwoven with the hospital in that it had been the place where my grandmother had been cared for prior to her death. I had also been a patient there for appendicitis in my high school years. It was both strange and comforting to see this version of the building still welcoming and accommodating guests, but in a much different manner.

The rooftop terrace is located on the fourth floor of the hotel. From the terrace, there is nearly a three-hundred sixty-degree view of Santa Fe and the surrounding area. Because of zoning ordinances, no building can be built over five stories. This allows for panoramas that are unobstructed and expansive. The diminishing sunlight creates beautiful sunsets to the west with the shadow of the mountains contrasting with the lingering blue skies. It would have been a perfect setting for a date night if I did not have a meeting scheduled with Julia later.

Maria joined me and, as we sipped our wine, we began to discuss my upcoming meeting with Julia. Because we already knew Julia's identity and I would be meeting her at El Farolito, it did not make sense for Maria to accompany me or be on "standby" as she had been at the Farmer's Market.

We discussed what I needed to find out from Julia, especially to identify and understand any enemies she may have. Given the information we had received from Roberto about Julia's temperament, she may have pissed off the wrong person.

I found myself so preoccupied that I was not able to fully engage with Maria or fully enjoy our time together. After about an hour of talking and planning my next step, Maria suggested we return to the house so I could prepare for the meeting.

I paid the tab, and we returned home.

24

It was approaching the time for me to get to El Farolito to meet with Julia. Normally the walk from my house on East Alameda to El Farolito would take about twenty minutes. Santa Fe tends to roll up its sidewalks at about six every night. Unless there is a special event at the Plaza, the shops all close, the Native Americans selling their wares at the Palace of the Governors wrap up their goods, and downtown becomes quiet.

In the fall and winter months, the Santa Fe Plaza can seem almost eerie at night with an absence of people and all of the stores having closed. This part of Santa Fe has a very low crime rate, mostly because both the police and the locals are vigilant, knowing that it must remain safe for the tourist population. Nevertheless, since I was going to be with Julia until late, I decided to take my car and drive the short distance to El Farolito.

The small shops and a bookstore near the restaurant had already closed for the evening. As I approached the restaurant at eleven, I noticed that the parking lot was empty and the lights inside the restaurant were already turned off. The area around the restaurant was absent of people and strangely quiet. I began wondering if I had made a mistake on the time. Should I have been there earlier? I assumed, given the secrecy of our meeting, that Julia would want our meeting to be private, but I expected at least one light to be on.

As instructed by Julia, I walked around to the back of the restaurant. In the dark, I could make out the back door, but the light above the door was off. On further inspection, I saw that the bulb was broken, and the back door was ever so slightly ajar. I began to feel apprehensive and knew I needed to tread carefully. I cautiously made my way down the three stairs from the alley and knocked lightly on the open door.

No response.

I pushed the door just enough to squeeze in.

"Is anyone here?" I asked softly.

No response.

"Julia, it's Scott Hunter, are you here?" I questioned.

No response.

It was pitch black and I probably should have turned on my iPhone light but didn't. The back door opened to a small hallway that led to the kitchen. It was dark and I did not want to switch on an overhead light. Finally, turning on my iPhone light, I made my way down the hall. It was very quiet without anything stirring.

Suddenly, my progress was halted by a loud noise. It sounded like a pan or metal object falling from a shelf. I stopped in my tracks.

"Hello, Julia, are you there? Is anyone there?" I asked tentatively.

Again, no response.

After what seemed like an eternity, I slowly went forward. The light on my iPhone was practically useless in this abyss. Just then, in the dark, my foot hit an object on the floor and I almost tripped. Kneeling down, I could see the shape of a body lying on the floor. With my eyes adjusting, I found the person's carotid artery on the neck and felt for a pulse.

Suddenly, I could hear the side door exit of the restaurant open and close and the sound of someone fleeing. I was confused and a little scared. What the hell was happening?

"Who's there?" I yelled out, but the person fleeing was already gone.

Feeling no pulse, I made my way to the nearest wall, and felt for a switch. Finding one, I swiped at it and the kitchen was immediately flooded with light, temporarily blinding me.

As my eyes adjusted to the light, to my horror, I could see there lying on the floor was Julia Gomez. Her face was placid, eyes open, and her body was on its side. She still had on her chef's jacket, and she had vomited onto the floor. I could see her cell phone slightly visible underneath the table near her body.

I felt a wave of nausea overcome me and I had to grab onto the side of a preparation table to steady myself.

On the same metal preparation table near Julia's body was a bottle of mezcal distilled alcohol, bitters, and agave nectar. Next to the bottle of mezcal were two cocktail glasses, each with a single large melting ice cube sphere, an orange peel, and liquid, likely the mezcal and bitters which were the makings of an Oaxaca Old Fashion. One of the glasses had what appeared to be about two ounces of liquid. The other glass was almost empty with a lipstick smudge on the rim.

I knew better than to touch them and also knew that I needed to call nine-one-one, but I wanted to look around first.

I noted that her opened purse sat on another metal preparation table with a shawl draped near it. The purse did not appear to have a wallet or money in it but did not seem to have been rummaged through. Could this have been a robbery? I saw no obvious wounds on Julia's body nor any other evidence of a struggle.

I found the staff lockers and all but one was closed and appeared to be locked. As I peered into the only open locker, I could see another unopened bottle of mezcal with the same label as the one on the metal preparation table. On the inside door of the locker were taped some faded photos of what seemed to be family members in a house. The locker also held a chef's apron hanging on a metal hook, some hand lotion, and several small bottles of eye drops. Other than that, it was orderly and empty.

I made my way to a small office in the back of the kitchen. The door was open and behind the desk was a small safe, presumably to hold the day's cash. It was not open and the papers on the desk had not been disturbed. Whatever the intruder was after, they had not bothered the office.

Finally, I made my way to the check-out area where credit cards were used and money from cash paying customers was held. I saw the register unopened. If this had been a robbery, either Julia had interrupted the intruder and was killed in the process, preventing them from opening the safe and money register, or it wasn't a robbery at all. In either case, it appeared that a murder had taken place, but forensics would have to confirm that.

Searching further, I found the source of the earlier noise. A pan sat on the floor, apparently having fallen from the metal shelf nearby. The shelving was next to a side door that was slightly ajar. This was obviously where the intruder had exited.

What was going on here?

I called nine-one-one to report the murder. The police arrived and quickly secured the crime scene, including the alley behind the restaurant, the dining room, kitchen, and staff locker room. They carefully bagged the two glasses, Julia's iPhone, and her purse, being careful not to disrupt any possible prints.

It wasn't long before Sergeant Ed Apodaca appeared on the scene. I brought him up to date on Julia's leaving the note at my house, my meeting with Julia at the Farmer's Market, and her request to meet me at El Farolito after it closed for the evening.

Ed looked at me puzzled, and said, "Scott, since you were here and called nine-one-one, I will have to take your fingerprints and confirm your story, too. We need to make sure to follow protocol here. Understood?"

"Understood," I replied. Even though Ed and I had worked cases together before, I appreciated his thoroughness and professionalism. Promising Ed that I would drop by the police station in the morning, I went home.

I was still shaky as I called Maria and told her about the mysterious death of Julia. It became clear to both of us that the note to Julia was not an idle threat, but a real one. I chastised myself for not taking this as seriously as I should have. But now I still had more work to do tonight.

I was dreading the next call that I knew needed to be made.

25

"This better be damned important, because you are interrupting our breakfast overlooking the Mediterranean," Miguel Montez said with only slight humor in his voice.

It was past midnight in Santa Fe, but eight in the morning in Marbella, Spain.

In my most regretful voice, I answered, "Miguel, I would rather have had my wisdom teeth pulled than to call and disturb you. But something has happened here that I wanted you to hear about it from me first."

Miguel was the Chief Detective at the Santa Fe Police Department. Originally from Santa Fe, he became an FBI field agent after college and headed up the Bureau's Atlanta Office at one time. Years later, he returned to Santa Fe and joined the Santa Fe Police Department. Soon after arriving, he uncovered corruption and graft at the Department that led to the resignation of the former Chief of Police and two of his lieutenants.

Miguel had then been offered the position of Chief of the Department but had declined it for both personal and professional reasons. He remained at the Department as the most senior Detective over many challenging and important investigations. We had become acquainted when he investigated the death of my ex-wife's husband. Since that time, I had assisted him with several cases and was now on retainer with the Department as a forensics psychologist.

I was glad that my colleagues at the Santa Fe Police Department had not already reached out to Miguel, honoring the fact that he was on vacation.

I gave Miguel an overview of the situation with Julia and explained how Maria and I had become involved with her. I mentioned the note Julia had received and the meeting she and I were supposed to have at the restaurant. I told him that I had already gathered a lot of information about Julia and was developing some hypotheses about the situation, but that I did not feel comfortable talking about them with anyone at the police station but him.

Miguel chastised me for not having reached out to either Sergeant Apodaca or himself before and said that he would think about what I had told him and call me the next morning, if not before.

By the time I completed my call with Miguel, the police had secured the area and there was little more I could do.

Driving back home after midnight, the roads seemed disconcertingly quiet and menacing. Maria greeted me at the front door, and we hugged. Sobbing and shaking she said, "Are you okay. I was so worried."

"I am fine," I said holding her, "just shocked at what has happened."

Maria replied, "I felt like I was getting to know Julia, even from a distance. In the short time she has been in Santa Fe, she has made her mark. This is going to really shake up the restaurant business."

Knowing that Miguel could call anytime because of the time difference, I suggested to Maria that we begin piecing together what we knew so that I could give him a coherent picture. We began by listing those individuals, known and unknown, that we knew had a relationship with Julia, in the order of her arrival in Santa Fe.

Pablo Ramírez, Julia's step-father
Larry Ulibarri, owner of the Rolling Burrito
Fernando Romero, owner of El Farolito
Michele Ronaldi, executive chef at El Farolito
Additional staff at the Rolling Burrito
Additional staff at El Farolito

There were also individuals that were considered but about whom we had no knowledge. These included:

The person exiting Farmer's Market
The individual at El Farolito when I arrived who quickly exited
Possibly unknown individuals with whom Julia may have been "intimate"

It was obvious to both Maria and me that there were a significant number of things we did not know and needed to find out. Before I could proceed further, I needed Miguel to decide how he wanted the investigation to be handled. Because he was with his lovely wife on their anniversary trip to Spain, he would probably want to handle this differently than when he was in Santa Fe in the past.

It was now three o'clock and we needed to get at least some rest before morning.

26

Once again, dawn came quickly, very quickly.

A call rang out on a mobile phone, not mine but Maria's. The caller ID identified the caller as Roberto Montoya, Maria's father. It was now six. Even with only three hours sleep, my adrenaline was pumping. Wishing it wasn't so early, Maria swiped the accept on the face of her iPhone on the last ring.

Groggily, Maria said, "Hi dad. Kind of early for a call, don't you think?"

Hastily, Roberto responded, "Maria, I need to see you. I just got a jarring call from Fernando Romero. He called to tell me of the awful murder of Julia Gomez last night. He was really shaken up and said he needed to talk to someone. I am meeting him here at the Guadalupe in two hours, and I need to talk with you first. Can you come down?"

Reluctantly, but curious, Maria dressed quickly and made her way down to the Guadalupe.

Later, Maria told me later that Roberto already had coffee ready for her when she arrived at the Guadalupe forty minutes later and they made their way down to the conference room. There were already a couple of sous chefs working in the kitchen, even though the restaurant would not be open for several hours. It was part of the work ethic that Roberto instilled in his staff and contributed to the great success of the restaurant.

As they sat down, Roberto was demonstrably upset. Roberto was a tall, confident, man who always seemed to be in control of the situation. Having been a state senator, he knew how to command a room and did so masterfully. It was highly unusual for Maria to see her father so uneasy and vulnerable. It was odd to have the tables turned with Maria being the one in charge and Roberto needing consoling.

Roberto began, "I was shocked to get a call from Fernando. First, he never calls me and, second, we aren't exactly close friends. In fact, I was surprised that he wouldn't have reached out to someone in his orbit, although I don't know exactly who is in his orbit. Finally, of all people to be murdered, I am stunned that it is Julia Gomez. She was such a talent and I wanted her to work here at the Guadalupe, but I was just too late to make her an offer."

Maria knew that, even though this was her father, the information that she and Scott had from Julia, the note, the conversation from the Farmer's Market, the plan to meet again with Scott, all had to be kept confidential. She could only listen and be supportive to him.

As they talked, it occurred to Maria that she should be with Roberto when Fernando arrived. Roberto was himself preoccupied and may not be at his best for Fernando. In addition, it would help for Maria to hear any information from Fernando first-hand and "off the books," prior to the police talking with him. Roberto was actually relieved when Maria offered to stay and listen to Fernando with him.

It was only a few minutes before Fernando had arrived.

As Roberto greeted him, Fernando lunged at Roberto hugging him and weeping. "Oh, mi compadre, estoy tan triste. Thank you for meeting me."

Roberto ushered Fernando back to the conference room and said, "Fernando, of course. This is so very tragic. I have asked Maria to join us and provide you even more support."

Fernando hesitated momentarily and then replied, "That will be fine, my friend."

Fernando acknowledged Maria, Roberto offered Fernando some coffee, and they all sat down around the conference table.

"Tell me what has happened," Roberto quizzed.

Fernando replied, "I got a call this morning at about four from Sergeant Apodaca of the Santa Fe Police. He informed me that there had been an incident at the restaurant and requested that I meet him there. He would not tell me what had happened over the phone."

"When, I arrived, he told me of the death, the murder of Julia."

Putting his head in his hands, Fernando began to weep. "Oh dios mio! What am I going to do?"

Roberto placed his hand on Fernando's shoulder to comfort him.

Fernando, gaining his composure, said, "Julia was like a daughter to me. When I first met her at the Rolling Burrito, I knew she was special. Her ability to cook was incredible. She brought to Santa Fe a new way of blending the cooking of her ancestors with that of Northern New Mexico. It was all splendid. What am I going to do? Without her, the restaurant cannot succeed."

Maria was struck both by Fernando's depth of grief and the fact that he seemed as concerned with the success of the restaurant as with Julia's death. The two emotions seemed to be at odds with each other.

Fernando said weeping, "Julia was like family. I did everything I could to make her feel welcome both at El Farolito and in Santa Fe. We included her whenever there was a festivity. Just last month, she attended my niece's Quinceañera. She even came to our house to celebrate with my family after Fiesta."

Again, Maria was taken back by the relationship Fernando claimed to have with Julia. He wasn't known to be an easy person to work for and his relationships tended to be more transactional than personal. Maybe it was because of Julia's culinary genius that he treated her differently. She thought to herself that this needs to be investigated further but, for now, just listen.

Fernando continued, "She was so important to El Farolito. You may have read the recent amazing review in the *Santa Fe New Mexican*. They had a review in Maestro's Musings highlighting the amazing fusion of Oaxacan and Northern New Mexico food that Julia created. The article praised Julia and immediately brought in more customers than we were even able to serve."

Silently shaking her head, Maria considered what she knew about William Maestro, the man behind Maestro's Musings. What a joke, she thought. Maria knew there was a price to pay for getting a good review in his column. Nothing coming from him was free. Maestro had a reputation in town that there were always strings attached to receiving a good review.

Unlike his predecessor, the beloved Martha Hays, whose reviews were always fair and even handed, Maestro's tended to be "over the top." His reviews were either effusive in their praise and absent of criticism, or effusive in criticism with little to praise. In fact, Roberto had time and again steered clear of Maestro, neither needing nor wanting his endorsement. Did this put Maestro in the frame for Julia's murder? Unlikely, but worth considering.

Fernando continued, "I am beginning to have problems with

Michele, our head chef. She came from New York and ever since Julia's arrival, Michele lost focus and has been more volatile. She seems to have been threatened by Julia. She has even considered leaving. Oh, dios mio, what am I going to do?"

Fernando's lamenting and wailing lasted for another thirty minutes, part grief, part self-pity, and all self-absorption. Roberto did his best to be supportive and was still curious as to why Fernando had sought him out. However, now wasn't the time to explore that question.

Maria said little, occasionally patting Fernando on the back and empathizing.

Once Fernando had finished, Roberto walked him to the front door, wished him well, and offered to be available in the future if Fernando wanted to talk further. They again embraced and just as quickly as Fernando had arrived, he was gone again.

For Maria, the meeting had raised more questions than it answered. She was anxious to reconnect with Scott.

27

Maria had just left to talk with Roberto when my iPhone buzzed. I could see on the face that it was Miguel calling me back.

Answering quickly, I said, "Miguel, good morning, or afternoon, what's up?"

Answering with an unusual irritation in his voice, Miguel said, "Hi Scott. You were right to call me. My cell phone started blowing up after you called. First, I got a call from the Police Chief Trujillo, then Sergeant Ed Apodaca and, also, one from a reporter for the *Santa Fe New Mexican*. I was glad that I had a heads-up from you first."

"Glad it helped," I said.

Miguel quickly replied, "Here is what's going to happen. This vacation is our twentieth anniversary, and I will be damned if we are returning early. If I did, it would be our last anniversary.

"We are staying here in Marbella and taking side trips during the day. Because of our eight-hour time difference, I will have calls with you daily at two in the afternoon your time. I have arranged with the local officials here at Policia Nacional to use their technology to video conference at that time. Because of the spike in drug traffic here, the police have beefed up their technological capabilities.

"The calls will be to my office with you, Sergeant Apodaca, and our forensics expert Dolores Griego. The three of you have worked well as a team on other cases, so I feel confident I do not need to rush back to Santa Fe.

"Here is the big difference. Because I am not there, you will have more latitude than you have had previously in scheduling any additional meetings needed with Ed and Dolores, determining what direction to go in, and what leads to follow. I have already confirmed this with Chief

Trujillo. The daily calls will be primarily updates keeping me in the loop until I return.

"Any questions?" he queried.

"Just one," I said. "Since Julia Gomez was a sous chef at El Farolito, and because Maria knows the culinary scene in Santa Fe like the back of her hand, I would like to use her as a consultant when it makes sense. No pay, of course. If Julia's murder is in any way related to the broader restaurant scene, Maria could be a very helpful resource. What do you think?"

I could hear Miguel taking a deep breath before saying, "Look Scott, I think Maria is great and she may have some important insights. It is really important that her opinions are to you and no one else. Otherwise, it could really screw things up."

"Great," I said, adding, "We will be discrete. In the meantime, I will meet Ed and Dolores prior to today's call and update them on what I know."

As we hung up, I was anxious to get started and relieved that Miguel was involved, even from a distance. I was also relieved that Maria would be working with me, even in a somewhat clandestine role.

I immediately set up a meeting with Sergeant Ed Apodaca and Dolores Griego and made my way down to the police station. I briefed them regarding the call I had with Miguel and what I knew about Julia. They had already been made aware of my leading the case on the ground and briefing Miguel daily.

I handed Dolores the initial note from Julia requesting my help and the second note that had been left for Julia by a patron at El Farolito. I also summarized the meeting Julia and I had at the Farmer's Market. I gave Ed Apodaca a print-out of the information I had uncovered on the national data base about both Sofia Lopez and Julia Gomez.

Finally, I gave them the initial list of suspects that Maria and I had considered along with possible motives. We began creating a plan of approach for the investigation including what needed to be done and by whom. We decided the best approach was to divide and conquer.

Next, I planned to conduct interviews with Fernando Romero, the owner of El Farolito, and his staff; *The Santa Fe New Mexican* Food critic William Maestro; current and former Rolling Burrito food truck personnel; and the usual patrons at El Farolito.

Dolores would focus on forensics, such as we had. That included the cocktail glasses on the kitchen preparation table in El Farolito; reviewing any other prints at the murder scene including any shoe prints out the side door; following-up with the pathologist on Julia's autopsy; and analyzing the notes for any prints or other unusual signs. Dolores noted that if Julia had a cell phone that was opened on the basis of her fingerprint, she would need to get it to the pathologist before her print became unrecognizable through decomposition.

Because Julia was deceased and had no known relatives, the Fourth Amendment regarding search and seizure could be bypassed. A search warrant was unnecessary. Ed would begin a search of Julia's world, including her home, locker at El Farolito, bank accounts, computer activity, emails, and texts. Ed would also begin to explore any other known relationships, data bases, arrest records, and so on.

By the time Miguel video called, the team had a plan to go forward. Miguel indicated that he would lean on Judge Gonzales to expedite any necessary search warrants for El Farolito and confirmed that this was unnecessary for Julia's house.

When we finished our call with Miguel, it was already late afternoon, too late to schedule anyone for interviews. I was interested in getting the next day set up, so I called Fernando and asked him to get his entire staff down to the restaurant first thing the next morning. I also set up a time to meet with food editor William Maestro at the police department. These interviews should be a good place to start.

I was interested in further debriefing with Roberto about his conversation with Fernando but, first, I wanted to accompany Ed on his search of Julia's house.

28

Julia's house was a small one-bedroom on Don Gaspar street, about a mile from the Farmer's Market. This neighborhood, like many close to the State Capitol Building, had houses in a Midwestern style with porches and small lawns. The streets are lined with deciduous trees and the neighborhood is largely residential. Houses here are very different from the architecture seen in many other parts of Santa Fe.

Julia's house was a rental, a guesthouse that was part of a larger compound in this older, but pleasant, neighborhood. Her house sat back off the street with a parking space but no yard. Inside the four-room house was sparse but tidy. It was a wooden frame house with rugs covering some of the wooden floors. There were a few framed photographs on the white walls but, otherwise, the decor was meager. In the closet she had a basic wardrobe, and everything was clean and neatly pressed. She had work clothes and some of her clothing looked to be more dressy, suitable for dates or parties. While her kitchen was small, it was clear that she had spent time here.

The kitchen counter and splash-back were covered in older yellow tile. The counter held a small coffee maker and a dishrack. The drawer under the older four burner stove and oven had a number of well-worn pots and pans. Covering two of the stove burners was a flat griddle. On the kitchen counter was a notebook that included what appeared to be some new recipes that she was trying out—Oaxacan with Northern New Mexico ingredients like red and green chile. The contents in the refrigerator mirrored some of the ingredients in the notebook, with several covered containers of what appeared to be the makings of different molé sauces.

On the small, two seat, kitchen table, there was an older and very basic computer that appeared to be little used. It was password protected, so Dolores and her IT forensics team would need to work on getting it opened. Julia's mobile phone, found at the murder scene, had already been taken to forensics.

The furnishings were all well-used and uncluttered. The living room consisted of an old loveseat, a coffee table squarely placed on a small rug, and an end table with a lamp. A small, older, television sat on what appeared to be a homemade console with two doors for storage. Again, it was very sparse. The overall feeling of the house was that it was much more functional than one used for entertaining. That was until I heard Sergeant Apodaca summon me to the bathroom.

"Scott," he bellowed, "you might want to come in here."

Taking the four steps across the living room to the bathroom, I asked, "What's up, Ed."

Standing with the medicine cabinet opened, he was pointing to a box of what appeared to be a box of loose condoms. "I thought this seemed strange and out of place," he said perplexed. "What do you think?"

Upon closer examination, I could see that the box actually contained several loose finger cots, which had the appearance of smaller condoms but were not. Smiling, I explained to Ed that finger cots were a staple in the chef's toolbox. In the midst of preparation, whenever a chef cuts a finger and needs to complete their work, they often quickly put a Band-Aid on the cut finger and cover it with one of these finger cots. It allows the chef to continue working until they can later more closely attend to the cut.

Embarrassed, Ed said, "Otherwise, nothing suspicious here."

I crossed the living room into a very small bedroom with a neatly made twin size bed covered in a Native American blanket. There was a single bedside table and lamp. In one of her bedside table drawers was a diary with a calendar. Knowing I would have to give this to Ed and his team upon leaving, I sat down at her kitchen table and perused the contents, holding it carefully with latex gloves. In scanning it, I was surprised to see several entries, all neatly written.

Consistent with her general tidiness, her notes were very orderly with dates and times of going to and from work, meeting friends, times of mass at the Cathedral, and the times she was to pick up fresh produce and baked goods at the Farmer's market. Most of the entries detailed her daily life and appeared to be mundane. However, as I turned the pages of the diary, I began to notice another entry, not explained by her routines. It was the letter "R" at different times and dates, seemingly without any consistency.

In addition, by each letter "R" there was a particular location cited. Hmm, I wondered. "R?"

Then it hit me. "R" was the single initial on the bottom of the threatening note left for Julia. Did Julia know the identity of the person who sent the note? Was "R" her assailant? If we found "R" would our case be solved?

I was curious about what Dolores and her team may find in the computer and cell phone, as well as the autopsy results. With what we had discovered at Julia's, a wave of excitement came over me because I thought we had found some clues.

Having completed my preview of Julia's house, I departed to prepare for tomorrow. Little did I know what a surprise I was in for.

29

Early the next morning, I arrived at El Farolito as planned. Dolores Griego and her forensics team had scoured the restaurant for prints, DNA, and other possible clues. However, they needed daylight time to complete the forensic review of the restaurant. As a result, they could not release the restaurant back to Fernando Romero. I asked Dolores to text Fernando requesting him, and his staff, to meet me at the Police Station.

By the time I got to the station, Fernando had gathered his staff into a waiting room we had reserved. In addition to Fernando, there were two other chefs, two dishwashers, eight waitstaff, and the maître d', Josef Castellano. Fernando requested to see me privately before we began. I had not previously met Fernando and only knew of him through Maria and her father, Roberto.

"Good morning, Mister Romero," I began, offering my hand to him. "I am Doctor Scott Hunter, a psychologist consulting with the Santa Fe Police Department and working with Detective Miguel Montez. Detective Montez is currently out of town, and he requested me to conduct any interviews necessary regarding the case. I will be the one interviewing you and your staff."

Extending his hand to mine, Fernando replied solemnly and almost tearfully, "A pleasure to meet you, Doctor Hunter. I have heard about you from our mutual acquaintance, Roberto Montoya. I wish we were meeting under different circumstances. I am at your service, here to help you any way I can. What has happened is tragic and I am devastated. I cannot tell you how shocked, and overwhelmed with grief I am. Anything you want, just ask. And please call me Fernando."

"Thank you, Fernando." I replied, "I will need to interview all of your staff and any other people you may consider having been acquaintances of Julia."

"Acquaintances?" Fernando asked with a puzzled look on his face. "Why? I thought this was a random act of violence, a robbery gone wrong, or something of the sort. Why acquaintances?"

I thought Fernando's question was a strange one. Why would he care who we interviewed. Wouldn't he want the investigation to cast a wide net? Not wanting to divulge any more information than I needed to, I simply replied that we wanted to look at all possible angles to get this solved.

Now, looking a bit sheepish, Fernando said, "It's just that Julia was like a daughter to me. She was so special. I cannot imagine that anyone she knew would have harmed her. I perfectly understand the need to look at everyone. You wouldn't be doing your job if you didn't. Again, let me know anything I can do to help."

I suggested that Fernando and I return to the room with all of the others and begin the process.

Upon returning to the waiting room, I explained to the staff that we needed as much information as possible to better understand who might have committed this heinous crime. The room was quiet and the atmosphere solemn. I asked them first as a group regarding anything they had noticed that might be helpful. Did Julia have any enemies? Did they know of anyone who may have wanted to harm her? Was she involved in any dangerous activities or with any "shady" people.

As I expected, no one offered any opinions. Either they knew nothing, they were afraid to mention anything publicly, or they did not want to implicate anyone in the room. I knew that talking in a group situation is more difficult than one-on-one, so I then spent thirty minutes with each of them separately while an individual on Dolores' team got their fingerprints and DNA swabs to "rule them out."

It has been my experience that when I identify myself as a psychologist, people tend to open up more freely than I expect. Such was the case with the staff.

As I talked with one staff member after another, a picture began to emerge that suggested that, in the kitchen, things were not at all as they appeared to outsiders. Similar to the information Maria had gathered from her friend Belinda, the staff portrayed Michele as talented but also very volatile. She regularly demonstrated an ability to be creative, even with mundane ingredients. They marveled at her ability to transform humble foods into dishes that were extraordinary.

On the other hand, all of them saw what one staff member referred to as "her evil twin." This Michele was characterized by yelling at staff, cursing, throwing pots, and tossing out dishes that she believed were poorly prepared. She publicly castigated and demeaned staff and, rarely, if ever, apologized. The more crowded the evening or important the event, the more these behaviors were evidenced. According to some staff members, Michele would even physically strike out at targeted staff with slaps or hits on the arm, always accompanied by choice words.

When asked why kitchen staff would continue to work in such an environment, they universally said that working at one of Santa Fe's finest restaurants carried a certain prominence in their peer groups. In other words, the status they had achieved made the abuse tolerable.

A couple of staff noted that the relationship between maître d' Josef Castellano and Michele had become increasingly apparent and troublesome. They noted that whenever Michele told the staff that she was going out in the alley to "take a break," it was code for spending a few intimate moments with Josef and for the staff to stay inside. One staff member unknowingly opened the door to go out to the alley and witnessed Michele and Josef groping and entangled. Fortunately, he was not spotted by Michele, or his job may have become history.

During such interludes, waitstaff had to cover the reception area for Josef until he returned. It was noted that the pressure in the front of the house was much less intense than in the kitchen. They also noted that any comments to Josef about the food or customer complaints had to be presented gingerly, lest he "chop their head off" in defense of the kitchen and Michele.

Finally, there was a unanimous belief among the staff that the relationship between Michele and Julia had worsened. While, as the staff noted, Michele had always treated Julia as her inferior, the deterioration of their relationship worsened following the restaurant's very positive review in the *Santa Fe New Mexican's* column "Maestro's Musings." Michele believed that the success of the restaurant had always been because of her genius and any belief to the contrary was heretic.

Since the review, Julia had become Michele's target. Michele found fault with everything she did and would not let her introduce new dishes or modify standard ones. Julia had been put in charge of selecting produce at the Farmer's Market, and Michele regularly criticized the quality of the fruits and vegetable Julia purchased.

The staff identified that the conflict between Michele and Julia had come to a head just days earlier when Fernando appeared in the midst of one of Michele's tirades. They reported that Michele stomped out of the kitchen, threw down her chef's apron, and departed with Fernando in pursuit. With Julia being put in charge, the staff agreed that a sense of calm had permeated the kitchen. Many were glad that Michele had gone and hoped it would be permanent.

30

As my interviewing progressed, I released folks one at a time. I knew that I wanted to have more in-depth interviews with Fernando and Michele. I decided to begin with Fernando.

As I began my interview with Fernando, tears came to his eyes and he quickly began sobbing, too quickly, I thought. As he had already related to Roberto, Fernando spoke about how important Julia had been to the restaurant and to him. He referred to her as being part of his family and discussed how he tried to help her make feel welcome. He referred again to the glowing review of her cuisine in Maestro's Musing and cited the many customers who regularly raved about her cooking. So far, he had not said anything to me that he had not already mentioned to Roberto in their conversation. I needed something more, so I used his own description of their relationship to probe further.

"Tell me, Fernando, given that you were so close to Julia, she must have confided in you about anyone with whom she may have had problems. Boyfriends? Co-workers? Family? Customers? Surely, she must have mentioned someone to you."

Looking toward the ceiling as if in deep thought, Fernando took a while before saying, "Well, she did mention having a bad relationship with her stepfather when she was younger. But that was several years ago and in Mexico. Other than that, I can't think of anyone."

I noticed his manner and the almost rehearsed way he answered. He had done some mental preparation for this. There was something he was not telling me. I decided to push a little harder.

"Fernando," I replied, "I know that in your business, there is a fair amount of competition in the back of the house. Every sous chef wants to be the head chef. Head chefs are often very demanding and even harsh. I know that employees in the kitchen of a fine restaurant like yours regularly experience a certain amount of tension, and this can lead to much frustration and anger. In fact, there have been altercations between some chefs that were so fierce they resulted in one chef hurting the other. Tell me about the atmosphere in the kitchen at El Farolito."

Sitting up and answering more confidently, Fernando replied, "Well, Doctor Hunter, our kitchen staff from Michele to Julia to the other staff runs like a well-oiled machine. Not only do they deliver a fine product, the do it on time and regularly exceeded expectations."

Knowing from the staff interviews that the "well-oiled machine" Fernando referred to was, in fact, clunky and full of friction, I had latitude to continue to press. I also noted that while his upper body was mostly still, his right leg couldn't stop shaking, up and down. He was definitely anxious about something.

"Tell me," I asked, "was there ever any friction between Michele and Julia? I am sure it would have been normal in an intense environment like the kitchen."

Pausing longer than he needed to answer a straightforward question, and one that I had already "normalized," Fernando said, "Oh, maybe a time or two, but nothing serious."

I knew that Fernando wasn't being forthcoming, but I didn't know why. Was he trying to protect Michele? Was he trying to protect the reputation of the restaurant? He did not want me to probe further, and he had dramatically underestimated the degree to which the restaurant staff had been cooperative. Should I push harder now or wait? I decided to push.

"Fernando," I said firmly, "I know what you are telling me is not accurate. Don't forget, this is a murder investigation, and we are trying to find Julia's killer. It's not in your best interest to withhold information. Now, I want you to be honest and tell me everything you know about Julia, her relationships to Michele and other staff, and her relationship to you. Can you do that for Julia?"

Hanging his head, Fernando replied, "Okay Doctor Hunter, you are right. Not everything between Julia and Michele was perfect. I just don't think that looking at Michele, or anyone who works at El Farolito as a suspect is the right way to go. In fact, I think it is a waste of time."

I responded, now becoming irritated, "You need to trust me and the team here at the Police Department to make the decisions about whom we need to interview and consider as suspects. Now, please tell me about Julia's relationships with any and all of the El Farolito staff."

At that point, Fernando began to open up, at least to a degree. He mentioned the recent altercation that Michele and Julia had in the kitchen resulting in Michele's storming out of building. It matched the observations the staff had made. He also admitted that the very positive restaurant review in the *Santa Fe New Mexican* created much more tension between Michele and Julia, with Michele believing she had not been given enough credit for her substantial work.

Even when pressed, Fernando denied that Michele's behavior toward the staff, or Julia, had been excessive or toxic. Also, he did not admit observing any behaviors between Josef and Michele that were inappropriate on the job. He related that he was aware of their relationship but, as far as he knew, they kept it professional while at work.

Either Fernando had blinders on with regard to the conflict going on in his own kitchen, or he was continuing to limit what he admitted to me, in hopes that I would not probe too much. I recalled in my own work with executives, how frequently they are ignorant of bad behaviors going on in their own organizations. They either turn their heads in hopes that things will get better or are totally unaware of the degree to which toxic behaviors exist.

I did not want to divulge what I knew about Michele's New York City history yet. It might be information that would be useful to me later. Also, if I let Fernando know now about her tendencies, he may do an "end around" to Michele to prejudice her for the interview I was to have with her.

Having all I needed for now, I terminated the interview with the reminder that we would likely talk again soon.

By the time I completed my interviews, I noted that it was nearly time for our daily call with Miguel.

31

I made my way to the room set up for Miguel's call. Dolores and Ed were already present and ready, and Miguel was on the video call.

We went through what each of us had discovered to date and, at this early stage, the report was fairly cursory.

I gave a summary of the initial interviews I had conducted and named the individuals with whom I wished to follow-up and have more in-depth interviews, including Michele, Fernando, Bill Dirschauser, aka "William Maestro," and a few particular staff members of interest.

Ed reported that Julia's small house was tidy, and nothing seemed to be out of place. The level of organization and cleanliness suggested that Julia was disciplined and did not appear to have regular guests. However, he did note the presence of an unusual number of bottles of eye drops. There were no men's clothing in the house and nothing to suggest she had overnight visitors. We were left with questions and no answers.

We also discussed other items found in Julia's rental, including information from her diary and a basic computer on which the forensics team was checking emails. In her diary, he had identified a mostly routine pattern of Julia's goings and comings with one exception. It was the same exception I had noted-her meetings with an unidentified "R" at locations identified by mysterious names rather than specific places or addresses. Finally, Ed had retrieved Julia's notepad with her recipes from the kitchen counter. It did not seem to be important but, besides the diary, cell phone, and computer, it was the only other item with any information.

Dolores Griego, the forensics expert, reported that her team was looking for fingerprints on the scene of El Farolito. They had also fingerprinted all of the staff. This was probably a long shot because they all worked there so their fingerprints would likely be everywhere. On the other hand, if staff fingerprints could be matched with any from Julia's house, that could suggest that she was more than just professional with one, or more, colleagues. For further comparison, Dolores had also taken DNA samples from the staff.

Julia was not a sophisticated user of technology in that she did not have any "Favorites" or "Bookmarks" set up on her computer. Her computer had mostly been used to send and receive emails. However, she had an internet browser, and appeared to be an avid learner with regard to perfecting her craft. She had several web searches focused on culinary themes. These ranged from how to best select fruits, vegetables, and seasonings to how to prepare foods that combined the local fixation on green chile with Oaxaca mole sauces. Her interest in learning about cooking confirmed Michele's observations of her being very proficient.

Dolores reported that her computer team had identified a number of files under a single master file titled "Recetas." Dolores translated this to mean recipes. The files inside this master file were titled hierbas (herbs), condimentos (seasoning), verduras (vegetables), chile verde (green chile), carne (meat), pollo (chicken), mariscos (sea food), and cerdo (pork). She believed these to be for her cooking and they were not explored further.

Julia made another group of internet searches that were intriguing. They all had to do with information about how to equip a new restaurant kitchen; how to refurbish and reinvigorate a restaurant; and how to hire and manage restaurant kitchen staff. These were puzzling in light of Julia having stable employment at El Farolito.

Some of Julia's emails had been to and from acquaintances in Oaxaca and also to a friend, Adelina Cruz. Julia had written emails in Spanish to her and her two siblings in Oaxaca. Some of the emails between Julia and her sister had a hostile tone to them, with her sister accusing Julia of having "left them behind." They appeared to be more of a desperate plea for Julia to somehow arrange for them to come to the United States. However, Julia's responses were to feign ignorance or inability to arrange for them to join her, rather than encourage their longing to leave Tuxtepec.

The emails from Adelina had a much different tone. On the one hand, they were like emails between two old friends, reminiscing about old times. However, in more than one email, Adelina referred to having either heard about, or run into, Julia's evil step-father, Pablo Ramírez. She indicated that Ramírez continued to blame Julia for his problems, often citing the scars from her splashing hot grease on his face as the reason he was unable to get a job. Adelina indicated that his anger, often bordering on rage, suggested that he planned to get revenge. No local emails were found.

"With regard to her phone," Dolores explained, "Julia never set up Contacts on either her cell phone or her computer. She had never even set up the voice mail on her cell phone. For all of the incoming calls, we had to conduct a reverse phone lookup to identify the callers. For the most part, the incoming and outgoing calls on her cell phone had a definite pattern. Most of these calls were to and from El Farolito where she worked there. However, she also received calls fairly regularly from Fernando Romero and Randolph Wyman.

"The calls from Fernando continued until the day before her murder. The calls from Wyman stopped about three weeks ago with no subsequent attempts to reach her. Other than these calls, she had received a few others that we have been able to identify as from friends or acquaintances. Many of these calls were to a phone number with a Mexico prefix and an Oaxacan area code. We have not determined whose number this may be.

"Also, there was a flurry of about fifteen calls in a short time period from William Dirschauser, all incoming. The pattern was interesting. The initial few calls lasted anywhere from two to fifteen minutes. Then, a few days after the last lengthy call, it appears that calls were not being picked up by Julia. Almost all of those calls lasted around twenty seconds, just enough for her phone to go to an automated message but Julia had not set up any voice mail capability. None of them were long enough for there to have been a conversation. It would imply that Julia identified his number but no longer wanted to answer his calls. Without any voice mail, there was no record of what he had wanted to tell her."

I said, somewhat disappointed, "That's too bad. It would have been very helpful to know what was on his mind."

"On her phone," Dolores answered, "Julia had a myriad of text messages that were still being analyzed, including to Randolph Wyman. The text messages were brief and mostly about where they could meet to talk. Interesting.

"A few of the text messages were from social friends, with messages like 'meet me at the mall,' or 'do you want to go for coffee?' As you would expect, the more substantive text messages came from Fernando, Dirschauser, Wyman, and a couple from Michele Ronaldi. One was from Josef Castellano, the maître d' at El Farolito.

"We are also able to learn where an individual may have traveled using the cell phone's GPS tracking data. Based on Julia's cell phone GPS information, her traveling activity was primarily within a five-mile radius of her house. This includes areas like the Farmer's Market, the plaza, and El Farolito. Outside of this perimeter, there were only a few other places she went near shopping centers like DeVargas Center mall. The only other exception was Fernando Romero's house north of town. According to her GPS, she lived a fairly simple and consistent life. Basically, most of what we saw was routine and expected. A lot of the information had to do with her work."

"Anything else?" I asked, somewhat disheartened.

Dolores answered, "We are still waiting for the toxicology report. I will let you know just as soon as I do."

There was a lot for us to sort through. We all committed to a deeper debriefing the next day when we had more time to process all that we were reviewing. Satisfied and tired, Miguel signed off and we agreed to communicate with him again tomorrow.

32

I had scheduled a late afternoon time to meet with Bill Dirschauser, aka "William Maestro," at the police station. I had heard of people having stage names, or even pseudonyms for authors, but I have never heard of a newspaper columnist having one, especially one so flamboyant. I was curious to meet "Maestro."

I should have expected that with such a flamboyant pseudonym as "Maestro," Dirschauser would want to make a big impression with his entrance. True to form, he came ten minutes late and walked in with a flair that seemed intended to convey just how important he was. In addition to his air of stuffiness and self-importance, his jacket was draped over his shoulder rather than being worn through his arms over his long sleeve turtleneck. His shoes looked to be designer shoes and he wore a huge bolo tie draped around his neck with a large diamond that showcased a turquoise setting,. His attire was meant to portray personal uniqueness, and it did. Gauche, but definitely unique.

Without apologizing for being late, he reached out to shake my hand, but his wrist was limp, almost begging me to kiss his ring.

Narcissists have an inflated sense of self-importance and usually have a superior and dominant attitude when meeting others. They can be easily offended when their own sense of grandiosity isn't acknowledged by those with whom they meet. For these reasons, I elected to meet him in my office rather than in one of our interview rooms, not wanting to offend his sensibilities. I decided that the best way to interview him was to appear to be initially impressed and only slowly puncture his fragile ego. I showed him to my office and offered him one of two leather chairs, then sat down across from him.

"Well, officer Scotty, how may I be of service?" Dirschauser began, speaking in a slightly nasal tone with his chin raised, almost looking down on me. He seemed like a caricature of an English actor. His reference to me being a police officer, using a nickname for my first name, and trying to look down on me was his way of demonstrating his superiority. I was astounded at how transparent his defenses were.

"It is so nice to meet you, Mr. Dirschauser. And it is 'Doctor Hunter.' I am not a detective, I am a consulting psychologist working with the Santa Fe Police Department. Thank you for coming in," I replied, wanting to offer a welcoming tone while also correcting his misnomer.

"Of course, Doctor Hunter. And please, call me 'William' if you don't mind," he responded.

Knowing I had to salve his ego before I could make any real headway with an interview, I asked him to tell me about himself.

Dirschauser began with a smirk of self-importance, "I would be happy to tell you about my background, Doctor Hunter. I am sure you already know that I am the food editor for the *Santa Fe New Mexican*. I write a weekly column called "Maestro's Musings," about my experiences at various Santa Fe culinary institutions. I am told that my reviews can make or break one of these establishments. Obviously, what I write can change their history. I take my work very seriously."

The first part of the interview was primarily focused on how important he was, how well-connected he was, and how the interview was an imposition because he had more pressing matters to attend to. Like a politician not wanting to answer questions directly, he had become a master at deflection and distraction. I let him drone on until he believed he had convinced me of his prominence. I than began asking him about Julia.

"You have obviously made your mark in Santa Fe," I said with as much of a deferential tone as I could. "What can you tell me about 'El Farolito" and Julia Gomez?"

"Oh, poor child!" he exclaimed. "What a dreadful thing to have happen, and just as El Farolito was beginning to become noticed."

His remark indicated more concern for the reputational damage to the restaurant than the death of Julia. How screwed up was that. Nevertheless, I wanted him to continue.

"Yes," I responded. "Truly dreadful. Tell me anything you may know about either Julia or the restaurant. I know you wrote a very positive review about it within the past ten days or so. You must have researched it carefully."

"As I mentioned," he began with a knowing smile, "I know how important my reviews can be. I saw in Julia a very promising talent. She was also 'easy on the eyes,' if you know what I mean."

"Easy on the eyes?" I asked seeming to be perplexed but internally thinking what a slime Dirschauser was.

"Well," he answered with a smirk, "you must know in my line of work that I often have these young female chefs wanting to court my best opinion. In fact, it is not unusual for them to throw themselves at me in hopes of receiving a positive review."

Taken aback, I quickly countered, "Did Julia 'throw herself at you' to get that good review?"

Gathering himself, he replied, "You must know how it is Doctor Hunter. Women love to associate with powerful men. It happens all of the time in my line of work."

I was shocked. My experience with Julia was that her significant trust issues would not allow her to throw herself at any man, much less one like Dirschauser.

After a momentary pause, he winked at me and continued, "They call me 'Big Willy' for a reason."

Narcissists have great difficulty forming relationships, mostly because they have no empathy, and the relationship has to be all about them. They give little to nothing back. The only long-standing relationships narcissists have are with very dependent, compliant individuals. They regularly exploit people, sometimes to get their ego needs met, sometimes for currency, and sometimes for sex. Their attention spans and patience are always in short supply. Once they have fully milked the relationship, they are on to the next one.

Dirschauser was certainly conforming to the description of a toxic narcissist. It seemed that his Maestro Musing reviews were very transactional and "up for sale." They were a *quid pro quo* unrelated to the quality of an "establishment" or its cuisine. I needed to conduct better research on him and read his previous reviews to look for any additional clues.

I proceeded to ask him for specific information about Julia, but he continued to keep the discussion hypothetical and vague. He began looking at his watch and protesting that he had several other appointments that he needed to honor. I concluded the conversation and decided to think more about how I would approach him in a subsequent interview.

Following much frustration, I grudgingly secured William's

permission to get his fingerprints and a DNA swab to "eliminate him" as a suspect.

I knew that once he had been fingerprinted and a DNA swab had been collected, I did not need to play as nice with him. I would be ready next time.

It was getting close to six., and I was tired and hungry. I texted Maria who was still at the Guadalupe. She vowed to bring home take-out and we could talk over wine and pozole.

33

I decided to check out my private office in the Sena Plaza complex on the way home for any mail or voice messaged I may have received. I continued to maintain a private office for working with some of the corporate clients with whom I continued to consult. As I arrived at my office, I noticed the mail had been placed through the mail chute, mostly junk. The light was blinking on my office phone indicating a couple of voice messages. They were reminders of some upcoming client meetings I was to attend, nothing related to the Julia's case.

My office computer had a couple of recent emails, but nothing of consequence.

As I often do, I took out a note pad and reflected back on the day. There was a lot of information to process including Julia's diary, information from Julia's emails, the interviews with Fernando Romero and the staff at El Farolito, and the interview with Bill Dirschauser, now aka "Big Willy." Even in this early stage of investigation there was a lot to unpack.

First, the Julia with whom I had spoken at the Farmer's Market seemed to be multi-faceted. She was resilient, adaptable, capable, and clever. She had high expectations for herself that she seemed to meet. She could also be flirtatious, bold, and abrasive, and forceful. I imagined that the skills she developed and used to survive on the streets and alleyways in Oaxaca served her well in all sorts of environments. People seemed to look up to her, be threatened by her, and, in some cases, dislike her.

With regard to relationships, I was still uncertain. The abuse she had received in her childhood made her wary and cautious about getting close to people. Understandable, but this wariness did not seem to match the flirtatiousness she was reported to demonstrate on occasion. It also did not explain some of her finer clothing, suitable for parties and dating. Did she have a relationship with someone that we had not yet identified?

Julia's emails and diary also presented some additional questions. Foremost was the identification of "R." I assumed that it was the same "R" in the diary as was on the threatening note Julia had received. I hoped that the forensic team scanning her phone calls and messages would help us identify "R." The information from her emails did not rule out the possible involvement of her stepfather, although this seemed to be a low likelihood. What we had recovered from her computer seemed less promising, mostly recipes.

There was still a lot to uncover, but I was beginning to get a fuller picture of Julia than the one I had earlier. I had more research to conduct and more interviews to facilitate. I was looking forward to tomorrow's activities.

Before leaving to go home, I wanted to get a fuller understanding of Maestro's Musings. On my computer, I went to the *Santa Fe New Mexican* website. I had been a long-time online subscriber, so I was able to access it easily. Fortunately, they had created folders for several of their editors and reviewers' articles. There was one folder identified as Maestro's Musings. I opened the folder and there were several months' worth of reviews. I decided to save them to a digital file and study them prior to our next interview. I had been at the office for over an hour and was ready to go to our comfortable home.

I left for the short drive home. I was eager to be with Maria, have a good meal, and process what we had discovered that day. It had been a long day, and I was tired, but not too tired to take in the beautiful multi-colored sunset. Even having spent most of my life here, the beauty of Santa Fe and the surrounding mountains, sunrises and sunsets never escaped my delight and amazement. It was nice to have a moment's reprieve to enjoy nature's palate before relaxing and having a glass of wine with my beautiful Maria.

As I pulled into my driveway, I was unprepared for that I was about to see.

There, attached to the front door, was a large manila envelope. As I approached the porch, I could see "Scott Hunter-Confidential" written on the outside of the envelope. Since I had just been at the police station, I knew that it could not have come from there. Not having any texts or voice mails that would account for the envelope, I was perplexed and concerned. Who could have left this envelope and why?

Maria had not yet arrived, and I thought it would be good to have a witness to watch me open it. I also wanted to be careful about handling it.

As I exited the car I retrieved a pair of latex gloves out of my glove box. I went to the front door and carefully took the push pin out of the envelope attached to the door. I held the envelope carefully by the corner, opened the door, and took it inside, laying it on the dining room table.

Just about that time, I heard Maria's car in the driveway. Leaving the envelope on the table, I went to help Maria bring in the take-out bags she had with her. The powerful smell of the pozole and green chile momentarily took my thoughts away from the envelope. Catching myself, I told her about the envelope on the door and wanting her to serve as a witness as I opened it. Taking the bags into the kitchen, we went together to the table with me holding the envelope.

As a precaution, I had photographed the envelope with my iPhone prior to opening it.

The envelope was not sealed tightly but secured with a metal clasp. I carefully unclasped the envelope using a pair of tweezers. Holding the opposite corner of the envelope, I emptied the contents onto the table.

There on the table lay a small square envelope and two photographs. Maria shrieked, nearly falling to her knees as she saw the photographs.

Staring back at Maria, the photographs on the table were of her father, Roberto. One was of Roberto leaving the Guadalupe at what appeared to be dusk. He was exiting from the back door. The image was very clear.

The second image was that of Roberto in front of his house as he got out of his car. The time stamp of the photos indicated that they were both taken the same day and within twenty minutes of each other.

What was chilling was that on each photo there was a clear target on Roberto's head. It was the kind of target that would have been in the sights of a rifle.

In the envelope, there was a note, again in block letters, that read:

DOCTOR HUNTER,
IF YOU DON'T WANT YOUR GIRLFRIEND'S FATHER TO
END UP LIKE JULIA, BACK OFF!
NOW!

There was no signature or any other indication of who may have sent it.

Maria's breathing was quick and shallow. She was having an anxiety attack. I quickly got a small paper bag from the kitchen and told Maria to blow into it on the same cadence as my counting.

One, blow in.

Two, breath out,

One, blow in

Two blow out.

After a few seconds of this tempo, Maria's breathing became slower and deeper. Once her breathing had returned to a normal rhythm, she began to sob and grabbed me tightly to hold her.

Sobbing, Maria asked, "Scott, what does this mean? Who would have sent this? What is going on?"

Not having any worthwhile answers, all I could do in the meantime was to hold her as she collapsed into my arms.

After a few moments that seemed longer, Maria said, "Scott, I need to call my father to make sure he is safe."

Maria called Roberto and on the third ring he answered. "Oh padre," Maria cried out, "are you okay?"

Confused, Roberto answered, "Maria, yes, I am fine. Why are you asking?"

Knowing that she could not tell Roberto about the envelope or photos, Maria said, "I just had an intuition that you were not safe. Silly me. But please humor me and make sure you lock all of your doors and be on guard for anything unusual.

Roberto reassured Maria that he would be extra careful, and they vowed to see each other the next day at the Guadalupe.

Once Roberto and Maria finished their brief conversation, Maria sat down and said, "Scott, what have we gotten into?"

I wasn't sure, but this kind of escalation, a threatening note, and the photographs, told me we were agitating someone big time. I was baffled as to who, or what, we were uncovering that caused such a threat, but I knew we were onto something huge.

Now that we knew Roberto was safe, Maria and I decided to have that wine and discuss what we knew over dinner.

Once the adrenaline wore off and the wine took effect, fatigue set in heavily for both of us. We went to bed, cuddled, and fell into a fitful sleep, but not for long.

The ring tone on the incoming iPhone was familiar. It was "Malagueña," the one I had assigned to Miguel. While it was only 4:15

in the morning. Santa Fe time, it was 12:15 in the afternoon in Marbella where Miguel and his "bride" were celebrating. I answered wearily, and warily.

Without his customary greeting, Miguel was quick to exclaim, "Scott what trees have you been shaking? I just had a call from the Chief Trujillo. Mr. Dirschauser called him personally to complain about your interview with him. What the hell is going on?"

I took time to bring Miguel up to date on the interview as well as the envelope and the photos pinned to my door.

With a cautionary note, Miguel encouraged me to continue to investigate and asked me to let Roberto know of his concern.

Miguel continued, "You are clearly on to something. Poke as many bears as necessary, but very carefully. Chief Trujillo feels the same way. Go ahead and conduct all the necessary interviews."

I thanked Miguel for his call and encouraged him to get back to celebrating with his wife.

I elected not to tell Maria about Miguel's "poke as many bears" comment. She was already feeling anxious, especially for her father's safety. No need to stir the pot on the home front.

Because of Dirschauser's complaint to Chief Trujillo, I resolved to get "Big Willy" on my interview schedule as soon as possible.

34

Working with Miguel over the past couple of years as a consulting psychologist, I had learned that sometimes you follow leads, and try to uncover as many clues as possible. Most of this hard work leads to blind alleys but, sometimes, helpful leads or clues come to you unexpectedly. You just need to keep your eyes and ears open to possibilities.

Such was the case when I received an unanticipated call from Michele Ronaldi later that morning. She asked to meet me alone and privately at her home, a small casita in a secluded compound backing up to Canyon Road. Her timing was nearly perfect, following what I had recently learned about her and her employment record in New York City. Given that Maria had determined, through her New York City friend Belinda Brennan, that Michele had a reputation as having quite a temper and difficulty managing her anger, she had moved up on my list of persons of interest.

On my way to Michele's house, I dropped by the police station to deliver the envelope and the photos of Roberto that had been tacked to my door. I wanted forensics to take a closer look to see if there were any clues we might be able to use.

Getting to Michele's house was itself a little adventure. Alameda Street splits into two different roads with the same name, one on the north side of the Santa Fe River and one on the south side. It is a part of the Santa Fe river that is lined with trees and is peaceful. What differentiates the two Alamedas is that odd numbered addresses are on the north paved side of the river. My house is on the north side. Even numbered addresses are on the south side of the river. Very confusing. The Alameda on the south side of the river is a dirt road only three blocks long.

Near the end of this three-block street is an adobe walled conclave with two massive wooden doors, meant to give the appearance of being gated. Behind the open doors are ten small private casitas with a gated fence in back opening up to Canyon Road. It is a unique and unexpected gem of a neighborhood in this secluded location.

Michele's casita was midway between the entrance and the back fence. Her abode had a turquoise painted door with potted plants on either side. It was an inviting entry with a truly Santa Fe style appearance. I knocked on the door and it almost instantly opened, with Michele in a loosely fitting tee shirt, tight-fitting jeans, and her hair in a ponytail. Attractively casual.

The "Santa Fe Style look" continued inside her house with tiled floors, a corner fireplace, and low ceilings with pine vigas and latillas in a herringbone pattern between them. The small kitchen flowed into the living area separated only by a counter with stools tucked neatly into it. The rear wall had windows that looked out to a small, but cozy, enclosed back yard. It was small but definitely had the Santa Fe charm.

Michele directed me to a couch facing the fireplace. After offering me water, she sat down in a cushioned chair facing the side of the couch. Since she had called me, I decided to let her be in charge of the conversation.

I began, "I was interested in your call. Please tell me how I can be of assistance."

Michele responded, "Doctor Hunter, I am taking a real risk talking with you. That is why I wanted to meet you here and not at the restaurant or the police station. Our meeting must be 'off the record' if I am to tell you anything substantive. I am putting my job at risk and even my career. Can I count on you to keep this confidential?"

It is always a conundrum when someone wants information to be "off the record." Essentially the requestor is trying to tie your hands so that any information you receive either cannot be used or cannot implicate them. I view this tactic as passive-aggressive.

With these requests, I am always cautious about giving anyone a carte blanche pass, lest the information be so impactful and compelling that it has to be used and maybe the source revealed. I have learned to give a qualified condition, and I did so here.

"Michele," I began, "we are in the middle of a murder investigation involving Julia. I will keep what you tell me private to the extent that I am able. However, if what you tell me is material to the investigation, I cannot guarantee that what you say will be fully confidential. If this is agreeable to you, we can continue. If it is not, we should end the conversation here."

I knew that if she decided to end the conversation, I could always request that she come to the police station again. I was hoping we would not have to do that.

Michele shifted uneasily in her chair, sighing deeply, and looking down at the floor. After a few seconds, she replied, "Okay, but I expect you to treat what I tell you as a very sacred trust between us."

I agreed, somewhat reluctantly. I knew that I would have to be respectful of her need for privacy and balance that with the need of the investigation to pursue justice.

She had a lot to say, and it pointed me in a completely new direction.

Michele said, "I will start at the beginning. Several years ago, Fernando recruited me from where I was working in New York City to come to Santa Fe to be the head chef at El Farolito. He promised to significantly increase my salary and hinted at the possibility of my becoming a partner in the restaurant."

"A partner," I replied. "What did he mean by that?"

Answering slowly, she said, "It was never clear, but I took it to mean that I would become a part owner when the restaurant became more popular and more profitable. You have to understand that when I came here, the restaurant was a dump. It even had a different name, La Cocina."

"What happened," I queried.

With her face beginning to flush, her neck turning red, and her jaw clenching, she answered, "It took a hell of a lot of work to get the restaurant from really horrible to respectable. We had to change out virtually everything, the menus, the staff, the marketing, and remodeling the dining room. It was truly a redo.

"Once we seemed to be on track to be competitive and a restaurant where locals and tourists would like to come, I approached him about this 'partnership.' But did it do any good?"

"What happened then?" I asked.

Answering angrily, she said, "Every time we hit a milestone, like getting the customer volumes up to a certain number or improving the revenues by a certain amount, I would approach him about being a partner. But he would constantly have a reason to delay, always promising to have a proper conversation about it in the near future. But nothing ever happened."

"Why did you stay," I wondered.

"You have to understand," she said, "in Santa Fe, there are only a handful of restaurants where I would *want* to work. Each of the premier restaurants already had head chefs with a line in back of them to take their place. It is very competitive. Returning to New York wasn't an option, I would have been starting from scratch. Besides, Fernando was paying me well, so I decided to stick it out hoping that he would let me be a part-owner at some point."

"Please continue," I urged her.

Thoughtfully, she responded, "About four years ago, I thought I was close to convincing him. We were solidly a good restaurant. I worked my ass off and it had been a long, hard slog, but we were so much better than we had been. While we had not been able to crack the code of being one of the elites, we were good, but Fernando seemed to have some kind of inferiority complex. He always wanted to be in the 'inner circle' of Santa Fe's best leaders but felt like he was on the outside looking in, and it drove him crazy. He believed that by getting El Farolito identified as one of those premier restaurants, he would finally get the recognition he so desperately wanted."

"You said you were 'close to convincing him,' what happened?" I asked.

Shaking her head, she replied, "Fernando kept me from being a partner, always looking for a miracle that would make a difference. He would read something in a culinary magazine and the next thing I knew, he was wanting us to try some new dish, buy some new fancy kitchen appliance, or make a change to the lighting or ambience in the dining room. He was obsessed.

"He asked to talk to me, and I thought he was going to offer me a partnership but, instead, he told me that he was hiring Julia. I was terribly angry and disappointed, especially after waiting so long."

124

35

As I listened to Michele, I could see her becoming increasingly agitated. An agitated state is a result of "letting your guard down." From an information gathering standpoint, this was a good thing. When people are stressed like this, they tend to say what they are really thinking and feeling. I did not want to diminish her state of irritation.

"That must have hurt," I said wanting her to tell me more.

"You bet it hurt. That bastard Fernando was once again going after some shiny new object hoping to finally grasp the gold ring. This time the answer was Julia, someone that had been working in a food truck for Chrissake! A food truck.

"It not only hurt, but it was a damn insult to have someone with a food truck education in the same kitchen as me, a person with a proven track record and a degree in the culinary arts. Julia was an immigrant no less. I was pissed! What a damn joke."

"How did that work out?" I asked, wanting to continue to gently push.

Julia answered with anger in her voice, "I was so angry when Julia came, that I had her do menial chores. I would not let her cook. I would have her prepare vegetables, clean up the kitchen and, at times, even wash dishes. I was not going to let this uneducated little bitch do anything to screw up what I had worked so hard to achieve.

"She always complied without complaining. It took a while for me to realize that it wasn't her fault, it was Fernando's. I began allowing her to do more in the kitchen and found out that she had some skills that were very good and even complimentary to mine. In fact, she tried some of her Oaxacan recipes and they were very good. But I never quite got over my anger of her being there at all."

It was clear that Michele had not liked Julia, but she still had not told me the impetus for calling me. I needed her to move forward.

Michele continued, "A couple weeks ago," Michele started, I was walking across the Plaza to work. It was early in the morning, about eight. As I walked, something caught my eye that I could not believe. In fact, I had to do a double take in order to be sure."

"What was it you saw?" I asked, very curious now.

"Well," Michele answered, "there on one of the benches was Julia sitting and drinking coffee with Randolph Wyman. I was shocked that there, in broad daylight, Julia was talking with that self-absorbed jerk."

I had heard about Randolph Wyman from Maria and conversations she had with her father. I did not want to play that card just yet, so I feigned ignorance.

"Randolph Wyman?" I asked. "Who is he and why was this surprising to you?"

"He has a restaurant a few blocks south of the Plaza, named Rojas." Michele answered. "It is a building that has had several failures and resurrections as a restaurant but has never seemed to 'get over the hump' of being successful. It was in a great location but always seemed to be "on the verge" of collapse. In fact, it had been rumored that the restaurant had been a mafia front for laundering money, but I never saw this confirmed."

"Given that you referred to him as a 'self-absorbed jerk,' I take it you did not like him." I stated.

Replying with a smirk on her face, Michele said, "Randolph always came across as being wealthy, worldly, and important. He would brag about the great schools he had attended, how well-known his family was back east, and how much he had traveled. He could never see the incredible discrepancy between how he presented himself as being highly successful and now owning a dump of a restaurant. In fact, his restaurant made El Farolito look like royalty, even in its worst days. He seemed harmless enough and was really thought of as a clown behind his back."

"Why would he have been talking to Julia?" I questioned.

"Isn't it obvious?" Michele answered cynically. "He desperately needed a creative chef to pull Rojas out of the years of being in Santa Fe's restaurant hell, or should I say irrelevance.

"See, just like Fernando poached me out of New York to resurrect his pitiful restaurant into what is now one of significance, Randolph needed something similar for Rojas. Every successful restaurant has at its foundation someone in the kitchen who has strong culinary capabilities and can create dishes that are unique, creative and, most of all, pleasing to the palate.

"You can create all of the ambience you want in the front of the house, linen tablecloths and napkins, well trained and well-presented wait staff, a welcoming maître d', and soothing music. But if the food tastes like shit, you will not rise above mediocre and never develop a following."

"So, you think he was trying to entice Julia to become his head chef at Rojas?" I asked.

"Duh." Julia said sarcastically. "Of course that is what he was trying to do."

"Did you ever ask Julia about her conversations with Wyman?" I asked.

"Of course." Michele answered. "I ask her about her conversation right away and she denied there was anything serious to their meeting. I wanted to warn her that he was up to no good, but she did not want to talk about it, so I let it go. He had tried that same crap with me."

"What do you mean?" I asked, now more curious than before.

"He called me to drop by Rojas about a month ago," she started. I have no idea how he got my number, but I was inquisitive. So, one afternoon when I was out running errands, I dropped by Rojas and met with him briefly. He invited me to come to his small office off the kitchen and have a cup of coffee with him. In fact, it was really weird. Both the dining room and the kitchen looked old and tired, but his office looked like a lawyer's or an executive's office."

"How so?" I enquired puzzled.

Sneering and shaking her head, she replied, "His office was large with a polished wood floor that was covered with Navajo rugs. The walls were covered with high end southwestern art. He had a very nice desk with a fancy executive chair, and two comfortable leather chairs in the front of the desk. It was completely unlike any kitchen office I had ever seen. It looked like he had created an office to show any visitors how successful he was, but it had the opposite effect. It was like seeing a mansion in the middle of a neighborhood with poor shacks. The weirdest thing was that he did not see just how crazy this was.

"After talking about nothing important for a few minutes, he pointed to the kitchen and said, 'This could all be yours if you came over to join me. We could do great things together.' He could not see the incredible difference between his opulent office and the shabby kitchen, much less what he was asking me to do. It was bizarre.

"Besides, I had already been through this once with Fernando at El Farolito. Why in God's name would I want to do it again? I felt like laughing at his offer, but I simply told him I already had a job."

"Did that seem to satisfy him?" I enquired.

"Not at all." Michele answered. "In fact, he tried harder to sell me on the idea. He initially looked for similarities we both had, both of us being from the east coast and both of us being ambitious. Then he hinted at a possible partnership in the future, just like Fernando had done. I was struck by how similar their tactics had been. The difference was that after not having been able to 'close the deal,' with me, he started getting angry and threatening."

"Threatening?" I probed.

Now, sitting on the edge of her seat, Michele said, "He threatened that if I didn't work for him, he would make my life hell. He said he would spread rumors that I was a slut and had 'slept my way to the top' with Fernando. He would also tell people that I was a bitch and impossible to get along with. It was striking how quickly he changed from being nice to becoming menacing.

"Little did he know that his methods were solidifying my determination that there was no way in hell that I would work with him. Just before I was about to leave, he became more conciliatory, said he was just kidding about the threat, and he would love to have me as his business partner. He asked me to, at least, take time to consider his offer before saying 'no.' But by then, I had already made up my mind."

Just then I heard my iPhone ping, indicating I had a new text message. Looking down at my phone, it was from Dolores and said, "Important. Call me as soon as you can."

I said to Michele, "Please excuse me, I have a quick call I need to make."

Michele graciously led me to her back patio to make the call.

36

Dolores answered on the first ring.

"What is it, Dolores?" I asked.

"I just received the toxicology report from the lab, and we have some very interesting results. Remember that I ordered toxicology screens on Julia as well as on the contents of the two cocktail glasses found on the table near the body. I received the results from those screens and was able to piece together a clear summary of what has been found."

"What did the lab results tell you," I asked eagerly.

"As we expected," Dolores began, "Julia had ingested a copious amount of the distilled alcohol mezcal. In addition, the lipstick on the cocktail glass found on the table near Julia's body matched her DNA. It is clear that Julia had been drinking prior to her death.

"Also, the autopsy determined that, prior to death, Julia had experienced difficulty breathing, likely a seizure, vomiting, and finally death. Her body also had *cyanosis*, or blue lips and fingernails."

"Did the ingestion of copious amounts of mezcal cause all of this?" I asked perplexed.

"Did I say, 'copious amounts?'" Dolores responded. "Actually, the cause of these symptoms, and her death, surprised even me.

"The toxicology screen indicated that Julia had an unusual chemical in her body, tetrahydrozoline, that was the likely cause of death. Tetrahydrozoline is a compound often found in over-the-counter eye drops and nasal sprays. It belongs to a family of compounds known for their ability to induce chemical reactions that either relax or constrict blood vessels. It is this effect on the nervous system which puts tetrahydrozoline in the "neurotoxic" category."

"You mean that eye-drops killed Julia?" I asked incredulously.

Dolores replied, "Tetrahydrozoline poisoning can occur only when the product is swallowed. In sufficient amounts, it can cause death. Julia ingested a large enough amount at one time to have killed her. We found traces of the tetrahydrozoline in both cocktail glasses as well as in what was left in the bottle of mezcal."

As Dolores explained these findings, I thought about what Ed, and I had discovered. There had been several bottles of eye drops in her medicine cabinet at her house and in her locker at work. Was it possible that Julia had mixed her eyedrops with her drink and committed suicide? If so, who was the other glass on the table for? Why then was her purse opened? Had there been money or credit cards stolen?

Shivers ran down my spine. Since Julia was expecting me, could the other cocktail glass have been for me? It did not make sense that she would be trying to harm me or harm herself.

Wanting to return to Michele, I indicated to Dolores that we could discuss the case further when I returned to the station.

It was shocking and confusing information.

37

Returning into Michele's house, I apologized for the interruption. Remembering where we had left off, I was still very confused by what she had told me. If Michele did not like Julia, why would she want to warn Julia about Wyman. In fact, why wouldn't she encourage him?

"Help me understand this a little better. If you did not care for Julia, why would you want to warn her about Wyman? It would seem like you would encourage her to go?" I asked.

Slowly, she replied, "I was beginning to warm up to Julia. We had incorporated some of her recipes on the menu and customers seemed to like them. It was shortly after another incident that things between us changed for the worse."

"What happened?"

With her tone suddenly becoming harder, Michele said, "It was after that absolutely false and bullshit review in Maestro's Musing in the *Santa Fe New Mexican* that I really got pissed."

Again, feigning ignorance, I asked "False review?"

With vitriol in her voice, Michele said, "That asshole gave the restaurant a five-star review, citing that Julia's Oaxacan-infused recipes had taken El Farolito from an also-ran to one of the best culinary experiences in Santa Fe. He went on and on about what an outstanding chef she was and how she had almost single-handedly put the restaurant on Santa Fe's food map. I barely got mentioned, and it had been my hard work that had saved the restaurant in the first place.

"I was furious. When I confronted Fernando, all he did was try to placate me. I was sure that Julia must have made some kind of kinky promise to the reviewer, 'Big Willy' as he is called, in order to get this great review. I was ready to walk, leave El Farolito, and even leave Santa Fe altogether."

I queried, "What kept you here?"

"You can guess. Once again, Fernando promised that he would soon offer me some kind of equity in the business. So, I relented." She said halfway defeated.

"Okay," I replied and asked, "but why did you refer to Bill Dirschauser as 'Big Willy?'"

Michele responded, "In the restaurant business, evaluations by well-read reviewers can make or break both restaurants and chefs. Dirschauser was known in Santa Fe circles to trade 'favors' for positive reviews. In addition, when these 'favors' were not granted, you could expect to see scathing reviews in his column. While he was not highly respected, he was feared. The name 'Big Willy' was meant to be a behind the back joke because he was known for trading sexual favors for good reviews. He got wind of this nickname, and it was rumored that he actually took pride in it.

"I was sure that Julia had negotiated something with Dirschauser, or 'dirt bag' as we called him, to get such a great review. There had been rumors that Julia would occasionally flirt with customers and others to win their approval. I thought she had done the same with Dirschauser. I was beside myself with anger. I wanted to strangle her."

Realizing what she had just said, she corrected, "I never would have done that, but I felt like it."

Embarrassed for having let her guard down, Michele said, "Anyway, I thought you should know about Julia's talk with Randolph Wyman and my suspicions regarding 'Big Willy.' It could be nothing, but that is for you to decide. I know that if it gets out that I am the source for any of this information, I could be the next bad review in Maestro's Musing."

With that conclusion Michele looked at her watch and said she had to get to the restaurant. She showed me the door, and I was on my way.

Just before leaving, as an afterthought, I asked, "Michele, did Julia ever complain about her eyes? We found eyedrops in her locker."

Laughing, Michele replied, "She was always using eyedrops. She said that the climate in Santa Fe was so much drier than in Oaxaca, so she needed to lubricate her eyes. In fact, we joked behind her back that she used the drops so much that they might ruin some of her best dishes."

I thanked Michele for the information and departed. She had confirmed, to some extent, the high number of eyedrop bottles we had found in Julia's locker and at her house. Because everyone knew about

Julia's high usage of eye drops, anybody could have poisoned Julia. This did not answer specifically how the tetrahydrozoline poisoning occurred.

Even though I had not taken Michele off my list of suspects, I now had others to consider, which confirmed the importance of my meeting with Bill Dirschauser, a.k.a. 'Big Willy.'

I knew what my next move had to be. I called Sergeant Apodaca at the police station requesting that he "invite" Dirschauser to the station for an additional "informational interview."

38

I made my way to my Sena Plaza office to do some research prior to interviewing Dirschauser again, still pondering my interview with Michele.

Although Michele seemed convincing, I was not ready to rule her out. The reputation she had in New York city about not controlling her temper, competitiveness, and manipulation of others, still kept her in the frame for Julia's murder. She even said to me that she had felt like "strangling" Julia. Whether that was just metaphoric or real, she was obviously very angry with her. Angry enough to murder her? A big step.

The Restauranteur Randolph Wyman added a new twist to the situation. There was a desperation about him. The fact that he had spoken with Roberto to try and develop some kind of restaurant alliance between the Guadalupe and Rojas was strange, to say the least. Wyman had very little to offer Roberto and much more to gain, but it seemed like a frantic long-shot for respectability or success. Wyman seemed to be a pitiful person in so many ways.

I wondered if Wyman had an angry disposition like Michele described. What kind of relationship did he and Julia develop? Business or personal, or none at all? Was this another dead end or maybe the lead we had been looking for? I would have to revisit Wyman's involvement in the near future. Right now, I had something more pressing to focus on, as I was about to interview "Big Willy" again, and I wanted to be prepared.

I prefer conducting computer research in the quiet of my office rather than at the police station, surrounded by hustle, noise, and drama. I had electronically archived several articles from Maestro's Musing to identify any trends that could be revealing.

I had already identified Dirschauser as having strong narcissistic tendencies. Narcissists deceive, manipulate, and exploit without regard for the truth or facts. They are very skilled at twisting and massaging information to justify their behavior, with little regard as to how they hurt or offend. At their core they are highly insecure. Their behavior is always in pursuit of shoring up their weak egos, trying to impress and to get others to admire them, no matter what the cost.

When narcissists imagine they are challenged, they have strong urges for retribution and long memories. Heaven help the person who gets in their way.

I wasn't sure what I was looking for as I scrolled through the Maestro's Musing reviews. I typically look for themes that paint a picture of what an individual is like. Narcissists can't hide their tendencies, either in person or in their writing. They can't keep from regularly citing their self-importance, nor can they refrain from criticizing those they despise.

The veracity of this behavior was evidenced time and again in Dirschauser's reviews. He regularly used exaggerated language to either praise or condemn restaurants, food, recipes, waitstaff, and chefs. Nothing went unaddressed in his appraisals. He also never failed to have at least one reference to the expertise he claimed to possess, the accolades he had received, and how fortunate the establishment was to have him as their reviewer.

Even when he seemed to post something positive in a negative review, the effect was "damning with faint praise." He wrote things like "at least the soup was hot," or "I didn't have to wait too long," to get his plate delivered. There was a viciousness when he condemned and an ebullience when he praised.

When I researched his column on El Farolito, it followed the same pattern. However, he was effusive in his praise of both Julia's culinary genius as well as the exquisite flavors he experienced in her dishes. He gushed about the presentation of his plate as "a piece of art that challenged the Mona Lisa." He was also very positive about the ambience. He added one sentence citing Fernando for "his foresight and visionary thinking" in hiring Julia.

Not a single mention was made about Michele or any dishes that were created by any employees other than Julia. It was easy to see why Michele felt slighted and angry, especially in light of the years prior to Julia's arrival that she had worked successfully to raise the restaurant's standards and profile in the community.

I wanted to understand Dirschauser better. First, I wanted to understand if his reviews actually had a real impact on both restaurants and chefs. I also wanted to understand more about his personal history. I went to two data sources for this information.

First, I wanted to see how his reviews actually impacted restaurant volumes. I visited the Santa Fe Restaurant Association's (SFRA) data base. Restaurants of any consequential size were members of SFRA. It was a members-only website to which I had been granted access. The restaurants did not report financial data like revenue, margins, et cetera. They did report percentage changes in customer volume, both month over month and month compared to the same month in previous year. It was a treasure trove of information.

I categorized his reviews into one of three groups as either exceptionally good, exceptionally bad, or mediocre. I was interested in whether there were customer volume changes in those restaurants as a result of his reviews.

It did not take long to see a strong pattern. Those restaurants rated exceptionally good had between a twenty and forty percent *increase* in customer volumes over the following four to six months.

On the other hand, those establishments rated exceptionally bad reported between a thirty and fifty percent decrease in volume. Furthermore, it took these restaurants more than six months to recover back to pre-review volumes, and some never did. I was shocked.

I remembered a business guru once saying that when people have a good experience with a business, they will tell three to five others about it. However, those having a bad experience will tell between ten and fifteen others. This also seemed to be the case with Dirschauser's reviews.

I was stunned to see the impact of his words. The data confirmed that, even though he was a despicable narcissist, he had a huge influence in the local restaurant world. I could see why people would want to curry his favor and, especially, not want to cross him. When narcissists are "winning," they begin to believe that they are bullet proof and can't be deterred. I wondered if Julia had somehow crossed Dirschauser and may not have "paid" for her exuberant review.

Second, wanting to understand more about William Dirschauser, the man, I went to the National Criminal Information Center database. This was always my go-to source for tracking criminal-related information. It was the same one I had used when looking at Julia's past. I did not expect to find anything on Dirschauser. How wrong I was.

I searched "William Dirschauser" in the NCIC database. To my astonishment, his name came up several times and all at different locations.

Prior to coming to Santa Fe, there had been arrest warrants for Dirschauser in Davenport and Des Moines, Iowa, and Lincoln and Topeka, Kansas. Dirschauser had been a very busy and very bad, boy. Accusations ranged from simple assault to domestic violence and, even, attempted rape. Every occurrence involved Dirschauser and a single female.

In each case, police reports identified a different woman with whom Dirschauser had gotten into altercations, both parties claiming that the other was at fault. The women were all unmarried and the typical clash appeared to have been preceded by outings at bars ending up in either Dirschauser's or the women's homes.

The exception was the one attempted rape charge which occurred at night and in a parked car. In all instances, the woman had initiated a nine-one-one call. However, all charges had ultimately been dropped with the women failing to file charges. The details of each police intervention were remarkably similar. I was able to download photos of all of the women complainants from the database. Some of them were accompanied by pictures of bruises on their bodies.

There had been one outlier in Davenport. There had been a heated exchange between Dirschauser and an unhappy restaurant owner over one of Dirschauser's reviews. The exchange became physical and while the charges were dropped, there had been a restraining order requiring Dirschauser never to go to the restaurant or discuss the restaurant in his column again.

I then looked at Dirschauser's employment record during this same time period. Unsurprisingly, Dirschauser had been working for a number of small local newspapers and was somewhat a "jack of all trades," writing various stories of local interest. However, he had not been restaurant reviewer, at least not on a regular basis. His employment duration always coincided with his legal problems, and it appeared that he had either been dismissed or had resigned from his positions shortly following the reported altercations.

Of particular interest was that, in three of the newspaper positions, he also authored the "Police Beat," reporting on any criminal activity followed by the local police department. I wondered if he had been able to charm his way into the hearts of the local police officials to assist getting charges dropped. His call into Chief Trujillo may have been his way of trying to undermine our interviews and attempt to elicit the Chief's favor. Regardless, it hadn't worked.

I now was prepared for our meeting and looking forward to learning just how Dirschauser would react.

39

Living up to his reputation, Dirschauser was again "fashionably late" by ten minutes. He strode in as he had done previously but, this time, with more of that attitude that suggested he was "one up" on me, having complained to the Chief. I had not noticed earlier the strong scent of cologne on Dirschauser. With his cheap aftershave, slicked back greasy hair, brushed leather sport coat draped over his shoulders, and his faux alligator shoes, he fit the definition of sleazy.

He was clearly agitated, and the previous air of self-importance had been replaced by a clear sense of anger. With narcissists, when they can't "baffle you with their bullshit," they try to "bluster you with their bravado." He was now in a full-blown state of self-righteousness and indignation, challenging me as to why a person of his statue and importance should be subject to yet another interview.

Little did he know that Chief Trujillo was secretly delighted that our previous interview had bothered him enough for him to register a complaint.

I was ready. I led Dirschauser to an interview room. No special treatment this time. I had with me a file folder with information I had gleaned from the NCIC database, incriminating photos, and a pen and pad to take notes.

During the initial part of the interview, I massaged his ego just enough to get him to let his guard down. He actually began to tout how his position as a food critic gave him great access to the "lovelies" as he called women whom he had reviewed. He seemed to take delight that his status allowed him great liberties with women.

As I feigned marveling at his ability to manipulate women, particular restaurant owners, sommeliers, chefs, and sous chefs in exchange for favorable reviews. He couldn't seem to help himself from being braggadocious and forthcoming. He justified his exploitations by explaining how lucky these women were to have received any attention from someone of his stature and influence. In other words, they were fortunate to have been the recipient of his attention at all. Unbelievable.

After allowing Dirschauser some time to gloat, we discussed his involvement with Julia. Smirking, he said that his review was intended to set off an internal firestorm at *El Farolito*. He wanted to see if he could "stir the pot" and influence Fernando to promote Julia to the head chef while dispensing with Michele. Winking at me, he indicated that he and Julia had "created an alliance."

"An alliance?" I asked.

Leering at me, Dirschauser said, "Well, a quid pro quo if you prefer. I give her an outstanding review and the opportunity to move into the head chef position in exchange for something I would like in return."

"And that would be what?" I queried.

Folding his arms across his chest and leaning back in his chair grinning, he responded "I think that is obvious, don't you Doctor Hunter?"

Unable to stop himself, he continued, "I thought my intentions with Julia were clear when we first discussed our 'alliance.' But somehow, she misunderstood. The language difference I presumed. When I approached her after the rather gushy review in my column, she did nothing but rebuff my advances. I was pissed to say the least. I am sure you can understand."

I decided that now was the time to push Dirschauser. As most narcissists are skilled at doing, he was an expert in getting under the skin of people to get the responses he wanted. I had to admit to myself that he was beginning to get under mine. He was despicable, but I knew I had to keep my cool and lead with my mind and not my emotions.

"Tell me, Mister Dirschauser, have these advances in the past ever been discouraged?" I started, knowing the multiple arrests but no convictions.

"Of course not," he replied, almost indignant.

Then opening his arms wide, he said with an evil look in his eyes, "Who would ever want to refuse this. My 'agreements' with the recipients of my favorable reviews have been willingly and greatly appreciated."

Trying hard to keep my composure, I continued, "I wonder if you could help me with the identities of some photos I have? This may help me better understand Julia's situation."

I knew that, in reality, the photos had no direct tie to Julia's homicide.

I wanted to see how Dirschauser would behave when presented with the photos of women he had been accused of having abused. Would he deny? Obfuscate? Get angry? I wanted him to know that I was on to him and that his manipulative ways had met their match. I also wanted to see if his anger could have escalated with Julia to the point that he could have murdered her, even accidentally.

Believing, as narcissists do, that he was the smartest person in the room, he answered confidently, "I would be happy to help the police any way I can. Julia's death has been such a shock to all of us. With all of the people I know, I can probably provide you great assistance."

On that note, I reached into my file folder and pulled out the photo of the first woman, the one who had alleged that Dirschauser had raped her in Davenport, but later dropped charges. I slowly pushed the photo of the woman, covered in bruises, in front of Dirschauser.

As he pulled the photo closer, I could see his body stiffen as he examined her facial features. He turned a ghostly white, his breathing became shallow, and he promptly stood up.

"I don't know what the hell you are trying to do here, doctor," he said stiffly, "but this interview is over. If you want to see me in the future, it will have to be with my attorney present."

Then he gathered himself and walked briskly out of the interview room. It looked like I had once again 'poked a bear.'

As Dirschauser left, huffing his way down the hall to the exit, Dolores Griego spotted me and reminded me it was time for our daily rundown with Miguel.

40

Ed, Dolores, and I met for our afternoon debriefing, having reached Miguel on a video call.

Upon further study of the crime scene, one of Ed's men discovered one unusual finding on the door opposite the one which I had entered. I had related having heard someone exiting a side door, and Ed's team had identified a scuff mark on the recently repainted door frame and a thread attached to a splinter on the door.

The big finding from Dolores' people was that the note paper and envelope that Julia had received at the restaurant, and the note paper and envelope inside of the larger envelope tacked to the door of my house, came from the same place. They were unmistakably the same high-end paper and envelopes and had likely come from the same stationery store. She was following this lead, maybe the most promising so far.

I briefed everyone on the discussion I had with Michele Ronaldi and my intent to follow up with the individual Michele had named, Randolph Wyman. We discussed the contentious relationship between Michele and Julia as well as Michele's history in New York. They were particularly interested in the pattern that Michele had of periodically blowing up and either quitting her job or getting fired. In fact, as far as I could tell, Michele's employment at El Farolito was the longest she had in over a decade. Either she was learning to manage her temper, or she was past due to erupt.

I also reported my research on Dirschauser and our subsequent interview. His prior run-ins with vulnerable women and subsequent arrests definitely kept him at the top of our list as a suspect. The fact that, in his opinion, Julia had not fulfilled her end of their "agreement" made him an especially strong person of interest.

We were beginning to assemble a critical mass of clues and hypotheses, but we still had a long way to go.

Miguel encouraged us to follow our leads. He was especially interested in the content of Julia's emails. He also requested that we look deeper into her calendar for any regularly scheduled meetings she may have been having. He closed by saying he believed the trees we were shaking were beginning to yield some fruit. I hoped he was right.

41

I had a strong sense of fatigue come over me. It was late afternoon, but it already seemed like it had been a long day. I texted Maria to meet me at the Patio Restaurant at *La Posada*, not far from my office where I needed to make a stop. Early in our relationship, Maria and I agreed that even though her family owned the Guadalupe restaurant, we would not let that keep us from going to other places to dine. In fact, we often felt like we did not have any privacy at the Guadalupe because of Maria's father, Roberto, owning it. Tonight, I needed to talk to Maria without any distractions.

I planned to visit Randolph Wyman the next day and, before dinner, I returned to my office to conduct some research on him.

I am always surprised by what you can find out on the internet, even without accessing the NCIC database.

I typed Wyman's name into my browser and was surprised to see several references to him and his family. I was able to determine that Wyman had come from a "blue blood" family, one of wealth, privilege, and power. His father, Jackson Wyman, was the CEO of Security Insurance, a national insurance company headquartered in Boston. The company had been founded by his great-grand father and had been in the family ever since. Jackson had been involved in Boston philanthropy and politics.

Randolph's journey had not been one that followed that of his family. In fact, he had been in and out of trouble since his youth. It appeared that he had been "removed" from several schools, including college. Trouble seemed to follow him wherever he went. Of note was an incident that took place when Randolph was in high school in a private academy outside of Boston. There was reference to the death of a co-ed, a girl of sixteen, at which Randolph and three other male friends were present. The circumstances of the death were hazy, and the involvement of Randolph and the other males was unclear. Nevertheless, he did not survive that school term and went to another shortly thereafter.

His teenage years into his early twenties were characterized by several incidences of DUIs, shoplifting, loitering, and petty theft. In every case, it appeared that charges were not brought, and he had served no probationary or jail time. There was a period of time when there were no references to him. However, in the six years, prior to coming to Santa Fe, he had been involved in some minor drug use and bar fights. Since he had been in Santa Fe, his record was clean. I believed I had enough background information on him to conduct an informal interview the next day.

Now it was time to meet Maria. La Posada is located near our house, so I elected to drive the short distance rather than walk.

La Posada is an upscale Resort and Spa located just three blocks from the Santa Fe Plaza. The hotel dates back to eighteen hundred eighty-two when Abraham Staab, a merchant, built a three-story brick mansion on the property that now houses the hotel and a series of pueblo-style adobe casitas. The hotel has restaurants, bars, and an outdoor patio which are very popular with locals and tourists. It is a convenient and comfortable place for us to meet.

When I arrived at the Patio Restaurant, the evening was still warm enough to eat outdoors. There were a couple of kiva fireplaces already glowing and warm. The red umbrellas protecting the small cozy tables provided a lovely romantic ambience. Maria had already arrived and ordered a margarita for me. I needed something to help me relax. Maria and a margarita were just the ticket.

For the time being, I took my mind off the events of the day while we dined and enjoyed being together again. I felt like I could breathe again, at least for a while.

42

The next day, I decided to try and catch Wyman on his own territory rather than have a formal interview at the police station. When interviewed in familiar surroundings, people tend to let their guard down and present themselves less defensively. I went to his restaurant, Rojas, at a time that I thought would be the end of their lunch crowd, hoping to catch Wyman as activity slowed down. Little did I know that crowds of diners were never a problem at Rojas, and it appeared that I could have come at any time.

As Michele Ronaldi had cited in our previous conversation, the restaurant was in a prime location, just a block south of the plaza and adjacent to the Saint Julian hotel. Surprisingly, as I entered through the front door, the interior seemed "tired" and had seen better days. The floor had aged Saltillo tile and the booths had benches of faux leather. Old fans hung down from the faded tin tiled ceiling. It had the appearance of a seventy's scene with neither the traditional Santa Fe style nor a more modern, sleeker look. It was begging to be refreshed.

The restaurant was mostly empty, late for lunch and too early for happy hour. There was no maître d' and I had to wait until a staff member approached me. When she did, just mumbling, she guided me to a corner booth and handed me a menu on yellowed wrinkled paper that also seemed old and worn. The room was dimly lit and there was only one other booth occupied by customers that appeared to be ready to depart.

The menu was as sparse as the surroundings and, not wanting a heavy meal, I ordered a bowl of chile and an Arnold Palmer. The service was slow, the waitstaff minimally attentive, and the drink seemed to be watered down. The experience was odd and quite lacking to be in such

146

a competitive culinary market as Santa Fe. The ambience was obviously neglected, needing freshening up and down. I wondered if the conversation that Michele had witnessed between Wyman and Julia included plans to update the restaurant as well as bring it to life with her exemplary dishes. Hmm.

As I was finishing my meal, I asked the waitress if I could speak with Mister Wyman on the pretense that I wanted to personally thank him for my fine dining experience. She stared at me, maybe in amazement that I could have found the experience rewarding in any way, then gave me the check and said she would get him.

In just a few minutes, Wyman appeared. He did not look the part of what I expected from either a blue blood easterner or a restaurant owner. He seemed to be in his forties, was a bit disheveled, and was wearing faded blue jeans, untucked denim shirt, and scuffed loafers. His wrinkled, drawn face gave a despairing air to him, like he had lived a rough life. And from my research, I knew that he had.

I introduced myself and my relationship to the Santa Fe Police Department. I explained my interest in talking with him, especially about Julia. I tried to sound casual, wanting the conversation to seem informal so as not to provoke him to lawyer-up.

With some hesitation, he agreed to talk and then encouraged me to look around at the restaurant. He said that the meaning of Rojas, derived from "rojo" meaning red in Spanish, is often associated with passion and vitality. However, the restaurant showed no signs of vitality.

After a very brief tour, he invited me back to his office. As Michele had described, his office seemed out of place. The rest of the restaurant was worn and shabby, but his office was more fitting for a law firm. The walls had polished dark wood wainscoting going half-way up each wall. On the walls above the wainscoting, large Native American paintings were hung, and the floors had strategically placed Navajo rugs. I noticed that the office was completely absent of anything of a personal nature, no family photos, diplomas, or citations. In that sense, it was more like a museum than an office.

He invited me to sit down in a plush chair opposite his desk and asked me if I would like a drink. I noticed on his desk a highball glass with a clear liquid and a sphere ice.

He offered, "I have vodka, gin, bourbon, mezcal, and scotch. I'm having gin and tonic. What's your pleasure?"

It was mid-afternoon, too early for a drink. I wanted to be clear headed and declined for the moment. I also thought it was notable that he was already drinking. I had not smelled alcohol on his breath, so I surmised that he was drinking either gin or vodka.

Behind his desk was a credenza with several bottles of alcohol partially hidden behind a sliding door. Only the best, including Beefeater gin, Smirnoff vodka, Woodford Reserve bourbon, and Johnnie Walker Gold Label scotch. I was certain his selection of alcohols was a vestige of his affluent upbringing. Only the best and meant to impress. I also noticed the mezcal he had was the same brand I had seen in Julia's locker. I wondered if this could this simply be a coincidence, or was there something else to consider?

Even though I had been prepared for the contrast between his office and the rest of the poorly tended restaurant and kitchen, it was still a shock. Even more appalling was Wyman's apparent nonchalance or lack of awareness of how the opulence of his office contrasted with the rest of the interior.

This gave me some insight into Wyman's emotional intelligence, or lack thereof. It was like driving a Lamborghini through the ghettos. There were people making minimum wage working in Wyman's restaurant while he flaunted his affluence just steps away. I wondered why anyone would want to work for him since I doubted he could pay them well.

His situation especially brought to mind the difficulty that sons of very successful fathers often had making their own mark in life. Having to live up to their father's affluence, status, and expectations could be both grueling and personally crushing. Sons of very accomplished fathers often had identity problems. They carry their father's name so there was likely to be the expectation that the son would live up to the father's reputation. It could be very difficult for these sons to develop their own identity and they may even rebel instead.

Secondly, the careers of very successful fathers often do not allow for them to spend much time at home. One of the reasons for their success is that they have poured themselves into their work. In these instances, they inadvertently become absent parents. Their demands and expectations of their sons are not met with a commensurate level of support and guidance, leaving their sons to fend for themselves.

As I sat in Wyman's office, I wondered if it had been a tribute to his father. Was it a way in which he could show his father how successful he was and that he had established himself independently? Unfortunately, it was more of a "putting lipstick on a pig" analogy.

I actually felt sorry for Wyman. He was a very emotionally damaged, and angry, individual whose unfortunate way of garnering attention was to act out and rebel. Buying Rojas had been his lame attempt to prove that his father was wrong about him. Unfortunately, so far it had backfired. He knew nothing about the restaurant business but was determined to show that he had not made a mistake. Instead, he was confirming all of his father's doubts.

As we began our conversation, Wyman acknowledged that he had become aware of Julia's cooking prowess and had reached out to her to consider being the head chef at Rojas with the possibility of becoming an equity partner. She was initially interested, and they had several clandestine discussions about how Rojas could become one of Santa Fe's best restaurants. They had discussed drastically upgrading the kitchen to accommodate an equally upgraded menu, one suited to Julia's skills.

Wyman reported that Julia had insisted on refurbishing the entire dining room, including floors, ceilings, seating arrangements and décor. Wyman said that Julia often cited *Los Danzantes*, a restaurant she had worked at in Oaxaca, as her reference. According to Wyman, they had worked it out, at least theoretically. He figured out how he could secure financing and said he was genuinely excited, until it all fell apart.

"What happened," I asked.

Slowly, and with a halting, slightly shaky voice, Wyman answered, "I texted her, like I usually did, to meet me at our usual place to finalize our plan. She didn't respond. I texted her several more times, and she never replied. Then my text messages began to show 'Not Delivered.' At that point I assumed that she had blocked me."

"That must have been disappointing," I said.

"I was gutted," he responded. "I felt like Julia was my best chance for making Rojas really special. I felt like she had led me on. To tell you the truth, I was really angry! I had gone out on a limb to secure financing, spent numerous hours planning, and then I got dumped."

I was aware that he had not yet alluded to Julia's murder, but rather how much he had been "wronged." It was a very interesting series of comments and I had to follow up.

"Can you tell me when you heard about Julia's murder?" I asked.

I knew this should have been an easy question regarding the recency of her homicide, and one which I thought would have elicited a quick response. Instead, Wyman lifted his head to the ceiling as if he had to think about it.

"I think I heard about it the morning after her death." He replied haltingly. "Yes, now that I think about it, I had just gotten up, was brewing some coffee. I always like to hear the local news when I get up. There on the screen was a picture of Julia and the newscaster mentioned that she had been murdered. I was dumbfounded. I couldn't believe it."

"Do you know of anyone who may have wanted to hurt Julia?" I probed.

Again, thinking before talking, Wyman responded, "A month ago, I wouldn't have believed anyone would have wanted to harm her. But after what she did to me, I am not so sure."

Persisting, I asked, "Well, is there a person you know, or have heard about, that would have wanted to have hurt her?"

"No, not anyone in particular. But with the way she dumped me, " he said, arms out and hands to the ceiling, trying to demonstrate that he had been victimized. I decided to press him to see how he might react to a more direct question.

"Mister Wyman," I challenged, "I know that in your past, you have had some run-ins with the law and even some that have involved physical altercations. I also know from what you just told me that you were very angry with Julia. Did you kill her?"

For a moment, the air was thick with anticipation and the room very silent. Wyman turned pale, slumped back in his chair before raising his head and saying, "Doctor Hunter, Are you trying to accuse me of Julia's murder? I think I am going to need my lawyer and so this conversation is over."

Without saying another word, he rose from his chair and pointed to the door of his office, indicating it was time for me to leave.

I found my way out, through the now vacant kitchen and dining room and out the exit to the street.

As I thought about what I had just learned, Wyman acknowledged that he had known Julia, had tried to entice her into the business, and that she had backed away. By his own admission, he had been very angry with her. I wondered if he was the "R," Randolph, who had written the note to Julia that had been left at the table at El Farolito. He had been desperate to communicate with her and may have been bold in reaching out. Having someone leave the envelope at a table in the restaurant was desperate. I needed more information before I could conduct a formal interview with him, but his behavior led me to believe that I was on the right track.

43

I was on my way out of Rojas when my iPhone rang. It was Sergeant Ed Apodaca and Dolores Griego. They had some news for me, including that our afternoon call with Miguel had been canceled until tomorrow. But there was more.

Upon further study of Julia's emails, Ed found that the emails had not all been between Julia and Adelina or either of her siblings. Many emails to Julia were from her step-sister Fatima, the daughter of the abusive step-father, Pablo Ramírez. The emails were characterized by threats with allegations that Julia had caused all of the problems their father had following Julia's hitting him with a frying pan and hot grease. The emails threatened that Fatima, and her step-brother Raul would find a way to "even the score." They threatened do this by finding Julia or taking revenge on her natural siblings.

The emails became increasingly threatening, claiming that they "knew where she lived and were coming her way." They demanded that she send them money as a way to compensate them for their misery, or else. Julia's return emails were increasingly frantic and pleading. There was a very fearful tone to them. The emails from Fatima had abruptly stopped just two weeks prior to Julia's death.

Ed noted that in her emails to Fatima, Julia had not given her any information about where she lived. Fatima had used Julia's given name, Sofia. It appeared that Fatima's ability to track Julia had been through repeated and random attempts at trying various combinations of her given name and using a number of internet providers until she had a hit. Ed also said that there were also some emails to Julia from mysterious unidentified sources that seemed to be local and difficult to track.

While I believed it was unlikely that her step-siblings would be able to legally cross the border, much less find Julia, their threat could have been the main reason for her fearfulness. And she may have believed the message signed "R" came from Raul. This new revelation caused me to question my previous belief that the "R" in the note to Julia may have been from Randolph Wyman. I thought that Raul added an unexpected twist to explore further but Dolores soon put that hypothesis to rest.

Dolores had been researching the note that had been left for Julia at the restaurant just a week earlier and signed "R." It was the same threatening note that Julia had given to me at the Farmer's Market the night just prior to her murder. Dolores and her forensics team had been able to determine that the high-end stationery used in that note matched the stationery of the note I had received tacked to my door.

As Dolores told me that, a cold chill went down my spine. This all became more frightening to me than it had been before. Dolores' research had also determined that the stationery was not something to be found in a typical office supply store, but more likely to be sold in a high-end stationery store. That suggested that the same person likely had been responsible for both notes. If that was true, the same person had also been responsible for the threatening photographs of Roberto with a target on his back. This clue had the potential to point us to the author of those notes and to also dismiss Julia's siblings as suspects.

Dolores closed by saying that she would continue to investigate these notes and photographs and, like Ed, would keep me posted.

My mind was spinning and my adrenaline pumping. It had been a very intense day.

I needed to process this with Maria. I texted her to meet me at the Guadalupe for dinner and asked if we could have the private room to talk and digest everything I had going through my mind.

44

Night was falling as I entered the Guadalupe and was escorted back to the Private Conference room by Albert Gonzales, a former Marine and law student that was serving part-time as Roberto's protective "muscle" until Julia's murder had been solved.

"Good evening, Scott. We have been expecting you," said Albert, shaking my hand firmly. "Maria is waiting for you in the private Conference room.

"Good to see you, Albert," I replied. "Glad you are staying close to Roberto. I know he appreciates it."

"My pleasure. It is a small thank-you for all he has done for me." Albert concluded as he opened the door to the conference room.

As I entered the room, I had to smile to myself. The Guadalupe was everything that Randolph Wyman wanted Rojas to be. It was a very fine restaurant with a high-end but comfortable ambience, a great menu, excellent servers, and attentive service. It was a place that was welcoming to many celebrities and commoners alike.

The only thing that was remotely similar to Wyman's restaurant was the lavish private Conference room that equaled Wyman's opulent office. There was a sadness in the comparison.

The sconces on the walls with the sculpted art in the nichos gave the hallway to the private Conference room the feeling of being in a lavish Santa Fe home. It felt warm, cozy, and unpretentiously affluent. The small conference table had been set with a lovely linen tablecloth, two place settings with *Nambe* dinner ware, and a space where we could lay out any papers we needed to review. A bottle of my favorite Malbec stood at the end of the table, open and breathing. The waiter, Jerome, had already dimmed the chandelier adding to the coziness of the room. I had to remind myself that we were there to work as well as dine.

Maria looked gorgeous as usual, and I gave her a big hug and even bigger kiss. She had brought a dimension to my life that I had lost and did not believe would ever return. After my divorce and the infidelity of my ex-wife, I doubted that I could ever trust anyone again. Being patient, and accepting me for the flawed person I am, Maria helped me believe in love again. It had been a journey from despair to joy, and one for which I would be forever grateful. In addition to being the love I had always hoped for, she was my equal in every way, intellectually, romantically, and her love of adventure and justice. She had become my best friend as well as my lover. How wonderful is that?

There in front of me was my scrumptious-looking plate with a chile-rubbed rack of lamb, fingerling potatoes in a garlic aioli sauce, and a fresh beet and goat cheese salad. We ate slowly as we discussed the case.

I went through my list of suspects and motives with Maria. When solving a homicide, there are five motives to consider: love, lust, loathing, loot, and lunacy. I wanted to take a step back to consider what motive could be in play for Julia's murder, given the suspects that we were considering.

With Michele, there was obviously hatred and jealousy. The same might be true for Josef Castellano, Michele's lover, whom I had yet to interview. It seemed clear that Michele was threatened by Julia's ascendance in El Farolito and the Santa Fe culinary scene. The possibility that Michele would soon find herself unseated as head chef was unthinkable after having turned her back on New York City to come to Santa Fe. The same logic held true for her lover Josef who was a protective and, maybe, vindictive partner. But were these grounds for murder? I wasn't sure but, in the case of a "folie a deux," or shared delusions, it was possible that Michele and Josef could be contributing to each other's hatred of Julia and her potential for unseating Michele from her elevated role. I had to keep them on the list.

Considering William Dirschauser, the exposure of his tactics of using sex and exploitation in return for writing positive restaurant reviews in the *Santa Fe New Mexican* stood to dethrone his position in the community as well as his job. In his case, being slighted and fearing loss of income could have played a role. Interestingly enough, sex has very little to do with love or lust for a narcissist. It is about exploitation and control. Dirschauser's sexual demands had nothing to do with any feelings of attraction or intimacy but were all about his ability to dominate. Could he have felt some sort of narcissistic rage at being rejected?

Randall Wyman had much to lose. First and foremost, the failure of the restaurant would be a serious blow to Wyman's chances of being seen as a success in his father's eyes. At least, that is what Wyman would have believed. Traumatic shame and humiliation have been identified as factors behind the rage of some killers. Such failure would have had serious financial implications and a sense of disgrace in Wyman's mind because he was unable to succeed as his father had. If Wyman's relationship with his father had been toxic enough, could it have resulted in the kind of rage behind killing someone?

Finally, Julia's step-brother, Raul, believed that she was responsible for the harsh challenges that afflicted his father, her step-father. From the emails, it appeared that Raul's life had been difficult and that he had been involved in some measure with the drug cartels surrounding Oaxaca. The threatening nature of Raul's emails evidenced a desperation, including a willingness to blackmail and, possibly, even kill Julia if she did not deliver on his ransom request.

While his emails suggested anger and desire for money on Raul's part, it seemed unlikely that he could easily cross the US/Mexico border, at least legally. Given what Dolores had determined about the notes to Julia and those tacked on my door being of the same stationery and probably from the same person, Raul seemed a much less likely suspect. Maria agreed with me about dropping him from the list of main suspects.

There were definitely a couple of loose ends. First, who actually left the threatening note for Julia on a table in the restaurant and the one with pictures of Roberto on my door. This was the most promising lead. Second, who was it that slipped out the side door of the Farmer's Market the night I talked with Julia? Could this have been the same person who knocked over the pot in the El Farolito kitchen the night I was to meet Julia again? Was this the person that had spiked Julia's mezcal? I felt the pressure increasing to get the case solved quickly and to get it right.

Maria suggested that one person I should talk with again was Fernando, the owner of El Farolito. Fernando touched all of the other suspects in one way or another. He had been on my list to contact again, and Maria's nudge elevated the importance of doing so. She referenced his prior discussion with her father, Roberto. At the very minimum, he might know something about Julia that could either exclude, or implicate, any of the suspects with whom I had talked.

I was already planning what I would do tomorrow and was adding

Fernando to the list when, at that moment, the restaurant went dark. The electricity had gone out and the room became pitch black. I could hear sounds of startled customers panicking in the main dining room. There were echoes of glass and ceramic shattering as they hit the floor from waitstaff carrying dishes. It was spooky and unnerving.

Suddenly, Kaboom!

The window of the conference room erupted with an ear-piercing sound. Maria screamed and glass shards permeated the room. It was as if a grenade had gone off. I could hear the loud "thump" of something hitting our table, followed by the shrill tone of the Security Alarm and a repetitive electronic voice, "Warning, intrusion Sensor 26. Warning, intrusion Sensor 26..."

I grabbed Maria and we ducked under the table. I wasn't sure what was happening, but I knew we needed to get out of direct sight of the window. I held her close, covering her head and wondering what the hell had just occurred.

I heard it before I saw its effect. It was the low rumble of a generator followed quickly by light cutting through the darkness in the room. I realized that the loss of electricity had triggered the automatic ignition of a back-up gas generator. Roberto had installed both a sophisticated alarm system and the back-up gas generator following the arsonist-set fire to the Guadalupe just a couple of years before. He had also installed both exterior and interior video cameras to monitor traffic. I hoped these might help now.

As the lights came on, the piercing sound of the security system stopped. Someone had entered the code to disarm it. I could now see Maria shivering with fright. In just moments, the door of the room opened.

"Maria, Scott, are you okay?" shouted a very concerned voice, it was Albert.

"Down here, Albert." I said requesting his assistance.

Maria was still shaking when Albert and I helped her out from under the table and we surveyed the wreckage. The window of the conference room had a large hole in one of the panes. Glass slivers were everywhere. It looked like the remains of an explosion.

Then I saw it. There on the table was a red brick with a note tied to it. Cautioning Albert and Maria not to handle it because of possible prints, I asked Albert to get some rubber gloves from the kitchen.

Albert arrived momentarily and gave me a pair of the latex gloves. I carefully untied the note from the brick. On the backside of the note in the now familiar large black block lettering was written:

DOCTOR HUNTER,
SECOND WARNING!! NOW BACK OFF!!!!
I KNOW WHERE YOU ARE AND YOU WON'T BE
SO LUCKY WHEN THE LIGHTS GO OUT NEXT TIME!

I simultaneously felt anger and fear. Even with a bodyguard, we weren't safe. Nor was Roberto. Maria, Roberto, and I would all have to exercise much greater vigilance and caution.

If I felt a sense of urgency to solve the case before, I was frantic to solve it now.

The police arrived within minutes followed closely by Sergeant Ed Apodaca. I was relieved to see him. The incident had shaken me up more than I realized. It was only when Ed arrived that I was able to let my guard down and really breathe normally again.

Patrons quickly vacated the restaurant, and the staff were busy in the dining room cleaning up. It was a mess with broken dishes and food all over as a result of the blackout.

I asked Albert to take Maria and Roberto to the police station until we could best determine how to protect them. I also wondered if I was the one that really needed protecting.

The private Conference room where we had been sitting had glass shards all over. The brick that had been used as a projectile lay near the place where it had initially landed, in the middle of the conference table. I had been careful to relocate it where I found it for forensic inspection.

The polished hardwood table was dented and scratched, but repairable. The entire glass window, not just the pane, would have to be replaced.

I handed the threatening note that had been attached to the brick to Ed for evidence and for Dolores to review. Ed would also be studying any video tape that the Guadalupe's cameras may recorded.

It had been quite an evening and I needed to take care of Maria and prepare for tomorrow.

45

I woke up early, on my own. It had been a lonely and restless night. I had convinced Maria and Roberto to stay with her cousin, Angela Montoya. Angela lives in a small, gated area just off of Hyde Park road, north of downtown. Sergeant Apodaca agreed to place police protection near the house. It was a temporary solution, but one that we would all have to live with for the time being.

I telephoned Fernando and asked him to meet me at my office at the police station. I still wanted to keep things as informal as possible, for now. I was tired, but knew we needed to press on.

The officer on duty escorted Fernando to my office when he arrived. I offered him a seat and a cup of coffee, which I probably needed more than he did.

Fernando began the conversation. "What's going on at the Guadalupe?"

My first thought was what a small-town Santa Fe was. Secrets cannot be kept very long.

"Why do you think something is going on there?" I asked.

"When I drove to El Farolito this morning, there were several police cars and some yellow crime scene tape on one side of the Guadalupe. Was there a robbery or disturbance there? What happened?" he replied.

Not wanting to provide him any substantial information, I simply responded that the local window repair shop was replacing a side window.

"I hope everyone is okay. I will try to give Roberto a call later," he offered.

Wanting to move forward, I told Fernando that we had not had enough time to talk earlier. I wanted to get a fuller picture of Julia to determine if there were issues I had yet to identify regarding her homicide, especially because it was in El Farolito.

He responded, "We went over everything the last time we talked. I do not know how much more I can add."

I assured Fernando that our previous conversation had been very helpful, but I just needed more a detailed understanding of Julia and the environment in which she lived. He then acquiesced.

Fernando Romero described his relationship with Julia as someone he had "rescued" from the streets and given her a real chance. He detailed how he recognized her talent at the Rolling Burrito food truck and offered her a job, part-time initially. He explained that the relationship had become one like a father-daughter relationship where he "took her under his wing" to teach her the ins-and-outs of the restaurant business.

He acknowledged how her Oaxacan influence began changing the culture of the restaurant, both positively and negatively. Patrons loved the Oaxacan-fusion food in which Julia had creatively mixed the local affection for green chile with her Oaxacan herbs and spices. Customers especially enjoyed her various mole sauces, paired with different meats and vegetables.

However, as I pressed Fernando further, he admitted that not everything was as rosy at El Farolito as it seemed to be, even before Julia's death. On the negative side, Fernando cited that some of the staff, especially Michele, were jealous of Julia. Some even believed that Fernando had given her preferential treatment. In fact, he suggested that not only did Michele have a grudge with Julia but there were certain other waitstaff who thought ill of her, including Michele's lover, Josef Castellano.

According to Fernando, Josef believed that Julia was trying to get Michele's job as head chef and was purposely undermining her work both by turning waitstaff against Michele and by a "whisper campaign" with the patrons. Josef had even accused Julia of sabotaging some of the food that went to the guests by adding too much salt. As Fernando described, it was evident to him that Josef was furious.

Then, doing an about-face, Fernando tried to downplay these interactions as typical politics, evident in any fine dining kitchen where egos were big and the competition often fierce. It was almost like Fernando suddenly felt that he had revealed too much too soon and began backpedaling.

I was perplexed by Fernando's answers. Was he really trying to help me by providing more information or was he trying to influence the direction of the investigation by giving me mixed signals? It was very strange.

I needed to explore with Fernando the degree to which he had known about Michele's background in New York as a chef.

"Tell me, Mister Romero, how did you find Michele, and what reference checking did you do prior to hiring her?" I probed.

Squirming in his chair and obviously uncomfortable, he related the story of going to New York City and, by chance, eating in the restaurant where she was the sous chef. He said her dishes were amazing and he knew that he needed a great chef in his Santa Fe restaurant. He acknowledged that on his third visit to the restaurant over a three-day period, he offered her a position as head chef in Santa Fe with a substantial increase in her pay. To his surprise, she accepted and within just a few weeks she was in Santa Fe. That was four years ago.

"Did you do any reference checking prior to making Michele the offer?" I asked.

Lowering his head and shaking it sheepishly, he admitted that he had not.

"How has her being the head chef at El Farolito been for you?" I quizzed.

Fernando replied, "Well, mostly good. The restaurant definitely benefitted with her leadership in the kitchen but there was always one point of tension between us. For some reason, Michele thought that there would be a time when I would offer her equity in the restaurant. I assure you that I had not offered that. It was just in her mind, but it came up fairly often. Then when I hired Julia, Michele began to push harder for an answer. It was almost like she was jealous of Julia."

"So, you never indicated to Michele that she might become a part-owner of the restaurant?" I queried incredulously after what Michele had told me.

"Absolutely not. The restaurant is my legacy. I wanted to pass it on to my family when I retired or died. I would never allow an outsider to have ownership. In fact, I wanted to branch out by opening other locations but that never happened," he responded firmly.

I was reflecting on my discussion with Michele, and it was obvious that her recollection was different from Fernando's.

I pulled a file out of my desk drawer with the label "Michele Ronaldi." I deliberately let Fernando notice her name on the label. I opened the file and spread my notes over my desk.

"Mister Romero," I began, "you indicated that you hired Michele without having done any reference checks. If you would have investigated her background you might have proceeded more slowly."

With a puzzled look on his face, he simply said, "How so?"

I then went on to summarize my reference checking on Michele and the research Maria had also conducted in the New York City restaurant scene. I detailed the multiple positions from which she had been fired, her volatile temper, and the unfounded sexual harassment charge she had levied against one of the chefs. I also offered that the reason she had been successful at all was because she was such a great cook. I suggested to Fernando that Michele's ongoing push to become a partner and the jealousy she evidenced toward Julia were part of a pattern of escalating anger.

At that point, Fernando sat back in his chair, held his head in his hands, let out a big breath, and said, "Damn! My wife always says I make impulsive decisions. She never liked Michele. I should have been more careful and done the research that you did. Damn"

Now I asked him the big question, "Mister Romero, do you think that Michele could have murdered Julia?"

After a long pause, he responded, "Before you told me about her experiences in New York City, I could not put it all together but now, it begins to make more sense. The escalating anger she expressed toward me about becoming a partner; the intense jealousy she felt toward Julia; and Josef's anger toward Julia. Could they have both killed her? I never would have thought so before, but now, I'm not so sure."

I thought the conversation had yielded all I needed for the moment. It looked like Michele could be a prime suspect for Julia's murder. I wanted to circle back with Ed and Dolores before proceeding.

I concluded the conversation and Fernando offered to help with anything he could do to solve this horrendous homicide.

I still felt that there was something about Fernando's description of events was a little off, but I wasn't sure what.

I escorted Fernando out of the station and proceeded to Dolores' office for a forensic update.

46

Walking into Dolores' office and before I could sit down, she said solemnly, "Well, we are three for three."

"What do you mean?" I asked.

Pointing to her worktable, I could see three evidence bags with envelopes in each bag.

Dolores explained, "The evidence bag on the right holds the envelope and threatening note that Julia had received from the waiter at the restaurant and given to you that night at the Farmer's Market.

I nodded, asking, "And the other two?"

"The second bag holds both the larger manila envelope, the smaller envelope, and the note to you which was tacked to your door along with the photographs of Roberto with a target on his back. The third bag holds the envelope and note that were tied to the brick thrown through the window at the Guadalupe last night," Dolores answered.

Understanding where Dolores was headed, I exclaimed, "And the three envelopes all match likely having come from the same stationery store."

Dolores winked, pointed at me, and said, "You got it. The envelope on the brick last night matched the other two. They came from the same batch, and almost certainly from the same individual. The only outlier, of course is the manila envelope. It is fairly standard."

Wanting to make certain I was understanding Dolores' assertion correctly, I asked, "How do you know all three of the envelopes are from the same batch? Couldn't the similarities be just a coincidence and could at least one of them be from a different grouping of notecards and envelopes?"

"When the forensic team compared the notecards and envelopes," Dolores began, "there were several things we looked for that are differentiating features. Size, weight, texture, coloring, design, paper quality, and any other unique features help determine if the stationery is closely related. Unfortunately, the manufacturers only stamps stationery codes on boxes and not on individual envelopes or notecards."

"Then how did you determine that these were a match?" I questioned.

Confidently, Dolores replied, "The paper weight on all of them is eighty pounds, the notecards are thirty-two-point width thick and about the same as a bankcard. They all have a distinctive ecru color, and the notecards have a double-edged design of outer gold and inner maroon. The envelopes all have liners that are the same maroon color.

"Make no mistake, these envelopes and notecards are of luxury stock and are often custom monogrammed. This is likely a special custom order, not one you would find on the shelves of any of the local stores."

"So, if we find anyone who has stationery with these same features, we may be able to find our killer?" I asked.

"The stationery being the same is only circumstantial, but if we could identify the person who has such stationery it could help us begin to make a case," she answered.

Sergeant Apodaca had entered Dolores' office halfway through our conversation. I was curious about what he may have uncovered.

"What about your team, Ed, anything new?" I asked.

With a heavy sigh, he said, "As in any high-profile case, we have had hundreds of calls from people offering their thoughts about who may be involved and their ideas about avenues to pursue. All of the calls are screened for potential clues, but most of them are from crackpots wanting their fifteen minutes of fame.

"However, we do have a couple of items that are of interest. The video cameras from the Guadalupe last night provided some footage that may be helpful."

When the brick blasted through the window, I recalled that after an arsonist destroyed the restaurant a couple of years ago, Roberto had a sophisticated security system installed including external cameras.

"Tell me," I said anxious to hear, "what did you get?"

"It was unusual," Ed began. "We were expecting to see something akin to a drive by shooting, or in this case a drive by lobbing. We thought we would be looking at a car stopping with a person quickly emerging, throwing the brick through the window, and getting back into the car for a quick getaway."

"And?" I asked.

Ed began in his typical methodical manner, "You have to understand that it was very dark outside the restaurant. That side of the restaurant is adjacent to the street and the nearest streetlight was a block away. It would have been tough even under the best of circumstances and with a high-quality camera."

"For god's sake, Ed," I said impatiently, "tell me what you saw."

He replied, with frustration, "Not what we were looking for. Instead of a car driving by, we saw an individual in dressed in dark clothing and with a hoodie and tennis shoes walk up slowly to the building and heave a brick. Just when he was just about in decent camera range, the electricity went off. Then, as a result of the brick going through the window, the security system, including the outdoor cameras, also went out for about twenty seconds until the generator kicked on.

"When the generator came back on and the security cameras returned to full functioning, we could make out the same individual walking, not running, away from the building. We wondered why he wasn't running until we noticed that he had an uneven gait or limp. The person seemed to be walking as quickly as he or she could, but not running.

"We were also able to view from another camera at the rear of the restaurant looking further down the street. That is when we saw the individual get into a small dark colored car and drive off. It was too dark and too far away for us to see the license plate. We are doing more research to determine if we can identify the make and year of the car."

As Ed described the individual, I was reminded of the person Maria had seen leaving the Farmer's Market the night I had spoken to Julia. She mentioned that the person had an uneven gait and was driving a small dark colored car. I wondered if this could have been the same person.

"Good work, Ed. Thanks," I said.

"One more thing," Ed interrupted. "I conducted a database search of all of the employees who worked at El Farolito."

"And...?" I asked, impatiently.

Answering slowly, Ed said "There were a couple of DUIs, including one for Fernando Romero. The only other staff member to have had any record was Josef Castellano."

"You mean the maître d' who is in a relationship with head chef Michele Ronaldi?" I asked.

Smiling, Ed said, "Bingo. That's the one. Before moving to Santa

Fe, Castellano had a long rap sheet, mostly small stuff. He came from Albuquerque and, for a period of time, had been involved in some gang activity there. He was also charged with more than one assault and served about six months jail time for illegal drug possession and having a firearm without a permit."

"This could be huge, Ed." I said emphatically. "When was he last in trouble and how long has he been in Santa Fe?"

Ed replied, "There are notes in the database from his parole officer. Six years ago, Castellano went through a drug rehab program as well as anger management training. He left Albuquerque, moved to Santa Fe, and worked in hospitality. There is nothing on his record to indicate that he has had any additional incidents. He has been off parole and clean since coming to Santa Fe."

Thinking about the conversation I had with Michele, her dislike for Julia, and now her boyfriend having a record, I wondered if they could have conspired to kill Julia. Could Josef have thrown the brick through the window? Could Michele inviting me to her house have been a ruse to throw me off track?

I gave Ed and Dolores a brief description of my meeting with Fernando and suggested that we keep an eye on him, along with Michele and now, also Josef Castellano. I asked them to be my proxy in our afternoon call with Miguel because I had an important follow up I needed to make.

47

It was early-afternoon, and I had not yet had lunch. I decided to drop by the recently re-opened El Farolito. Forensics had completed their final review of the property, and it was now open again for business. Since I had just talked with Fernando and Michele, it would not seem too unusual for me to be there. Also, I reasoned, I could kill two birds with one stone. I could have lunch and work in a conversation with Michele, ostensibly to follow-up on our previous conversation.

The walk from the police station to El Farolito was about six blocks. The afternoon was glorious with the deep blue skies, only a few stationary clouds, bright sun, and the crisp air. I always enjoyed the walk in any direction from the police station. The sidewalks were lined with unique galleries, southwestern clothing stores, and exceptional restaurants. Santa Fe was a very special place with the nickname, "The City Different."

It was the first time I had been back to the restaurant since the morning after Julia's murder. At that time, it had only been a crime scene for me. Now, I could actually take in the full ambience of the restaurant. It did have an upscale feeling to it with the linen tablecloths, fine dinnerware, southwestern wall art, and lovely polished dark wooden floors.

Josef Castellano was not on duty as the maître d' and another member of the waitstaff guided me to a corner table. She obviously recognized me and was cautious, professional, and said only few words. She gave me a menu and indicated who my waiter would be.

The menu was sophisticated, and expensive for lunch. I opted for soup and salad and ordered the Southwestern Chowder with corn, green onions and crème fraiche and a kale and quinoa salad. I requested water to drink. Because this part of the southwestern United States is so arid, water is rarely served automatically upon being seated and only brought to the table upon request.

As I waited for my lunch to be served, I thought how eerie it was that I was to have met Julia in the kitchen just a few nights before. I wondered if it was also eerie for the chefs, sous chefs, and others working there to walk over the exact spot where I had found Julia's lifeless body. Looking around the restaurant, it was impossible to detect that a crime had so recently been committed here. Everything was in its place, and it was immaculate. Very strange.

Upon being served my chowder and salad, I asked the server to please let head chef Michele know that I would like to talk with her when she was available. I wanted my visit with her to appear as informal as possible.

Michele popped out of the kitchen shortly and let me know that she would be available momentarily, just needing time to get everyone else sorted.

When she came back to the table, she had traded her chef's jacket and apron for her street clothes, a loose-fitting sweater, jeans, and sandals.

The restaurant was nearly vacant and my table in the corner gave us ample privacy.

Beginning the conversation in a friendly tone and noting that I had just completed my lunch, Michele said, "I am surprised to see you here. I hope you enjoyed your chowder. I would have added some protein if I would have known it was you."

"It was delicious," I said honestly. "Michele, I need a little more information based on our discussion at your house but don't want to inconvenience you. I thought coming here at a slower time might be the best way to accomplish both."

"Sure," she said in a helpful tone. "How can I help?"

"It must be strange being back in the kitchen where Julia had been murdered." I commented, wanting to see her reaction.

Staring at me, her smile now gone, she said, "It really is. You know from our last conversation that Julia and I had our issues, but the kitchen feels really weird without her. Everyone feels the same. It will take some time to get over it."

I told Michele that I needed a bit more information from her about others in the restaurant, unhappy patrons, Randolph Wyman, and anyone who may have had a beef with Julia. I asked her to let me know about anything out of the ordinary that she may have thought of since we last met.

Michele shared of a number of very minor issues and incidents, but nothing that would rise to the level of anyone wanting to hurt Julia. She again referenced the talk she had witnessed between Randolph Wyman and Julia. She had given it more thought and still believed that there may have been a disagreement between the two of them but nothing of substance.

I decided that I should go ahead and let her know about the research I had done on her from her New York City days. I told her that I had knowledge of her history of getting fired from several restaurants because of her inability to control her temper. I mentioned the jealousy she had evidenced when working with other chefs and also the event when she had threatened the executive chef of a fine New York restaurant for sexual harassment.

As I continued to reveal my research, I asked her if she had ever had physical altercations with Julia. The more I talked and asked pointed questions, the more fidgety she became. Finally, I asked her point blank, did she want Julia dead?

Immediately, I could tell that Michele was shaken by the question. Her cheeks had turned pale, and her breathing was quick and shallow. I hoped to leave before she either stroked-out or came after me. At that point, she said she would not talk any further without her lawyer present. She abruptly got up from the table and exited through the kitchen and the back door. It was the same door I had entered just a few nights earlier when I had discovered Julia's body.

After this and the previous conversations I had with her, I felt like I might be finally getting somewhere. But where?

Just then, my iPhone buzzed. The caller ID showed Sergeant Apodaca's name. Strange since I had just finished talking with him.

"Scott," Ed exclaimed. "we just received a nine-one-one call. It looks like another unusual death. Can you meet me at the corner of Water and Guadalupe ASAP?"

I thought immediately that was the location of Rojas, Randolph Wyman's restaurant.

"You bet, Ed," I said urgently. "I'll be there in ten minutes."

48

I walked briskly from El Farolito on the north side of the plaza to the location Ed had given me a couple of blocks south of the plaza. As I feared, the location was that of Rojas, Randolph Wyman's restaurant.

Sergeant Apodaca met me at the front door accompanied by a tall thin man dressed in dark slacks, a long-sleeved white shirt, and a dark buttoned vest with a hotel logo and his name tag.

Ed greeted me with, "Hi Scott, this is Dennis, the night manager of the hotel next door. Dennis was responsible for the nine-one-one call. Dennis, please tell Doctor Hunter what precipitated your call."

"Of course, Sergeant Apodaca," he began. "I am Dennis Peck, the evening manager of the Saint Julian hotel. I usually come on shift at about four in the afternoon. When I arrived, I noticed that Rojas had what appeared to be a note on the front door, a sheet of paper taped to a glass pane on the inside of the entrance. The restaurant appeared to be closed and, while that is unusual, I didn't think too much about it at the time."

"Why didn't the fact that it was closed with a note on the door surprise you?" I asked.

Smiling and shaking his head, he said, "We at the Saint Julian have a mixed relationship with the restaurant."

"How so?" I queried.

"Unfortunately," he began, "while the restaurant is in the same building as the hotel, the hotel does not own the space. Apparently, there was a time in the past when the hotel and restaurant were owned by the same developers, but the restaurant portion was sold off over twenty years ago. Since that time, the restaurant has had a variety of different managers, it has never been open and operating continuously for very long periods. Such a shame, given its great location.

"At the Saint Julian, we consider ourselves to be a high-end boutique hotel. The current hotel ownership has tried on numerous occasions to purchase the restaurant, but to no avail. They finally gave up. You may have heard rumors over the years that the restaurant may have even been owned by the mafia as a way to launder money. It is so sad, because we never felt like we could recommend the restaurant to our guests. It did not seem to cater to our level of clientele."

"When Mister Wyman actually bought the restaurant, we were hopeful that things would change. He changed the name to Rojas and told us he had big plans for us. He seemed to come from money and always told us how well-known his family was in the northeast. We were initially glad to have him as an owner."

Becoming impatient, I asked, "What led to you making the nine-one-one call?"

"Well," he said, "when the hotel and restaurant had a single owner, they shared a common door in the back. It was there for staff and maintenance workers to go freely between the two businesses. Years ago, when new restaurant owners came, they boarded up the doorway. On the hotel side, there are still storage closets and a break room reserved for the hotel staff. But even now when the restaurant is open, you can still smell food cooking through the boarded-up wall.

"When I was getting my hotel clothes out of my locker in the break room, I could smell a peculiar odor. It wasn't food and really smelled putrid. My first thought was that it could be a dead rat somewhere, so I searched the area in and around the break room. Then, it seemed that the only place the odor could have come from was under the boarded-up wall to the restaurant.

"I went and checked the note on the front door. It was a handwritten note that said the restaurant was closed for repairs. So, then I knew that something must be wrong and made the nine-one-one call."

Dismissing him, Ed said, "Thank you Dennis. I know you have to get to your shift, but we may need to check back with you in the future."

As Dennis left to go back into the hotel, Ed began briefing me.

"When we got here," he said, "we searched around the building and detected a rancid smell in the back. We could smell the same thing in the break room of the hotel, the same one Dennis noticed. Because of the note on the door, we were concerned that the people doing the repairs may have cut a water or left the freezer open. I made the decision that we needed to get into the building unsure of what we would find.

"There was no contact information on the note, so I tried the number listed for the restaurant and it just went to voice mail. I believed we had to act, so my men forced the front door open. Once the door was opened, the smell was overwhelming.

"We made our way back to the kitchen area from which the smell seemed to emanate. Once back there, the scene was shocking. We saw the cold dead body of Randolph Wyman hanging from a rafter with a rope around his neck. His feet were dangling about three feet off the ground and a barstool lay on its side on the floor not far from his body. The scene had the appearance of a suicide."

As Ed gave me the details, I was stunned, having just spoken with Wyman the day before.

"Needless to say, Ed," I replied, "I am shocked! We just met yesterday. I knew he was disheartened, but I didn't suspect that he was suicidal."

"There's more," Ed said. "There was an empty bottle of vodka and a cocktail glass on a table near the hanging. It appeared that he had been drinking before hanging himself. In addition, there were two envelopes on the table near the empty bottle of vodka.

I knew that depression and alcohol are a deadly mix, literally. With alcohol being a depressant on top of feeling hopeless about one's future, bad things can happen. In Wyman's case, I also thought about one of Freud's beliefs about depression being anger turned inward. Freud postulated that depression involved self-loathing, self-dislike, or self-blame. In talking with Wyman, it seemed like the restaurant was his latest, and now last, failed attempt to justify his checkered life. Could this have been Wyman's motivation?

Guiding me back to the kitchen, putting on his latex investigation gloves and handing me a pair to use, he pointed to the two notes still on the table. One envelope was addressed simply 'POLICE,' and the other envelope had the name William Gaylord Wyman written on it.

"Take a look at the kind of envelopes," Ed said. "Look familiar?"

Both envelopes matched the other three envelopes that Dolores had laid out earlier in terms of size and their ecru color. Could Wyman have been the author of the other notes? My mind was racing now, and I was anxious to view the contents of these envelopes.

<h1 style="text-align:center">49</h1>

Ed handed me the first envelope with the inscription: TO MY FATHER, WILLIAM GAYLORD WYMAN

From the research I had conducted on Randolph Wyman, I knew that his father had been a powerful Boston business magnate. I also knew that Randolph had spent much of his adult, and pre-adult, life rebelling against the very things his father valued and believed in. Paradoxically, his recent desire to prove to his father that he was a success after all, was pushing him to be motivated by the same values of success, status, recognition, and affluence that he had spent much of his life fighting.

I recalled that the great psychiatrist, Carl Jung, described how our denial of suppression of unwanted or hurtful feelings creates what he termed the "shadow self." We try to banish these feelings and beliefs to our unconscious underground rather than deal with them. Unfortunately, the banished shadow demands to be heard and can emerge in harmful ways including addictions, anger, a history of relationship problems, and, in extreme cases, even suicide. I wondered if Randolph had become the victim of those buried hurtful feelings and that they dominated his later life, and now his death. I was curious to see the envelopes content.

As I took the envelope from Ed, I carefully opened it. Inside the envelope there was the same maroon lining as the ones Dolores had examined. The envelope contained a notecard that also had the same double-edged gold and maroon design as the others. I was cautiously optimistic that we may have actually found Julia's killer.

I pulled the notecard from the envelope. It was both very sad and telling:

DEAR FATHER,

YOU HAVE ALWAYS THOUGHT THAT I WAS A LOSER AND WOULD NEVER AMOUNT TO MUCH. WELL, YOU PROVED TO BE RIGHT. YOU SENT ME TO THE FINEST PREP SCHOOLS, INVOLVED ME IN THE BEST SOCIAL CLUBS, AND INTRODUCED ME TO ALL OF YOUR SUCCESSFUL FRIENDS. ALL TO NO AVAIL. YOU EVEN LEANED ON YOUR FRIENDS AND USED YOU INFLUENCE TO GET ME OUT OF TROUBLE.

I CAME TO SANTA FE TO TRY AND PROVE YOU WRONG. INSTEAD, I FAILED ONCE MORE AND CONFIRMED ALL OF THE DOUBTS YOU HAD OF ME. WELL, FATHER, YOU WILL NOT HAVE TO WORRY ABOUT ME ANY FURTHER. I CAN ONLY SAY HOW SORRY I AM THAT I COULD NOT LIVE UP TO YOUR EXPECTATIONS AND HAVE BEEN WHAT, AND WHO, YOU WANTED ME TO BE.

LOVE,
YOUR SON,
RANDOLPH WYMAN

The note was tragic, and angry. These demons that Randolph had to live with had accompanied him daily. The reproach and rebuke from his father had not only failed to serve as motivators, but had totally torn down his sense of self, making him a very desperate and sad human indeed.

I thought of a psychotherapist observation I once heard that "suicide is often a case of mistaken identity." With Randolph's anger toward his father this could have been true.

I also wondered, if in his desperation, he had lashed out at Julia when she had rejected his offer.

I put the notecard back in the envelope and the envelope in an evidence bag.

Picking up the second envelope, it was the same ecru color and shape as the first one. On the outside of the envelope was a single word: POLICE

I carefully opened it from the same kind of maroon liner and withdrew the second gold and maroon designed notecard. This one was also in bold block letters, but not as carefully as the note to his father.

TO WHOM IT MAY CONCERN

I CAN NO LONGER LIVE WITH MY INVOLVEMENT IN ACTIVITES THAT HAVE HURT, AND DESTROYED, THE LIVES

OF INNOCENT PEOPLE.
I AM SO ASHAMED AND VERY SORRY. MAY THEY, THEIR
FAMILIES, AND GOD PLEASE FIND A WAY TO FOGIVE ME.

RANDOLPH WYMAN

While the note was not exactly a confession, the fact that he used the same stationery as the other notes suggested that he could definitely be our culprit. The two notes together painted a picture of a desperate and angry man who may have seen the walls closing in on him. Placing the notecard back into the envelope and putting them both into an evidence bag separate from the first note, I summarized to myself.

We now had a fairly substantial amount of data to suggest that Wyman had the motive to kill Julia. He saw her as the last possible chance of making a success out of Rojas, and himself. The significant overlay of the anger and shame he had regarding his father could have been a basis for despondency and rage. It is often the case that jilted lovers, fired employees, and publicly humiliated individuals get their revenge by killing those who have offended them.

The mezcal in his liquor cabinet being the same as that found in Julia's locker and the open bottle on the preparation table suggested they knew each other more than just casually. But did he have the means and wherewithal to poison her? As for opportunity, being late at night in a vacant restaurant kitchen gave any number of people the chance to have murdered Julia. In any case, Wyman rose to the top of the suspect list.

I was feeling confident that we were about to wrap the case up. We had a few loose ends we needed to take care of.

Just then, my iPhone rang, and the caller ID indicated it was Dolores Griego, the forensics expert at the SFPD.

"Hi Dolores," I answered, and before she could talk, I said "I am down here at Rojas restaurant. I am sure Ed has already briefed you on Wyman's death and the notes he left behind. They look exactly like the others that you have in evidence. I think we are about to close in on solving this case."

"Hey Scott," Dolores replied. "Not so fast. We may have a problem with that theory. I have some new information I need to review with you down here at the station. Its urgent."

I thanked Ed for the work of him and his team, excused myself, and was off to see Dolores.

50

I walked briskly the eight blocks from Rojas to the police station. The plaza was busier than usual and getting across it took longer than I expected. It gave me time to reflect on what I had just experienced. I was puzzled by Dolores' comment about having a problem with the theory of Wyman having been behind all of the notes and, quite possibly, the murder of Julia. I could not imagine what she had that would modify my thinking.

The fifteen-minute walk gave me a chance to refocus and my adrenaline to quiet down. When I reached Dolores office, she beckoned me in with a worried look on her face.

"Well," I said. "What's up?"

Pointing to a chair beside her desk, Dolores indicated that I should sit down.

She began, "After we met and determined that the custom stationery likely came from the same batch, I wanted to find out where they had been purchased. I did a quick scan of high-end stationery stores in Santa Fe and found only two that carry, or could order, luxury stationery. I believed the stationery to have been purchased fairly recently, so I visited both stores.

"I was able to take high-definition photos of the stationery with me to show store employees. The manager of the first store I visited recognized the stationery, but he said they did not carry it nor were they distributors. The manager said they were probably a custom order.

"At the second store, Write Impressions, Nelda Baca the manager looked at the stationery photo and confirmed that it had been a custom order stationery and that they were distributors of that brand. I asked her if she could recall any custom orders in the past few weeks. She indicated that this brand was a favorite of many businesses and law firms. In fact, she suggested that the law firms typically like the stationery to be monogrammed or have their logo as an additional customization.

"I was both exhilarated and feeling overwhelmed by the work that would be involved in tracking down the prospective buyers. I was about to leave when Miss Baca just happened to mention that the store has surveillance cameras and digital videos. They had them installed because shoplifting had been a problem in the past. She pointed to a small, darkened glass ball in the ceiling, indicating the hidden camera. They had digital records going back three months. And here are our videos."

Smiling, Dolores held up a USB containing digitalized videos for the past two months. Inviting me to sit down in front of her computer, Dolores said that she had been through the entirety of the videos. She was able to isolate one of special interest.

She inserted the USB and began to play the timestamped video. The pictures were very clear. From the images, I was able to see a three hundred sixty-degree view of the store. I could clearly see up and down every aisle including customers and staff walking by displays and checking inventory. Most importantly, I could see customers at the checkout stand paying for their merchandise.

Dolores was playing the video at an accelerated speed. The first customer was a man purchasing some greeting cards and postage stamps. The second customer was a woman buying some wrapping paper and some kind of ornament. At this point, Dolores slowed the video.

Walking up to the checkout station was a trim brunette woman dressed in a loosely fitting sweater, jeans, and sandals. It did not take much imagination to realize that this was, to my surprise, Michele Ronaldi. The timestamp on the video was just three weeks earlier.

Michele spoke with the cashier who momentarily went to what appeared to be a storeroom at the back of the store. She came out with a small box that she put on the counter. Michele looked at the box and nodded her head suggesting that it was hers. She paid for the supplies and had them bagged. As she walked away, you could see her reaching for her cell phone in her purse and appeared to be answering a call. Then she was out of sight.

In addition to the box, Michele was purchasing a large generic manila envelope, and some additional office supplies including a red stapler, a package of ballpoint pens, some black markers, a package of yellow lined note pads, and file folders. Upon checking the register tape for the same day, Dolores was able to determine that the box given to Michele contained the same brand of stationery that was currently in evidence. The manager was also able to confirm this. Dolores was able to take a screen shot of all of the supplies on the counter that Michele was purchasing.

For the second time today, I was stunned. What Dolores had uncovered again changed the direction of the investigation. I immediately thought of myself having been a victim of confirmation bias. With Randolph Wyman's hanging and the stationery he had used for his notes, I had been seeking out information to support what I believed: that Wyman was guilty of Julia's death and all of the nefarious acts surrounding it. I was cuing into things that would support this theory rather than keeping an open mind about other possibilities.

Now I was confused. If Michele purchased the stationery and Wyman had been using it, were they in this together. They both had a bone to pick with Julia. Was it possible that they had conspired to kill her?

I knew that the next step was to secure search warrants for both Michele's and Randolph's residences.

51

As I suspected, the videotape of Michele purchasing the custom stationery at *Write Impressions* was sufficient for Sergeant Apodaca to secure a search warrant to search her house. Ed put in a call to Michele at El Farolito and told her to meet him at her house. She protested until Ed told her that the alternative was to pick her up in a police car at the restaurant where she would endure public humiliation. Michele relented and agreed to meet him at her house.

A disgruntled Michele Ronaldi pulled up to her house, very unhappy that two Santa Fe Police Department cars were there waiting for her. Before she even exited her car, she was cursing and angrily questioning Sergeant Apodaca about why they had to make such a scene, particularly in full view of her neighbors. Once he showed her the search warrant, she realized she had no choice regarding the search, but not without a lot of grumbling.

Without having to inform Michele about what Dolores had found, Ed and a couple of his team conducted a thorough search of Michele's house. Using the screen shot Dolores had of the purchases Michele made at the stationery store, Ed's team was able to locate several items she had purchased on the counter. These included a red stapler, a package of ballpoint pens, some black markers, a package of yellow lined note pads, and file folders, but not the custom stationery.

Michele was with Ed and became increasingly annoying and pesky asking about what he was looking for. He did not tell her directly, but indicated he needed to conduct a thorough search for anything that might help in the investigation of Julia's murder.

Upon hearing this, Michele got on her phone to her attorney. Ed could hear her talking in the background, but only on her end. Michele referred to her as Phyllis. From what he surmised, when her attorney realized that the police did, in fact, have a search warrant, she told her that there was nothing she could do to intervene. Michele began a litany of expletives aimed at her shouting "why in the hell do I have an attorney if you can't do anything for me?"

Ed continued the search surprised that he couldn't find the custom stationery. He wondered if she had hidden it somewhere else or if she had destroyed it. He knew that the case would be much more difficult without the stationery.

He began rummaging through a two-drawer file cabinet in a small room Michele had been using for an office. The top drawer contained odds and ends like receipts, warranties, and other important papers normally kept for future reference. There was nothing out of the ordinary or of interest to the case.

In the bottom drawer, Ed found three file folders. The first was labeled "JG recipes." In the folder were printed copies of photos taken of hand-written recipes. Many of the recipes had been written in Spanish. In the margins of the printed copies were the English translation of the recipes. There were over twenty-five copies of recipes, all translated into English.

In a second file labeled "Cookbook," there were several typed pages. The initial page had the title, centered on the page, "Fusion Recipes of the Southwest." Under the title was the name Michele Ronaldi. The second page had a Table of Content that listed Appetizers, Entrées, Side Dishes, Deserts, Salads, and Vegetables. Each of the categories had recipes that were accompanied by photographs of the prepared recipe. The recipes had all originated from those in the "JG" file.

The last file in the drawer was labeled "Contract." In it was a letter from Southwestern Cuisine Publishers. The letter read:

Ms. Michele Ronaldi
902 Alameda Road
Santa Fe, New Mexico

Dear Ms. Ronaldi,

After reviewing you book proposal, it is with great pleasure that I, and the editors of *Southwestern Cuisine*, have enthusiastically elected to publish your new cookbook, *Fusion Recipes of the Southwest*. We believe that there is a wide audience for this kind of cuisine. With Santa Fe having received so many accolades as one of the most sought-after travel destinations in the United Stated, we think that there is a market that will be "hungry" for your recipes.

Within two weeks, you can expect a contract from us stipulating the terms of engagement. We are particularly interested in putting your book in the hands of Amazon and various other distributors within the next four months.

Please read the contract carefully and, if you agree to the terms, sign it and return it to me. Once we have the signed contract, we are available for any assistance we can offer to help you get you book quickly to market.

We look forward to working with you.

Warmly,

Marjorie Taylor
Senior Editor
Southwestern Cuisine

Upon seeing this, Ed said to himself, "Well, I'll be damned! She is using Julia's recipes as if they are her own and writing a cookbook. Michele had copied Julia's recipes and was attempting to put them into a cookbook as if she were author. It was now obvious that the "JG" file contained photos of recipes from Julia Gomez own recipe notebook. It was probably the notebook that had been passed down to her from her grandmother.

This could be an important to the puzzle. Michele's dislike and jealousy of Julia could have been a motive for trying to get her out of El Farolito. If Michele was behind the threatening notes, maybe she believed that killing Julia was the best way to expedite the process. With a boyfriend like Josef Castellano who had a record of physical assaults, maybe she had help.

None of this explained where Wyman fit into the picture. Nor did it explain the tie between the custom stationery at the crime scene and the video of Michele purchasing the stationery.

Ed took the three file folders and Michele's computer with him and promised her that he would return them when the investigation was completed. When she saw what he was taking, she turned red, stiffened, and began shaking her fist at him and yelling, "Those are mine, you bastard. Give them back to me! My attorney will have your badge."

Ed and his team quickly made an exit and returned to the police station, computer and file folders in tow.

52

I was still at the police station when Ed returned. He briefed me on what he had found at Michele's house. It was now after seven, and it had been a very eventful, tiring day for everyone. We were all exhausted, I recommended that we reconvene in the morning and conduct a comprehensive review of what we knew so far. I also asked Ed to schedule Michele for a formal interview at the police station tomorrow morning.

Knowing that we had totally missed our daily update with Miguel, I texted him and promised to give him a rundown tomorrow.

Maria and Roberto were still staying with her sister, Angela, or so I thought. I was surprised to learn that Maria was safe at our home. I called her and she was ahead of me, as usual. She had already returned to our home and sent the security guard away that Ed had provided.

Roberto had also moved back to his home, but Maria insisted that he continue to have both Albert Gonzales and an off-duty police officer as security. I texted Maria and offered to pick up take-out from Thai Kitchen for us. Being with Maria plus having a good meal and a nice glass of Malbec was exactly what I needed right now.

It was good to see the lights of the house on as I pulled into the driveway with our Thai take-out. We both liked Thai Kitchen's Crispy Egg rolls, Wonton Soup, and Panang Curry with shrimp.

I didn't realize just how emotionally draining the day had been until I collapsed into Maria's arms. I had not comprehended how much pressure I had experienced in Miguel Montez' absence. Her hug meant everything to me, being with my lover, best friend, confident, and now undercover sleuth. It was so good to have her back home. It was hard to believe that she had only been away one night.

Always anticipating what we needed, Maria already had the table set and Malbec poured. She directed me to the dinner table, and, for the moment, the cares of the world were off of my shoulders. Miguel's giving me the authority to run the investigation made me believe I had to prove that he'd used good judgment.

The news of Randolph Wyman's death had not yet hit the airways but definitely would be on the ten o'clock news. Maria had not yet heard about it. I wanted to get her thoughts on his death, particularly in light of Wyman's previous visit to Roberto in a failed attempt to forge some kind of business alliance.

I reviewed the details of Wyman's suicide with Maria, including the content of two notes he had written. I discussed the highlights of my meeting with Fernando, especially his observations of Michele. I told Maria what we had seen on the video tape of Michele purchasing the custom stationery. Finally, I went over the scene at Michele's house as described by Ed.

For most of my update, Maria just sat and listened, letting me get the full story out before saying, "Jeez Scott, this is all terrible. I can't believe Randolph is dead, much less by suicide. What the heck is happening? Two people, both in the restaurant industry, have died the same week, both under very strange circumstances. All this, plus the envelope with the threatening note on your door, the brick through the window at the Guadalupe with the note attached, and the other notes written to Julia is enough to give me the willies."

"What do you think about Wyman's death?" I probed.

"Well," she began, "even though my father had a low opinion of Wyman, he would be shocked to hear that he had taken his own life. Restaurant owners in Santa Fe never wish for others to fail, even in Wyman's case. In fact, when I spoke to other owners in the city, they revealed they were secretly hoping Wyman would be the one to succeed in a restaurant that had not had any real success in any of our lifetimes.

"I know that Wyman had not made many friends and was only peripherally involved in the broader business community. People mostly thought he was odd. He was always quick to let folks know that he was from a powerful family, had traveled the world, and that he was going to make Rojas a great restaurant. Honestly, he was never seen as a viable owner who was capable of turning the restaurant around. But no one I have talked with would have wanted him dead, much less by his own hands.

"The notes he left behind are both sad and perplexing. I especially wonder what he was referring to in the note to the police."

"I wish I knew too," I responded.

Continuing, Maria added, "I can tell you that when Wyman's murder becomes public, it is really going to shake up restaurant owners and chefs. In Santa Fe, we are not used to scandals or tragedies in our industry. In fact, because food is such an important part of our culture, we work hard to keep any unsavory business issues private. These are both public, very public. What a mess!"

Pursuing the subject further, I said, "I know that the only shocking event I am aware of was the arson at your family's restaurant, the Guadalupe, a couple of years ago. I know first-hand that it was not specifically related to anything in the food industry but was motivated by a personal grudge."

I asked Maria if she knew of any reasons why Wyman would have wanted to take his own life.

Shaking her head, Maria said "None."

After a pause, Maria shifted and said, "The information about Michele Ronaldi certainly shows a side of her not seen by the dining public. Of course, I knew from my friend, Belinda, in New York City about her anger issues, but they had not surfaced here, at least not publicly. I have heard that her relationship with customers was congenial and basically pleasant. I will be interested to see what she has to say about the video you have of her purchasing the custom notecards."

We continued to discuss other aspects of the investigation, reviewing again interviews with both Fernando and William Dirschauser. What we reviewed, we had discussed before, but it was always good to step back and get Maria's perspective.

We were both tired and called it a night. I knew tomorrow would be another long day. We went to bed, collapsed in each other's arms, and quickly fell asleep.

53

When I arrived at the police station, Ed and Dolores were already there. I redeemed myself by bringing them Java Joe's bagels and fancy coffees. They had gotten there early and were eager to get going.

Sitting down at the conference table with a whiteboard on one wall, we began reviewing what we knew so far.

Ed's team had searched Rojas after Wyman's body had been taken to the police morgue. Ed was surprised to find the paucity of food in the pantry or in the freezer. It almost appeared that Wyman had been operating the restaurant on a day-to-day basis. This was confirmed when they found the schedule for the staff being crossed out for the rest of the month. It seemed clear that Wyman was preparing for the restaurant to close.

The staff lockers were all empty and the dining room had been swept and cleaned. In Wyman's plush office, they found a file drawer with a number of "Past Due" notices stuffed in a blank file folder.

Passing a file folder to us, Ed said, "Here are the top delinquent invoices that we found."

Merchants Bank of the Southwest (Mortgage Payment): $43,498
Xcel Energy (Electricity): $ 6,012
City of Santa Fe (Water): $1,004
Sysco (Food): $122,697
Premier Distributing (Alcohol): $76,795
Jones Facility Management (Maintenance): $4,266
Alarid Luxury Motors (Finance Payment): $ 15,695

Continuing, Ed noted, "We found many more past due notices, but I just wanted to give you a view of the most expensive ones. Based on what we have seen so far, we believe that Wyman also may have owed unpaid back taxes. It looked to me like the restaurant was indeed on its last legs. The combined amount of the delinquent invoices we found totaled over two hundred and fifty thousand dollars. Who knows how many other unpaid invoices are out there.

"When we took a look at his bank accounts, including both his business and personal accounts, there was about sixty-five hundred dollars. We do not yet know if there were any other accounts that Wyman may have had under other names. We have a team working with the bank now to try to determine that. We also do not know if Wyman had any stocks or other investments. We will be looking into that as well."

Sighing deeply, I said, "This definitely helps understand why Wyman would choose to take his own life. He may have thought that he had run out of options. The note to his father suggests to me that he would not attempt to go back to that well for water. That well had probably run dry. It still does not explain the other note he had written for the police."

Dolores chimed in, "We ran fingerprints on the crime scene, the envelopes, and the notecards, and found several partials, all matches for Wyman. This confirms that he had written the notes and not someone else, after his death. All this continues to indicate that Wyman took his own life. I only say that so we do not waste time generating any theories that this could have been a 'set up' homicide.

"Furthermore, the rope burns on his neck and the absence of any scratches or defensive wounds anywhere on his body are consistent with Wyman having taken his own life. An analysis of his blood found a blood alcohol level of point forty-two percent. This is very high, nearly lethal blood alcohol content amount."

Ed thanked Dolores and finished his summary saying, "We also confiscated Wyman's cell phone and computer and turned them over to Dolores' team for analysis. We will be conducting a search of his house today."

"Thanks Ed. I want to summarize on the whiteboard what we know about Wyman," I said.

On the whiteboard I wrote:

Randolph Wyman suicide
Failing restaurant
    Financial difficulties

Few identified financial resources
Note to father
Note to police
Matching partial fingerprints on both notes
Same custom stationery as notes written to Julia and tacked to my door
Confirmation that Michele purchased the custom stationery
Julia – conversations about employment with Wyman
Michele – conversations about employment with Wyman
Wyman history of personal failures and legal issues

"Is that about it?" I asked Ed and Dolores.
Both nodded their heads.

54

Michele Ronaldi was in the police station waiting room as Sergeant Apodaca had requested. She was accompanied by her attorney, Phyllis Borland. Phyllis was a well-known defense attorney in Santa Fe who had a reputation of being a bulldog in defense of her clients. The fact that Michele selected Phyllis to represent her made me even more suspicious about Michele. If she had nothing to hide, why would she need someone as forceful and, probably, as expensive, as Phyllis? Hmm.

I was also surprised when Ed told me how angry Michele had been with Phyllis over the phone when Phyllis let her know that there was nothing she could do to stop the police search of her house, given that they had a warrant. I would not want to be on Phyllis Borland's bad side, especially if she was going to represent me. Either Michele did not realize the power of the attorney she had employed or, like the reports of her behavior in New York City, she was unable to manage her anger when under pressure. Either way, I thought she'd made a big mistake by provoking Phyllis Borland.

I led Michele and Phyllis to the interview room and invited them to sit at the interview table. On the other side of the table, I sat with Sergeant Ed Apodaca. I had prepared for the interview by collecting photos of the custom stationery that had been used in the threats to Julia and me and was also present at the scene of Wyman's suicide.

Previously, I had met Phyllis at a few professional gatherings. In addition, Maria had gone to high school with her, and they seemed to have had a good relationship. I wanted to capitalize on any goodwill I might have with Phyllis by starting with some soft ball introductory statements.

"Good morning," I welcomed both of them. "Thank you for coming in. May I get you anything to drink? Coffee? Water? Coke?"

They both declined and Phyllis Borland began, "I am not sure what this is about or why you may have dragged us down here but, as you know, my client has a job, and she needs to be there. Could you please let us know what is going on? We both have better things to be doing."

Phyllis was very effective at trying to put us on the defensive immediately, deflecting any reason her client, Michele, would even need to be here. As she began the questioning, she tried to establish a conversation in which we would answer her questions rather than the other way around. It was a classic defense attorney's first move.

Not wanting to take the bait, I replied, "As you both know, we are investigating the recent murder of Julia Gomez at the same restaurant where Miss Ronaldi works. We have conducted numerous interviews and are collecting evidence that will help us solve this terrible homicide."

Interrupting, Borland challenged angrily, "So, because they both worked at the same place you have brought us down here to conduct a formal interview? Are you interviewing everyone who is now or has ever been affiliated with El Farolito? Why don't we just go ahead and get everyone who has ever dined at El Farolito interviewed as well. Yeah, that's it. Let's block off the plaza and do a group interview. This is absolutely ridiculous."

I had to admire Borland's moxey. She had no fear. It was also clear that any previous social interactions we may have had held no leverage. She was a freight train. Rather than respond to the assertion that we both knew was absurd, I began.

"It is important for me to proceed because we believe your client to be in a very precarious position regarding Miss Gomez's homicide. So, given your sensitivity regarding time, I will jump right to the concerns we have."

One by one, I brought photos out of my file folder and laid them side by side. There in front of attorney Borland and Miss Ronaldi, from left to right, were five envelopes and the backside of five notecards. I was not prepared to show either one of them what had been written on the notecards.

Borland quickly, and snidely, interjected, "Now what, Doctor Hunter, are you opening up a stationery store? What the hell does this have to do with my client?"

I explained, "These envelopes and notecards all came from the same batch of stationery. This has been confirmed by Nelda Baca, the manager of Write Impressions stationery store. Each of these envelopes contained the notecard pictured with it. On three of the notecards, there were threats related to Julia Gomez and the investigation. The last two notecards were found at the scene of Randolph Wyman's death yesterday."

Again, jumping in, Borland exclaimed, "Great! Congratulations Doctor Hunter and Sergeant Apodaca. It looks like you may have solved the case. Obviously Mister Wyman killed Julia and then killed himself. Case closed. May we leave now."

I was surprised by how relentlessly aggressive and sarcastic Borland was. She was very good on the attack. In the meantime, Michele Ronaldi sat back in her chair, arms folded, and with a smirk on her face. That would soon be erased.

"There are a couple more things I need to show you," I said, opening my laptop and putting it on the table. "Take a look at this."

I had already keyed up the video of Michele purchasing the custom stationery from Nelda Baca at Write Impressions. As I pushed the "Return" key on the computer, both Borland and Ronaldi moved in closer and focused their attention to the screen.

It did not take long for me to see Michele Ronaldi's complexion begin to blanche and her breathing increase. I let the video go on just to the point that it was clear that Michele was purchasing all of the items she had selected, including the box of custom stationery. As she drifted out of the scene, she could be seen reaching for her cell phone.

Sitting up, Ronaldi began "I, I...."

"Be quiet, Michele," Borland interrupted. "I will handle this."

Looking directly at me, Borland said, "This means nothing. I am sure many people and businesses in Santa Fe purchase the same stationery. Can you prove that the pictures of the stationery in front of came from the purchase Michele made? I'm guessing not."

"Wait, wait, there's more," I said imitating a host selling kitchen utensils on a television infomercial.

Smiling and turning to Ed, I said, "Sergeant Apodaca, can you help us out here?"

Ed began, "Certainly. As you know counselor, we had a warrant to search Miss Ronaldi's house yesterday. At her house, we were able to confiscate several items that could be of importance to the case."

Pulling out photos from his file folder, Ed said, "These are photographs we took of files we found in Miss Ronaldi's file cabinet. You can see there are three of them.

"One is marked 'JG' recipes. We have determined that Miss Ronaldi had photographed several recipes coming from a notebook belonging to Julia Gomez and having originated from her grandmother in Oaxaca. These are some of the recipes Miss Gomez was using at El Farolito.

"The second file marked 'Cookbook,' contained typed pages of a draft of a cookbook in the making. The book was to be titled '*Fusion Recipes of the Southwest*,' and the author was listed as Michele Ronaldi.

"In the third file marked 'Contract' was a letter from the Senior Editor of *Southwestern Cuisine* magazine. In this file was a letter indicating that the publisher had accepted Miss Ronaldi's submission and that a contract was on its way for Miss Ronaldi to sign as the author of a book of only Julia's recipes."

Not able to hide her irritation, Miss Borland jumped in and said, "So what. Everyone and their cousin want to write a book about something. Congratulations on my client for having had her book idea accepted. I can't tell that you have anything here. Just like the weak information on the stationery, you have nothing. I can't tell if you are simply incompetent or on some kind of a 'witch hunt.' In any case, this has nothing to do with my client."

Ed responded, "I had the opportunity to look at the contents of Miss Ronaldi's computer and there are some important entries that may interest you."

Ed placed in front of Borland and Ronaldi a typed sheet:

Activity on Michele Ronaldi's computer (past three months)

1. Emails

    a. Randolph Wyman (18)
    b. Fernando Romero (123)
    c. William Dirschauser (2)
    d. Josef Castellano (47)
    e. Miscellaneous in Santa Fe (247)
    f. Miscellaneous outside Santa Fe (122)

2. File folders

    a. JG recipes

b. Fusion Recipes

c. Book contract

3. Internet Searches of interest

a. Copyright laws

b. Getting rid of a competitor

c. Fatal Sous Chef mistakes

Ed continued, "With the combination of the stationery purchase and subsequent threatening notes, the book contract using Julia's recipes without any permission from or acknowledgement of her, and the information on Miss Ronaldi's computer, we believe we have significant grounds for motive for Julia's murder."

"Now Michele, please tell us where the rest of the custom stationery is," I interjected.

Michele stammered, "Wait, wait you don't understand..."

Again, Borland cut her off, "Shut up Michele! Doctor Hunter and Sergeant Apodaca, I would like a few minutes to talk with my client in private."

I collected the photos and my computer, and Ed and I stepped out into the hallway.

55

After a short break, Phyllis Borland stepped out of the interview room and requested that Sergeant Apodaca and I return.

Upon our entrance, we noticed a tearful Michele Ronaldi.

Borland began, "Michele has something she would like to tell you. Please kindly hold your questions until she has finished."

"Sure," I said, "we are very interested in what Miss Ronaldi has to say."

After being encouraged by Borland, Michele began, "Doctor Hunter, you already know that the circumstances in which Fernando brought Julia into the restaurant caused immediate friction between us, at least on my part. I hated Julia being there and I really hated Fernando more for having brought her in. I had already taken El Farolito to a level of excellence that it had never experienced in the past. There was no need to bring in another sous chef.

"I am not proud of how I treated Julia, but I didn't kill her. On one occasion, when Fernando sent Julia to the Farmer's Market to pick up some vegetables, she accidently left her locker unlocked with the notebook in it of her grandmother's recipes. I saw the opportunity and I took photos of her Oaxacan recipes on my iPhone. I wasn't sure at the time what I wanted to do with them, but I wanted to know the contents of her dishes that had become very popular.

"Yes, I admit that I was jealous. Actually, when Fernando kept pushing back the discussion about me having some kind joint ownership in the restaurant, I thought that he might be making such an offer to Julia.

"Quite by accident, I was looking at the magazine *Southwestern Cuisine*. I had not previously noticed that they also publish cookbooks. In fact, as I reviewed the magazine more closely, I saw several advertisements for cookbooks that they had published. Because my focus had always just been getting ideas for recipes, I had been oblivious to the ads."

"So, seeing the ads for cookbooks was the inspiration for creating one under your name using Julia's recipes?" I asked.

Hanging her head, Michele answered, "Unfortunately, yes. I knew that Julia's recipes were unique and that they could be the basis for a book. I thought that this would be my chance to market myself and open up opportunities outside of Santa Fe. I believed that any kind of ownership in El Farolito was not going to happen and there were no other options in town for me. So, I sent a proposal with a couple of recipes with photos attached to Marjorie Taylor at *Southwestern Cuisine*.

"I would give anything to take back what I have done. I was selfish and spiteful. I just wanted a way to get out of El Farolito. When Miss Taylor sent me the letter saying that they wanted to publish the cookbook, I couldn't stop myself. Did I hate Julia? Probably, but not enough to have killed her. Honestly, I had not figured out yet what I would do when she discovered that I had stolen her recipes."

I thought to myself, that being outed by Julia for plagiarizing her recipes was certainly motive for Michele to have killed her. I wanted to hear more.

Michele paused, wiping her eyes and for the first time showing some remorse. I still wasn't sure I was completely buying her story; her tears could be an act for having gotten caught. This still did not explain Michele's purchase of the custom stationery and the three threatening notes that had been written.

She had her chance to talk, now I needed some answers. I said, "I appreciate you having explained about essentially stealing Julia's recipes to further your own career. This still doesn't explain the video we have of you purchasing the custom stationery from the Write Impressions store. In my mind, this is more important since that stationery has been linked to a suicide and a murder. Do you have anything to tell us about that?"

Michele looked at her attorney and Borland nodded for her to continue.

"Doctor Hunter," Michele began, "do you remember that when we spoke at my house and I mentioned to you that, while running errands one day, I had gone to Rojas at the request of Randolph?"

"Yes." I answered. "You said that he wanted to speak with you about moving over to Rojas as the head chef and offered the potential of becoming a partner."

Now, her anger beginning to seep out and she said, "Yes, he was essentially offering me what Fernando had four years ago. I remembered the old adage, 'Fool me once, shame on you; fool me twice, shame on me.' I wasn't going to be anyone's fool again."

Just then I heard the sound of a text message arriving on my iPhone. Looking down at it, there was a note from Dolores. It said she needed to talk with me immediately in her office. I excused myself and asked Ed to continue the interview with Michele.

I exited the interview and made my way down the hall to Dolores' office. There, projected on a screen next to the whiteboard, were five documents and a photocopy of the recipes.

"What is this and why was it so important as to interrupt the interview with Michele Ronaldi?" I asked perplexed.

"Scott," Dolores began, "we have a problem."

"Really?" I asked. "What is the problem?"

Directing me to the projections on the screen explaining, "What I have projected are views of two different sets of envelopes and notecards and the photocopy from the "JG recipes" file that Ed confiscated from Michele's house.

"Okay," I said. "What is the problem?"

"The problem is that the handwriting samples do not match." Dolores explained.

When analyzing handwriting, you begin by looking for differences, not similarities. When comparing the handwriting between two documents, we try to determine if there are sufficient differences in the handwriting samples to rule out the same person as having written both documents.

"Once you determine that there are *not* sufficient differences to rule out that the same person wrote the document, you begin to look more closely at three main identifiers. The first identifier is letter form, including curves, slants, slope of writing, proportional size of letters. We then look at line form and how smooth and dark the lines are and indicating how much pressure is being applied to the writing instrument. Finally, we review formatting including spacing between letters and words as well as spacing between lines.

"At this point, if the documents seem to have met the criteria for similarities, we do a deeper dive into the handwriting such as looking at connecting strokes, pen lifts, size consistency, and 'diacritic' placement, meaning literally how the t's are crossed, and the i's are dotted.

"Notice the two envelopes and notecards on the left side. Those are the ones written by Randolph Wyman. The handwriting does match. However, our forensics' expert has determined that the handwriting on the other set of notes is not that of Michele's when comparing it to her written translation of Julia's recipes. None of the handwriting matches the notes given to Julia nor the two you received. This means that Wyman wrote the suicide notes but neither he nor Michele wrote the other ones.

"Damn, damn, damn," I exclaimed frustrated. "Just when I thought we were about to tie these things together, you are telling me that we have not identified matches to the threatening notes. That is the most important match of all."

"That is why I interrupted you," Dolores said. "It doesn't mean that Michele, or Wyman, or for that matter, Dirschauser, didn't kill Julia. It simply means that neither Michele nor Wyman wrote the threatening notes and there was one other feature that confirmed this.

"Look at the notes on the screen, left to right are the one to Julia, the one tacked to your front door, and the one attached to the brick thrown through the window at the Guadalupe. Notice that the writing on each note has a slight backward slant. That suggests that the writer was left-handed. We know that neither Wyman nor Ronaldi were left-handed, providing confirming that these notes were not written by them. Unfortunately, We still do not have any handwriting samples from Dirschauser or Josef Castellano to compare."

Now I was really puzzled. Why would Wyman have the same stationery as the notes to Julia and to me if he was not the author? Also, how could Michele have purchased the stationery but not have been the author of the notes either? As of now, we did not know who was in possession of the stationery nor the author of the threatening notes. I obviously needed to find out more from Michele.

I thanked Dolores and returned to the interview with this new information.

As I reentered the room, I could hear Michele still talking to Ed. They all looked up at me and I encouraged Michele to continue what she was saying.

"I mentioned to Doctor Hunter earlier that I had been running errands that afternoon. Those errands were, in part, for Fernando."

"What!" I exclaimed, "For Fernando, not for Wyman?"

She replied, "Yes. I mentioned to Fernando that I had to get some supplies for my home office, and he asked if, since I was going out, would I pick up an order that had arrived for him at Write Impressions. I needed to get some supplies anyway so I thought I would kill two birds with one stone. The video you just played was of me purchasing some supplies for myself and picking up the custom stationery and a manila envelope for Fernando."

I thought to myself how confusing this was. Just when I thought we had a Wyman/Ronaldi conspiracy, Dolores dashed that hope. Now, Fernando enters into the picture. Were the three of them in cahoots? It did not explain why Julia would have been murdered.

"Then why were the suicide notes left by Wyman on the same stationery?" I asked incredulously.

Michele answered, "On the video tape, after I bought everything and was walking away, you can see me reaching down to get my cell phone out of my purse. I could see it was Wyman calling. He asked me to come over to Rojas to discuss something important with him, but he wouldn't tell me what. That was the meeting I had with him that I mentioned to you.

"After Wyman and I talked for a few minutes, I got up to leave and he noticed that I had a bag from Write Impressions. He asked if I might have purchased some stationery, and if so, would I 'lend' him some. He said he had a few notes he needed to write and had just run out of good stationery.

"Grudgingly, I looked into the stationery I had picked up for Fernando. There were fifty envelopes and notecards in the small box. I did not think that Fernando would miss a couple, so I gave Wyman four envelopes and four notecards."

At that moment, Phyllis Borland jumped into the conversation. "Doctor Hunter and Sergeant Apodaca, my client has spoken freely with you about the concerns you had, and she did so of her own will and under the advice of her attorney. While she acknowledges that copying Julia's recipes for her own benefit was not the best thing she has ever done, no crime was committed.

"She has also explained to you why she had the stationery in question in her possession. Again, she has done nothing wrong. If you have no further questions, and you are not going to arrest my client, I think this interview is over."

From what I had learned from Dolores, it appeared that we had nothing on Michele allowing us to detain her further, certainly not to arrest her. I believed that she could still be guilty of having killed Julia, particularly in light of wanting to get rid of her before publishing her stolen recipes. The arrest records of her boyfriend, Josef Castellano, were also a consideration. Yet there was no reason to continue the interview at this time.

In response to attorney Borland, I said, "Yes, the interview is over, and we appreciate your assistance and cooperation. We request that you continue to make yourself available and not leave town until we have the case solved. You are free to go."

I was struck that Michele's ego, and her temper, had trumped common sense. Everyone in Santa Fe familiar with the culinary scene would know that the recipes in Michele's proposed cookbook were not hers, but Julia's. Her hubris and narcissism clouded her judgment. I wondered if they could have motivated her to murder Julia?

56

Following the interview with Michele and her attorney, Phyllis Borland, I huddled with Ed and Dolores. We discussed what we now knew and what our next steps would be. It was obvious that we needed a couple of items to clear up the issues of the owner of the custom stationery and the author of the notes. I asked Ed to secure handwriting samples from William Dirschauser, Josef Castellano, and now Fernando Romero.

I wanted to have a better understanding of Wyman's finances and how he had been keeping Rojas afloat. It was possible that the suicide note he had written to the police asking for forgiveness for the "activities" that have hurt and destroyed lives of innocent people could still be related to Julia's murder. The fact that Wyman had not written the notes that had been left for Julia and me did not absolve him from being the murderer. We also needed to better understand if Wyman had any involvement in Julia's life that we were unaware of.

Ed's team had just concluded conducting a thorough search of Wyman's house. In the process of turning Wyman's house upside down, they were particularly in search of evidence that could explain the content of the note to the police and exactly why Wyman wanted forgiveness. They were also looking for any possible indications that could link Wyman to Julia's death, including the presence large amounts of tetrahydrozoline.

Unfortunately, just like the restaurant, his house appeared to be barren and minimalist in its décor. They found a closet full of very expensive clothes. Aside from those, the rest of his house looked like he could have shopped at the Dollar Store. What little furniture he had was old, warn, and tattered. There were only what appeared to be inexpensive southwest prints on the walls with a notable absence of personal or family photos. On first glance, it suggested he had thrown what little resources he had into salvaging the restaurant.

The kitchen was equally absent of food or supplies. The refrigerator only had spoiled milk and sodas. The freezer had an ice tray. With the exception of a coffee pot, a couple of cocktail glasses, and a cabinet full of vodka, gin, and rum, there was nothing else. One exception was a small cache of cocaine in his bedside table.

It looked like Wyman was on a liquid diet at home and must have gotten most of his meals at the restaurant. There was no indication that he entertained. His house seemed like more of a crash pad than anything else. There were three notable exceptions.

Parked outside his house was a two-year old cherry red Maserati Levante S, usually selling for over one hundred grand. With his clothes and car, Wyman was more about superficial style than substance, always wanting to keep up the east coast rich kid image. With his house so destitute, it seemed to explain why he had such an opulent office. It was his office and restaurant in which he entertained people. However, he had not been able to generate enough income from the business to bring the remainder of the restaurant up to the style and comfort of his office. How sad, I thought.

A second item of interest was the accumulation in his mailbox of yet further invoices from creditors. These included Merchants Bank of the Southwest, Platinum Mortgage, Goldman's Gentlemen's Store, and another from Alarid Luxury Motors. The mountain of debt Wyman had must have been crushing, and it obviously was. Keeping up his façade of wealth and privilege finally caught up with him.

The most interesting find at Wyman's house was a box stuck in the corner of his closet. The box was filled with unopened first-class mail. They had all been addressed to "Mr. Randolph Wyman," and all had return addresses from the Boston area. The postmarks on the envelopes indicated that the mail had been sent during the time Wyman had been in Santa Fe and had continued until a week ago.

Return addresses in the box included mail from Jackson Wyman, Alastair Wyman, Felicity Wyman, Security Insurance Corporation, Withering Financial Group, and law firm Stearns, Cole, and Roberts LLC. There were over fifty first class envelopes in the box, and all unopened. It looked like Wyman wanted to cut all ties to his family and his past. It was a final statement of his anger.

Wyman's cell phone data told a similar story. He had received numerous Boston area code calls that had gone unanswered. Reverse phone number searches found the phone calls had originated from several of the same people that had been identified on the unopened mail envelopes. Most of them had come from his mother, Alastair Wyman.

One unhealthy, and often vicious, way people demonstrate their anger is to avoid or ignore attempts by others to make contact, hence the diagnosis, passive-aggressive. This had evidently been one of Wyman's ways of "getting back" at his family for whatever anger he may have held. When friends or acquaintances are ignored, they simply go away. Not so easy for family members, some never really go away.

In Wyman's case, it appeared that he wanted to inflict pain on them and, by ignoring their attempts to communicate with him, he was lifting his middle finger to them all. The problem with holding a grudge is that the grudge bearer is always the one doing the holding. Ultimately, the weight of Wyman's anger became too heavy for him to carry, leading him to end his life.

Wyman's outgoing calls had all been local. As we expected, he had called Julia Gomez on several occasions. Similarly, he had a number of calls to Michele Ronaldi. There were also a surprising number of calls to Fernando Romero. The remainder of the calls seemed to be routine calls to Rojas, with some to his creditors. The voice mail on his cell phone had been wiped clean.

The computers seized from Wyman's office and home did not provide any information of great value. He had done searches on "Successfully Managing a Restaurant, "Restructuring Debt," and some on "Selling a Restaurant." Other than that, both his cell phone and computer were set up with numerous video games including Grand Theft Auto, Spider Man Two, Madden NFL, Halo, and a couple of porn video games. He had spent hours on these video games, and by all indications, alone.

He had also conducted searches on dating websites, but it did *not* appear that he had ever submitted photos or a bio of himself.

The picture of Wyman that was beginning to emerge was a sad one indeed. It looked like he had been personally adrift, alienated from his family, and no evidence of close friends. Appearances were important and, while he presented himself with nice clothes and a fancy car, he was nearly bankrupt, both financially and personally.

I wondered if his reaching out to Julia and Michele was to revive

Rojas, to try to buy friendships, or both. In either case, he had failed miserably. Could his anger at not being able to win over Julia have resulted in killing her? The more I looked into his situation, the more I doubted it.

Just then I heard my iPhone ping. I had just received a text message. I didn't recognize the phone number and it appeared to be an international one. It looked like an out of the country number with a plus fifty-two prefix. I knew that prefix was Mexico. I wondered who, and why, someone from Mexico would be calling me.

<h2 style="text-align:center">57</h2>

I opened the text and the message read in Spanish, "Doctor Hunter, I need to talk to you. My name is Adelina Cruz. I am a friend of Sofia Lopez. You know her as Julia Gomez. I have been trying to reach her for several days. She told me that if I was ever unable to reach her that I should get in touch with you. She gave me your contact information. Please call me on the number with this text."

I was taken aback by the text message. It was unexpected and cryptic. It felt like Julia reaching back from the grave. I decided to call the number. I dialed the fifty-two prefix and then the rest of the number. After a few clicks and pauses, a female voice answered, "Hola."

"Hello," I answered back. "is this Adelina?"

"Si. I mean 'yes,' this is Adelina. Is this Doctor Hunter?" she answered.

Rather than try to talk in my broken Spanish, I decided to ask her to speak in English. Surprisingly, Adelina spoke fluent English.

"Yes," I answered. "This is Doctor Hunter. I just received the text message you sent, and I'm interested in hearing from you. How can I help you?"

"Doctor Hunter," she began, "I am a good friend of Sofia's, or Julia as you call her. I live in Oaxaca, and we grew up together in Tuxtepec, a city north of here. We talk or text regularly, but I have not been able to reach her for several days and I am worried about her."

"Why did you reach out to me instead of calling the police?" I asked.

Adelina answered, "Julia told me a long time ago that she does not trust the police. Her mother was killed in Tuxtepec, and the police did nothing to solve the case. I know that her step-father killed her mother, but the police did nothing to apprehend him. They acted as if her death never happened."

"I understand that," I replied. "but why did you call me?"

She answered, "Julia called me about a week ago and said that she had spoken with you about a note she received. She was really frightened and told me she was going to meet with you. She told me that she feared for her life and that if I couldn't reach her, I should call you."

I was surprised. Julia must have called Adelina after we met at Farmer's Market. This must have been something of a backup plan for her. I knew that I had to let Adelina know about Julia's death and I needed some more information from her.

"Adelina," I began in the most empathic voice I could muster, "I am sorry to tell you that your friend has been murdered."

There was a gasp and small shriek followed by obvious weeping. "Madre de dios. Por qué? Por qué? No Sofia! No Sofia."

I knew to let her cry and process Julia's death before asking question. I could hear her weeping and breathing in a halting manner, trying to regain her composure.

Finally, she said, "Doctor Hunter, when I didn't hear from her, I knew something was wrong. She was so afraid."

"What was she afraid of?" I asked.

"She called me late one night and told me she had discovered something bad by accident about her *jefe* and did not know what to do about it. She said that she told her jefe, and it was after then that she received the scarry note. She told me she was going to tell you all about it because she did not trust anyone else in Santa Fe. She was afraid to come back to Oaxaca because she believed her step-father would kill her just like he had killed her mother." Adelina replied.

"Her jefe? What does that mean, Adelina?" I questioned.

She responded weakly, still crying between words, "She was about to tell me when she said that she heard something outside of her house. She was frightened and had to make sure her doors were locked. She told me that she would call me later and explain, but that was the last I heard from her."

"Did she say if her jefe was a man or woman?" I asked.

"No," she replied. "I was going to ask her more questions, but I didn't have a chance. I wish I had more to tell you Doctor Hunter, but I can't think straight right now. I'm sorry."

"I completely understand, Adelina. If you think of anything else, please get in touch with me. I am so sorry for Sofia's death. Vaya con dios."

I said emphatically and hung up.

She had given me a lot to think about and I knew I could reach her again once she was less shaky and clearer.

Jefe? I wondered who Julia was referring to. It could have been Michele who was her boss in the kitchen. Maybe she found out that Michele had stolen her recipes and was going to publish them. That would certainly have been a motive for Michele to be alarmed and angry, but to kill her?

Thinking about Wyman's note, while he wasn't Julia's boss, he had made serious overtures for her to work for him at Rojas. What could Julia have discovered about Wyman or the restaurant that would have caused her to be frightened? Given Wyman's state of mind, could whatever she may have found, and her ultimate rejection of him have been the thing that threw him over the edge? Would he have killed her thinking that if he couldn't have her no one else could? With his impoverished state, he was certainly desperate, but was he so distraught as to resort to murder?

Finally, could jefe have referred to Fernando, the owner of El Farolito? He had hired her and while on a day-to-day basis she reported to Michele, he was really both of their bosses. Could Julia have discovered something sinister about Fernando? Could Fernando have uncovered attempts by Wyman to recruit Julia? Because of Fernando's obsessive need to elevate his status to become recognized as one of Santa Fe's elite businessmen, could he have seen Julia's possible departure to Rojas as an end to El Farolito's prominence in Santa Fe's culinary scene as well as a personal betrayal?

We had already conducted significant searches in both Wyman's house and that of Michele's, but we had not done anything serious with Fernando. Because he is well known in Santa Fe, I wanted to proceed cautiously. I did not want to conduct a search of his house before having time to interview him.

We were already reviewing the finances of Wyman and Rojas, so I decided to begin looking at Fernando's finances and that of El Farolito before interviewing Fernando. We still had an active search warrant to look into anything related to El Farolito. I asked Dolores to get her forensic accountants to look into all of the finances related to El Farolito over the past six months to determine if there had been any unusual activity.

58

It was now nearly lunch time and I needed to get some fresh air, stretch my legs, get some 'food for thought,' and have some time to think. I texted Maria to see if she could meet me for lunch and got a thumbs up in return. I was looking forward to reviewing what I knew with her. The Coyote Cafe as a place where I often go to think, reflect, and often write down my thoughts.

The Coyote Cafe is located about five blocks south of the police station on Water Street. The walk is just long enough for me to begin to clear my head. I stepped out of the police station and had to momentarily squint as the bright sun against the azure sky bathed my visual senses. I have learned to always wear sunglasses in Santa Fe. The elevation of seven thousand feet and the clearness of the skies makes the impact of the sun intense, but breathtaking. The air was crisp, the smell fresh, and it felt cool on my face.

The walk took me past the First Presbyterian Church, the first Protestant church established in New Mexico territory over one hundred fifty years ago. The church is built in the New Mexico pueblo style with a wide wooden entry door flanked by two massive columns and adobe walls with a traditional light brown stucco finish. It is rumored to have been the location of the marriage of Billy the Kid's mother, Catherine McCarty-Antrim. I am often surprised by feeling a sense of reverence and serenity when I pass by this historically significant building.

The cool air tickled my face as I strolled further down through Burro Alley, a short, narrow, and enchanting pathway, significant in Santa Fe's history. It was so named because it was the location where burros came into Santa Fe loaded down with firewood, the town's main heating source dating back to sixteen hundred and ten. The burros and their handlers were relegated to this alley, now home to a gallery and a Mexican restaurant. On the south side of the street, there is a life size wood-laden burro in bronze to commemorate the history of the alley.

Finally, I came to Coyote Café. The restaurant sits on the site where, in my youth. the Santa Fe bus station had occupied. I could still recall my parents' waving goodbye to me when at twelve years old, I rode a Greyhound bus all the way to El Paso, Texas, to visit family. It has been a restaurant for over thirty years, and I particularly like to sit out on its colorful Cantina rooftop. I found a quiet table in the corner with a view of Water Street and waited for Maria.

Maria arrived within a couple of minutes. Our waiter joined us, and Maria ordered the Cantina Chopped Salad with a glass of water. I needed some comfort food, so I ordered the Frito Pie, a staple in Santa Fe since I was a kid. I also had water. It had been an eventful morning, and I had a lot I wanted to review with her.

As I began telling Maria about the interview with Michele Ronaldi and her attorney Phyllis Borland, she grinned and said, "I'm guessing that Phyllis was a little different than when you saw her at the cocktail party at the Guadalupe last month."

I had to laugh and agreed. "Yes, she was quite unlike the Phyllis I saw then. She was charming at the party, but she definitely has a sharp edge, and it came out today. I can tell that as a defense attorney she represents her clients well."

Maria nodded in agreement and said, "Tell me more about the interview."

I proceeded to tell her about the highs and lows of the morning. I reviewed Michele's rationale for having bought the stationery for Fernando; her having given some of it to Wyman; and her admission of having copied and plagiarized Julia's recipes in order to write her own book. I told her that I thought we were headed in the right direction and nearing a close on the case.

"What about the lows?" she asked.

"Well," I began, "Dolores burst my bubble. Just when I thought we may have a tie-in to the stationery and the threatening notes, Dolores informed me that neither Wyman's nor Ronaldi's handwriting was a match."

Our food came and Maria suggested that we pause, enjoy our lunch on the outside deck, and take in the glorious view of Santa Fe. As usual, she was right to suggest a brief change of direction. I can become so caught up in the work that, as Maria says it, I forget to stop and "smell the piñon" in the air.

Maria had elected to eat healthy and indicated her salad was delicious. My Frito Pie was had several layers of wonderful tastes and took me back to my youth. When I was in high school, there was a Woolworth store on the plaza. One of their specialties was getting a small bag of Fritos, cutting it longways, and filling it with a mixture of ground beef, frijoles, and enchilada sauce. The mixture is poured over the Fritos and covered with cheese and diced onions. It was served in a paper bowl and with a fork or spoon. It is always interesting to me how the foods I grew up with still have a special meaning as an adult.

We chit-chatted through the meal and when we were about finished, our waiter brought us the final course, hot sopaipillas with honey.

Having taken time to "smell the piñons," I briefed Maria on what Ed's team found at Wyman's house, in particular the many unopened first-class letters from his family and Boston businesses. I finally told her about Adelina's call and the last distressing call she had with Julia. I told Maria that I was puzzled first about who Julia was referring to when she said she had found out something damaging about her jefe. And secondly, who she might have been referring to.

"Hmm," Maria responded. "Jefe can have several meanings. It can mean the 'boss,' as in your direct manager. It can also indicate the 'head,' as in the head of a department. Another meaning is that of 'manager,' like the most senior person in the dining room. Typically, it is used to describe either your immediate supervisor or, depending on context, the owner of the business.

"So, in Julia's case, jefe could be referring to her immediate supervisor Michele; or the owner Fernando, or even Josef Castellano since as maître d' he ran the dining room. There are a couple other possibilities. If Julia thought that she may bolt from El Farolito and go to Rojas, she could be referring to Wyman. It is also possible, but remote, that since Julia was responsible for purchasing food at the Farmer's Market, there could be a jefe there whom she discovered something about."

"Gee thanks," I said joking. "You have really narrowed down the list of suspects. I think I will probably stick with those we know best."

Turning more serious, Maria said "Something came up at the Guadalupe. It is probably nothing, but I thought I would mention it."

"Sure," I said expectantly, "what do you know?"

She answered, "One of the vendors that services the Guadalupe is Premier Distributing. They are responsible for much of the alcohol that Roberto purchases. In fact, the service many of the upper end restaurants in Santa Fe.

"Anyway, their area Manager, George Tsosie, periodically drops in and checks to see if Roberto is receiving the kind of service from Premier Distributing that he needs. It is the type of call you expect from vendors you are using. Kind of a quality check."

"How does this have anything to do with the case?" I quizzed her.

"Maybe nothing," she said, "but dad and George have known each other a long time and are just as much friends as business acquaintances. George asked dad if he knew of a company named Green Chile Enterprises."

"Green Chile Enterprises? Who the heck are they? Do the supply green chile to restaurants?" I said, becoming a little impatient.

"That is exactly what Roberto wondered," Maria said, "but it is actually some kind of payment or holding company. It seems that when servicing Rojas, Premier Distributing was instructed to send invoices to Green Chile Enterprises at a P.O. Box in Albuquerque."

"Why was George Tsosie asking you father about them? He doesn't have any affiliation with them, does he?" I asked.

"No, not in the least," she replied. "It seems that in the past couple of months, Premier Distributing has not received payment from Green Chile Enterprises for supplies that have been delivered to Rojas. George told dad that Rojas is over seventy thousand dollars in arears to Premier Distributing. In fact, George said that because his invoices had not received any responses, he had sent a letter directly to Randolph Wyman asking for payment. Having heard that Wyman was now dead, he was concerned about receiving payment."

A lightbulb went off as I recalled the invoices that Ed had discovered in Wyman's office. I recalled that one had been from Premier Distributing. But Green Chile Enterprises did *not* ring a bell.

"It may be a coincidence," I responded, "but I am aware of a delinquent Premier Distributing invoice being sent with a demand letter found in Wyman's office desk at Rojas. This may actually be some beneficial information.

"Maria," I said beaming, "you are the best. I will even pick up the tab for lunch."

After a little more small talk, we stood up, I gave her a big hug, and we were off.

59

Green Chile Enterprises. Green Chile Enterprises. I kept turning that name over in my mind, trying to make any connection, but I could not. I had no recollection of the name and could not make the link to any businesses.

I decided to walk to my business office to conduct some research on this new entity. I Googled Green Chile Enterprises, hoping to come up with a website and some other contact information. There was no website and no indication on the web that it actually existed.

Puzzled, I searched for the name on the Small Business Administration site. Nothing. I searched the Better Business Bureau site. Again, nothing. I searched the Albuquerque and Santa Fe Chambers of Commerce sites. Nothing. I was about to give up when I decided to search the New Mexico Secretary of State site to determine if the company had been established as a Limited Liability Company, or an LLC. Bingo.

On the New Mexico Secretary of State site I found Green Chile Enterprises, LLC listed as an outsourced billing company managing invoice payments for small businesses and operating in the "Hospitality and Food Services" industries. The site indicated it had only one employee, Ruben Benavidez, President and identified the company in the "one-to-five employee" range. I found it unusual that they had no website and only listed a single employee.

I was aware of such outsourcing companies operating in the small business space. For smaller companies not wanting the cost or hassle of back office administrative work, they would contract with such an outsource business to handle invoicing and collections. These collection and invoicing businesses typically had a small staff and were paid by the companies with whom they contracted. The usually had business accounts at banks for the inflow of fees and outflow of invoice payments. Once invoices were received, the outsourced business would collect from the contracted company and pay the invoice. In some respects, it was a substitute for a business having accounting staff. They typically charged a modest fee for their services.

So, it looked like Wyman's restaurant, Rojas, had been using Green Chile Enterprises as a third party for paying Premier Distributing. I wondered if there were other vendors that were receiving payments the same way. Typically, a restaurant, even a small one, would have vendors simply send invoices to the restaurant address. Someone, usually the owner or manager, would pay the invoices rather than invest in the third-party payment company. I was unsure why, or if, this had anything to do with Wyman's suicide.

I needed to dig deeper and find out who this Ruben Benavidez was. I also wanted call George Tsosie. I wondered if he would know anything else about either Green Chile Enterprises or Ruben Benavidez. I knew that I needed the police department experts to help on this. I called Dolores Griego, the forensics expert, to enlist her assistance.

I asked Dolores to research Green Chile Enterprises and Ruben Benavidez. I told her I was particularly interested in any connection to Rojas as well as any other companies, or vendors, that she could discover. In the meantime, I called George Tsosie.

The call to George Tsosie yielded some new information. George told me that initially, when he was developing a business relationship with Randolph Wyman and Rojas, the bills went straight to Wyman and the restaurant. After about a year, Wyman directed Premier Distributing invoices be sent to a P.O. Box in Albuquerque for payment from a third party, Green Chile Enterprises. He explained that he preferred to email invoices, but that Wyman expressly wanted invoice sent via snail mail to the P.O. Box.

Over the course of the following year, the process of invoicing and receiving payments generally went well with some payments late, but not terribly late. It had only been recently that invoiced payments had stopped altogether. At that point, Tsosie began asking other vendors whom he knew worked with Rojas if they were also have difficulty collecting on invoices. They reportedly had the same experience as Tsosie.

Because there was no way to contact anyone at Green Chile Enterprises, except via the P.O. Box, Tsosie and other vendors were faced with having to send their past due invoices directly to Wyman at Rojas, unfortunately with the same non-payment results. Tsosie said that Premier Distributing had discontinued their deliveries to Rojas two weeks earlier. He suspected that other vendors may have discontinued deliveries as well since there was no phone number or email address. Tsosie also said that he did not know anyone named Ruben Benavidez and had never been given the name of any contact person at Green Chile Enterprises.

I wrapped up with my call to Tsosie and was just leaving my office when my iPhone rang indicated Dolores was calling me back.

"Hi Dolores," I answered. "That was quick."

Without hesitation Dolores said, "Scott, I think you better come to the station. Ed and I have something to show you.

60

I hoofed it back to the station from my business office and got there in about fifteen minutes. I was met by an excited Sergeant Apodaca and an even more excited Dolores. She had already been able to research Ruben Benavidez and Green Chile Enterprises. Reviewing what she found was exhilarating.

Dolores had been able to secure a Financial Crimes Search Warrant allowing her department access to bank records for both Green Chile Enterprises and Ruben Benavidez. The warrant was granted due to the belief that transactions into and out of Green Chile Enterprises could be linked to Randolph Wyman's suicide and possibly some kind of fraud. The suicide was still under investigation along with the demise and possible bankruptcy, of Rojas.

Dolores had been able to identify one bank, the Merchants Bank of the Southwest in Santa Fe, as having accounts with both Benavidez and Green Chile Enterprises. The warrant specified 'any and all' records from these accounts for the past year. The Green Chile Enterprises account showed a relationship between invoice payments to vendors and Rojas bank deposits. Strikingly, Rojas, and Randolph Wyman, appeared to be the only client of Green Chile Enterprises. Why in the world would Randolph not have hired just a part time accountant to manage his accounts?

The payments had been sent to an average of about twelve vendors each month. The first nine months demonstrated a consistent flow of deposits and invoice payments. However, while deposits continued coming into the account for the past three months, there had been no payments made for invoices. In addition, the deposits tapered off so that a much smaller deposit had been made in the previous month.

Another anomaly was that deposits by Wyman far exceeded invoice payments for the previous twelve months. The balance of these excess funds was transferred monthly into yet another account named DBA EFR, following invoice payments. Dolores did not yet have a warrant to look into that account. Statistically, the amount going into the DBA EFR account was about twenty percent of the monthly total of all invoice payments. If it was the fee for the outsourced payment business, it was a very hefty fee indeed.

When looking into the Benavidez account, she noted that there had been a monthly deposit from the DBA EFR account into his of twenty-five hundred dollars. I guessed that this was Benavidez salary. But where was the remaining money gone, I wondered.

We were also missing the actual vendor invoices, so we were unable to match invoice payments to what had been billed. We wanted to know whether or not Wyman was being charged the definite invoiced amounts or if there was some kind of a 'management fee' that had been tacked on to them.

Dolores had already identified the vendors involved from their bank routing numbers. She was in the process of requesting copies of vendor invoices to Rojas that matched the same period for which she had Green Chile Enterprises banking records. She expected those soon.

As the three of us sat in Dolores' office, we noted with a combination of excitement and fatigue that it had been a very big day including:

> The interview with Michele Ronaldi and her attorney
> The determination of the handwriting analysis on the custom stationery
> The call from Adelina regarding Julia's "jefe"
> The conversation with Maria about Green Chile Enterprises
> The conversation with George Tsosie
> The information Dolores attained on bank accounts of Ruben Benavidez and Green Chile Enterprises

In thinking through next steps, we knew Dolores needed to secure a Financial Crimes Search Warrant for the DBA EFR banking account. She needed to receive all of the invoices from the identified vendors supplying Rojas for the past year. Then, her forensics accounting team could analyze the flow of payments and matching invoices to payments. Hopefully, they could identify where the remaining seventy-five percent of the excess billing was being allotted.

Ed and his team planned to make a visit to Ruben Benavidez to better understand the business of Green Chile Enterprises and how they charged their only client, Rojas, for services. He would also ask Benavidez about the owner of the DBA EFR account, and where the disbursement of funds from the account went.

Because Fernando Romero had been the purchaser of the custom stationery that Michele Ronaldi had picked up for him, and since we did not have a copy of his handwriting, I ask him to come to the station the next day for another "informational interview."

We were all aware that Chief Detective Miguel Montez and his wife were on a flight back from Spain to Santa Fe as we spoke. Depending on the severity of his jet lag, he might be joining us the following day. We all looked forward to his return, wisdom, and assistance on the case.

I volunteered to buy Ed and Dolores a beer at the La Fonda Bell Tower rooftop bar and they both accepted. Maria was able to join us and we discussed where we stood on the case over a Spanish Cheeseboard and drinks. The bar on the top floor of the iconic La Fonda hotel offers a picturesque view of the city and the mountains as well as the Santa Fe Plaza and Cathedral Basilica. I always felt grateful to be a part of Santa Fe when I was here enjoying a drink and a beautiful New Mexico sunset.

I was interested in the additional information that Maria had gleaned from the calls she made.

"Apparently," Maria began, "Premier Distributing wasn't the only vendor that Rojas and Wyman had stiffed. I spoke with six other vendors who serviced both Rojas and my family's Guadalupe restaurant. In each case, the pattern was the same. They had all been receiving steady, albeit occasionally late, payments from Green Chile Enterprises on a regular basis until about three or four months ago. Then, in every case, the payments stopped.

"They had each tried various ways to collect prior to discontinuing services. They all had the same frustration that reaching anyone at Green Chile Enterprises was a futile effort, given that all they had was a P.O. Box in Albuquerque. In the end, they all believed that Wyman was in deep financial trouble and unable to make payments. There was a feeling that Wyman's suicide provided verification of their assumption that the restaurant was failing."

As Maria spoke, Dolores, Ed and I nodded our heads in agreement that the information Maria provided was further proof that we were getting closer to answering some of our most pressing questions, but which ones, Wyman's suicide motive or Julia's homicide?

Maria and I decided to complete the evening by having dinner downstairs in the lobby of La Fonda at La Plazuela restaurant. The food was delicious, and I had the Filet y Enchiladas plate, topped with both red and green chile. This dish begged for a cold margarita, or two, to accompany the heat of the chile. The food and drink, along with my beautiful Maria's company, took my mind off of anything else but the moment.

Then it was off to our home for a well-deserved rest. Tomorrow would bring its own surprises.

61

I was awakened early the next morning with my iPhone singing Malagueña. I knew it was Miguel calling. I looked at the time on my iPhone before answering. I had slept in, and it was already seven. My throbbing head told me that I had one margarita too many as I answered his call.

"Good morning, Miguel," I said groggily.

"Don't you mean good afternoon, Scott?" I am jetlagged and still on Spain time. It is mid-afternoon for me, and I am wondering where all my team is. We have an interview with Fernando Romero in two hours. Do you think you could possibly get down here to the station by then? Or should I reschedule to a time more convenient for you?" he bantered sarcastically.

Even as tired as I was, it was great to hear Miguel's voice and have him back. "I will try my best to get there by that time," I bantered back.

I arrived at the station well before Romero, so Miguel and I had time to catch up. We decided that the interview with Romero needed to be low key and, ostensibly, for Romero to bring Miguel "up to speed" on everything he knew about Julia's homicide.

Shortly thereafter, Romero arrived. We engaged Romero with a brief discussion about Miguel's trip to Spain. Then, for "informational" purposes, we gave Romero a pad and pen to write down any observations or additional thoughts he had since we first met.

He was "happy to help" as he wrote down his recollections, using his left hand. We kept the interview relatively short and upbeat. We told Romero that we were closing in on a suspect for Julia's homicide and that the information he had provided had been very helpful.

As we got up to leave, Romero invited us to El Farolito for a meal "on the house." We told him we would take him up on it and escorted him to the exit. As he walked away, I noticed a slight limp and asked him about it.

"Doctor says I have a case of plantar fasciitis, the result of flat feet," he replied shaking his head. "It hurts like hell after I have been sitting a while. And, when I roll out of bed every morning, OMG, that first step or two is murder. Doc gave me a shot in the foot and told me to 'stretch and soak' and I would be back to normal in no time. Problem is that it is *not* getting back to normal."

We waved goodbye to him as he headed to the parking lot and got into his black BMW X2 SUV. We noticed that his car was small and could be difficult to pick up in the dark. Hmm.

I immediately took Romero's handwritten note to Dolores for analysis and comparison to the threatening notes that both Julia and I had received.

Miguel and I went to his office to discuss the case as well as Wyman's suicide and the notes he had left behind.

We had not been reviewing too long before Sergeant Apodaca poked his head in.

After greeting us, he said, "I was just about to go to Ruben Benavidez' house to talk with him when Dolores' tech guy, whom I had asked to take a second look at Julia's computer, came across a file that had been overlooked. The file was titled chile verde and in the folder called "*Recetas.*" Because Julia was a chef and had an interest in New Mexican recipes, we originally thought that the title of the file related to green chile recipes, so it was initially overlooked."

"What did he find?" Miguel asked.

"It appears," Ed began, "that Julia was using this file to catalog some information about vendor invoices. Come with me to the conference room and I will show you. Dolores also has some information that I know will help."

In the conference room, Dolores was already sitting with a file folder in front of her laid out on the table. Ed directed Miguel and me to seats in front of an open computer on the conference room table. Ed said that it had been Julia's computer. There on the screen was a photo of a document.

Ed explained, "The file had several photographs of vendor invoices to Rojas, obviously taken from a cell phone. In addition, there was a simple spreadsheet with the same invoice numbers but two columns showing different unit prices and totals. The photographed invoices had the higher unit prices and totals.

Our theory is that Julia either stumbled across the invoices and thought they were interesting enough to take pictures, or she could have been actively looking into them. It almost looks like she was planning to use this information, but for what purpose we do not know."

One of the photographs showed a chart with four columns: Vendor Name, Invoice Number, Actual, Billed. At the bottom was a cell titled "Profit" which tallied the difference between the "Actual" and "Billed" columns. The vendors' names were the same ones that Maria had identified as having served both Rojas and the Guadalupe.

"Notice," Ed clarified, "the heading for the chart is GCE, which we now believe to mean Green Chile Enterprises. When we put together all of the photos of invoices with the photo of the chart, this begins to look like an 'off the books' accounting of the profits.

"Furthermore, these were the same vendors identified in the Green Chile Enterprises banking account as having received payments for invoices sent to Rojas. It appears that Julia had discovered some kind of scheme."

Opening her file folder, Dolores added, "I spoke to all of the vendors identified in the Green Chile Enterprises banking account. I asked them to send copies of their past twelve months invoices billed to Rojas so I could compare them with payments. In every case, until about three months ago, the amounts paid to the vendors was the exact amounts they had billed."

"Okay," I said, "then what is the problem?"

Dolores smiled and replied, "When you compare the invoices that were actually sent to Green Chile Enterprises with the photocopies of invoices in Julia's 'chile verde' file, we see some serious discrepancies."

As Dolores put the actual copies of vendors' invoices alongside the same photocopied invoices from Julia's computer, the differences were obvious. On each vendor photocopied invoice, the description and amounts of the products were the same. What was different were the increases in both the unit prices and the totals. In each case, there was a difference of twenty to twenty-five percent. In other words, the photocopied invoices had been altered to show higher prices.

"We believe," Dolores started, "that someone at Green Chile Enterprises, maybe Ruben Benavidez, altered these invoices so that Wyman was unknowingly paying Green Chile Enterprises a significantly higher amount for the goods and services than the vendors had charged.

"We also believe that Wyman was receiving the altered copies of the invoices and was completely unaware that he was drastically overpaying.

Late last night we secured a subpoena to look into the DBA EFR banking account where some of the money from Green Chile Enterprises was being funneled. Our forensics' accounting team is now able to look into that account and should have information for us soon."

"Amazing work Ed and Dolores!" I said, very proud of my colleagues.

"Ed," I continued, "when you talk to Benavidez, make sure to learn all about the DBA EFR account in addition to everything else you are looking into."

As Miguel and I returned to his office, he put his hand on my shoulder and said, "I should take my wife to Spain more often. It looks like you have everything under control."

While I appreciated the affirmation, I knew we still had a long way to go.

62

Miguel requested time to catch up on paperwork, check in with Chief of Police Trujillo, and talk more with me later.

After another hour, as had been our tradition when in the middle of cases, Miguel and I went to Java Joe's to have a cup of coffee and an empanada.

As we entered, the barista, Carmen, came out from behind the counter and gave Miguel the biggest hug.

"I didn't know you were back from your vacation. It is so good to see you!" Carmen exclaimed. "We have missed you."

Smiling and hugging her back, Miguel agreed that it was good to be back.

Feeling like I was drifting into the woodwork, I said pleadingly, "What am I, chopped liver? Don't I get a hug too?"

Smiling sympathetically, Carmen responded with a hug for me and asked, "Shall I get you both your regulars," then added looking at Miguel, "or has Spain changed your preferences?"

We both stayed with our regulars, and, in no time, Carmen had brought us our coffees and a breakfast burrito.

Miguel and I talked briefly about his anniversary trip to Marbella, and what life had been like for Maria and me while he was gone.

As we began to discuss both Julia's homicide and Wyman's suicide, I noticed Miguel beginning to yawn. I knew that jetlag was now hitting him. He initially insisted that he was fine, but his head kept nodding and I knew it was time to get him back home to catch up on his rest.

As I was about to propose that he go home, my iPhone rang. I could tell it was Sergeant Apodaca.

"Hey Ed," I answered. "What's up?"

Ed replied, "My team and I have just been over to Ruben Benavidez house for the informal interview we discussed. He was really spooked by our presence and *very* willing to talk. He said that he wasn't going to take the fall for anyone, and he didn't even ask for his attorney. I have him with me in the squad car now and am about to take him to the police station. Are you available to interview him?"

"You bet," I said. "I can be there in twenty minutes."

"One more thing," Ed interrupted, "we are going to need search warrants for both Benavidez house as well as for Fernando Romero's house. I'll ask Miguel to make those calls before we interview him."

I was surprised at just how much activity there had been in such a short time. Miguel had quickly gotten the ball rolling with Judge Gonzales on the warrants.

I strongly suggested to Miguel that he go home for some rest, and he told me NO just as strongly.

We were back at the police department and in an interview room when Ed brought Benavidez into the building. Judge Gonzales indicated that the warrants would be ready soon, and we wanted to begin the interview with Benavidez now.

As Ed had observed, Benavidez was very anxious and fearful. I knew that the best time to get the most honest information from potential suspects is when they have the most to lose. Even when they fail to honestly answer questions, their "tells" give them away much more readily. The way they answer questions, their body language, and their mannerisms are much less guarded, giving the interviewers insights as to when to press and when to step back.

Benavidez was short and wary, looking from side-to-side and twitching his nose. He had difficulty making eye contact. He was wearing a hooded black sweatshirt, baggy torn blue jeans with a pant chain attached to a belt loop and ending in his pocket, and dirty and untied construction boots. He appeared to be trying to make up for his massive insecurity with his exaggerated punk look.

He was squirming in his chair, with his leg moving up and down nonstop, heavy breathing, fingers twitching, and sweat on his brow. I almost felt sorry for him, but believed whatever he had to say would be in the service of self-preservation. He did not appear to be a sophisticated individual, was compliant, and seemed to be someone who could be easily influenced and manipulated. His diminutive hands and limp handshake gave me the impression that he was someone who might have been easily bullied as a youth.

Because of his fatigue, Miguel elected to watch me interview Benavidez from behind the one-way mirror. I invited Ed to join me in the interview room.

Not wanting to move too quickly to specifics, the first part of the interview was more about background information, where Benavidez had grown up, jobs, family history, etcetera. It was in this part of the conversation that Benavidez told us of his connection to Fernando Romero.

Benavidez' mother and Romero's mother were cousins, part of a large extended family living in Santa Fe, Albuquerque, and Raton. While Benavidez and Romero had not grown up in the same place or gone to the same schools, they had been together frequently at family gatherings over the years. Romero was seven years older than Benavidez.

As Benavidez told it, Romero was seen as the "golden boy" of the family, admired because he owned El Farolito. The fact that, over the years, some of Romero's acquaintances had questionable backgrounds only added to Romero's reputation as someone who had power and status. Little did Benavidez know about Romero's failed longing to be among Santa Fe's elite businessmen.

When I began to ask questions more pertinent to the Green Chile Enterprises, Benavidez' led with "It wasn't my idea. I told him it would never work, and I am not taking a fall for the bastard."

"Hold up a minute, Mister Benavidez," I said trying to slow him down, "one thing at a time. First, what exactly was Green Chile Enterprises? What was the main purpose of it?"

Benavidez talked at length about how Fernando had come to him with a "job opportunity." Always in need of money, he accepted Romero's offer. Knowing that Benavidez had taken an accounting class in high school, Romero said he simply wanted Benavidez to set up a bank account and a P.O. Box in Albuquerque. Benavidez would go to Albuquerque once a month and pick up invoices sent to the P.O. Box. Using checks from the bank account, Benavidez would write checks to the vendors, make copies of the invoices, and send them to Romero.

Once copies of the invoices had been sent to Romero, Benavidez would receive cash payments from Romero for this service. Because of his anxiety, he tended to talk fast and in incomplete sentences. The more I pressed him, the quicker he breathed. I did not want him to stroke out in front of me, but I needed a little more information.

"How much was Mister Romero paying you for this responsibility?" I asked.

Benavidez replied, "Fernando paid me two thousand five hundred dollars per month."

"So," I began, "you opened an account at Merchants Bank of The Southwest in the name of Green Chile Enterprises. Is that correct?"

Benavidez nodded in agreement.

Continuing, I asked, "You also opened a P.O. Box at the main post office in Albuquerque under the name Green Chile Enterprises, is that also correct?"

Again, he nodded his head.

"Mister Benavidez," I said skeptically, "how were deposits made into the account to pay for the invoices and how did you know that you would have enough to pay for them? Did you receive bank statements?"

"Look, Doctor Hunter," Benavidez answered, "Fernando told me not to worry about money in the bank account. He said he would take care of that. And, when the account was first set up, Fernando wanted statements sent electronically to an email address he gave them. I never saw the statements, so I never knew the amount of the deposits. I just paid the invoices.

"Fernando told me the invoices were for wholesalers that were servicing Rojas restaurant. He told me that he had a contract with Randolph Wyman to take care of invoice payments. Fernando said he was doing Mister Wyman a big favor by doing this for him. I wondered if Fernando was doing something illegal or something like that, but I needed the money and did not want to ask too many questions. That's all I know."

This was getting stranger by the minute. Why would Romero be managing Wyman's invoices? "Do you still pay the invoices?" I asked.

"No," he answered, "Fernando told me to stop paying them about four months ago. I still went once a month to pick up the invoices, but Fernando told me just to keep the unopened envelopes and he would take care of them eventually. So, that is what I did, and I still have them in a box in a closet in my house."

"Did Fernando keep paying you after you stopped paying the invoices?" I asked.

"Yes," he said, "but he told me I needed to start looking for another job."

Then pleadingly, Benavidez said, "That's all I know. I promise. Now can I leave?"

"One more thing, Mister Benavidez," I said trying to keep him engaged, "what do you know about the DBA EFR account?"

"I don't know nothing about that. I ain't never heard of it. Now can I go?" he asked.

"Mister Benavidez," I said looking at him with disbelief, "it is hard to imagine that you have never heard of DBA EFR, because every month for at least the past year, money has been going from the Green Chile Enterprises account to DBA EFR, and you are telling me you know nothing about it? I find that hard to believe."

Now Benavidez replied assertively, "I'm telling you, I don't know anything about no DBA EFR. Besides, the only thing I did was write checks. I never even saw statements of account activity or balances. Fernando did all of that shit. Look, I have told you everything I know, can I go now?"

Remembering that we needed a handwriting sample from Benavidez, I asked him to write a paragraph summarizing what he had just told me so that we would have his observations "on file." He reluctantly agreed as I handed him a pen and a blank sheet of paper.

Once he had completed writing his observations, I explained to Benavidez that we had a warrant to search his house and that an officer would take him home and conduct a search with his team.

He wasn't happy about the search of his home but was glad to leave the police station.

I personally shuttled Benavidez' handwritten notes to Dolores for analysis and then went to meet with Miguel and Ed.

63

M iguel, Ed, and I huddled briefly after the interview and agreed that Benavidez seemed to be credible and telling the truth. His anxiousness and high attention to self-preservation suggested he was probably being honest about what he told us. What we didn't know was if there might be anything that he had not told us.

He had added some significant information to our investigation. If what he told us was the truth, it seemed like Benavidez was a pawn and an errand boy. The fact that he denied knowing anything about altered post-payment invoices suggested that he simply occupied a low-level role. However, his information did point to Fernando Romero big time, especially for his dealings with Wyman regarding Rojas.

We needed to understand the relationship between Romero and Wyman. Was there a written contract for Romero to handle payments of Wyman's bills? If there was, then the discrepancy between the original invoices and the "doctored" invoices suggested the potential for theft or fraud on Romero's part.

Having concluded the interview with Benavidez, I insisted that Miguel go home and get some rest. He finally agreed. I promised to get in touch with him if anything important happened.

Before moving on, Ed and I checked in with Dolores and found her huddled with two of her team.

"Your timing is perfect," Dolores exclaimed.

"Really?" I replied. "Did you get Benavidez' handwriting analyzed so soon?"

"Not that," Dolores stated, "but I can tell with just a cursory glance that Benavidez did not write those notes. He is right-handed and his writing does not have that same backward slant to it. So, we can rule him out.

"But I have even better news," she continued, "Fernando Romero's handwriting is a match to both the note written to Julia Gomez and the notes to you, Scott."

"You're kidding," I said skeptically. "Are you sure?"

Nodding her head, Dolores said, "We are certain. Remember the criteria I explained to you earlier about how we determine if the handwriting on two documents is from the same person? First you look for differences to rule out that the two documents have not been written by the same individual. If there are no key differences, you begin looking for similarities in the categories of letter form, line form, and formatting."

"Yes," I answered, "I remember. That is how you were able to determine that *neither* Randolph Wyman nor Michele Ronaldi had written the threatening notes to Julia and me."

"Correct." Dolores said. "Using those same criteria, we were able to determine that the handwriting on the notes to Julia and to you were an exact match with Fernando Romero's handwriting on the 'recollections' that you had him write."

Looking at her with a sense of astonishment, I asked, "And you are absolutely positive, Dolores?"

"Positive," she answered.

I was in a total state of shock. I knew about Romero's obsession to be widely admired as a successful businessman. I wasn't surprised that he could be manipulative and deceitful, but sending threatening notes and maybe even committing murder? Even with confirmation of the handwriting analysis, that still seemed far-fetched.

If all this was true, it meant that Romero was the jefe about whom Julia mentioned to Adelina. He was the one intimidating Julia with the threatening note. He had also nailed the envelope to the door of my house holding the note and photos of Roberto with a target on his back, and he had thrown the brick with the note attached through the window of the Guadalupe.

"There is one more thing, Scott," Dolores said, "and I think you are going to like this."

Half joking, I said, "What more could there be?"

She answered, "My forensic accounting team just made some interesting discoveries. They were able to determine that DBA EFR was another separate account at Merchants Bank of the Southwest account that had been set up by Fernando Romero. The monthly electronic transfers from Green Chile Enterprises into DBA EFR were going to Romero through this account."

I thought that this confirmed what Benavidez had suggested regarding Fernando Romero being behind Green Chile Enterprises and now, DBA EFR.

"We also determined," Dolores continued, "that, over the course of the past twelve months, about two hundred-seventy-five-thousand-dollars went from Green Chile Enterprises into the DBA EFR account, or almost twenty-three-thousand-dollars a month."

I thought to myself that, after paying Benavidez, Romero would still have a profit of almost two hundred forty thousand dollars, all on phony invoices. I was sure Wyman was unaware of this discrepancy.

Suddenly, I felt a strong sense of urgency to get Romero to the station for an interview, but we needed some further information first. After having obtained a warrant, I dispatched Ed to Romero's house to conduct a search about anything related to Green Chile Enterprises, Rojas, Randolph Wyman, or the notes that Julia and I had received.

It was clear that we needed to start circling the wagons around Romero.

64

It had been a wild twenty-four hours. Just yesterday morning I wouldn't have believed that Miguel and I would now be sitting across from Fernando Romero and his attorney, Max Brooks. This was the same Fernando that had recently invited Miguel and me to dine with him at El Farolito. His demeanor was no longer as friendly.

Following Sergeant Apodaca's search of Romero's house, a shed on his property, and a cabin near Pecos about thirty minutes from Santa Fe, we had gathered enough evidence to arrest Romero. The arrest was for the murder of Julia Gomez and the theft of thousands of dollars from Randolph Wyman.

We believed that the combined amount of evidence we had accumulated, though circumstantial, was sufficient to justify the arrest and the charges.

At Miguel's request, I took the lead in the interview.

"Mister Romero, as you know, you have been arrested for the murder of Julia Gomez and second-degree felony larceny for the theft of funds from Randolph Wyman. Sergeant Apodaca read you your Miranda Rights last night when you were arrested. Before we begin, do you have anything you would like to say?" I asked.

Romero, looking smaller than ever in his jail uniform, sat upright and said, "You have made a big mistake. This is all bullshit! All of it. You have nothing on me. You need to let me out of here or I will make real trouble for both of you."

I had heard this refrain before. It is a common one. Denial comes first, then angry attacks, and then a series of deflections providing alternate explanations for the presented evidence. I know that it is important in

231

the early stages of an interview to maintain a calm demeanor and simply lay out the facts. I decided to begin with what we had on the theft from Wyman.

At Romero's house, Ed found the contract between Wyman and Green Chile Enterprises to manage payments to vendors. The contract had been signed by both Wyman and Romero and it was notarized. In the contract, Wyman agreed to pay a monthly fee of two thousand-five hundred dollars in exchange for the management of vendor payments. Wyman would be required to make a monthly deposit into Merchants Bank of the Southwest for vendor invoices, copies of which would be provided to him. The contract itself was a straight up deal. There was nothing in the contract specifying additional payments to Romero other than the management fee.

I put the contract in front of Romero.

"Yeah," he said defensively, "so what? Wyman was an idiot when it came to business. He thought that he knew more than he actually did because he came from a big, rich family. He came to me begging to become some kind of a partner with him. He was failing at Rojas and needed some help. I did not want to become a partner, but I felt bad for him, so I offered to help him by taking care of his vendor invoices. I thought I could get him a better deal. So what?"

"Tell me exactly how the invoice management for Rojas operated. How did it all work?" I asked, baiting him to repeat what Ruben Benavidez had told us and what Dolores had discovered.

Romero gave much the same story as Benavidez had about establishing the Green Chile Enterprises LLC and hiring his cousin to manage the payments. He mentioned everything *except* having skimmed significant money "off the top" from Wyman's bank deposits.

Having gotten Romero's explanation of the business and confirmation about the agreement with Wyman, I put actual invoices in front of him and said, "Like *these* invoices? Here's one from Premier Distributing that was sent six months ago. Was it invoices like this you paid?"

"Exactly." Romero said quickly, "The invoices would come in and Ruben would pay them from the Green Chile Enterprises account. Wyman would make deposits into the same account and pay us a monthly fee for services as stipulated in the contract. It was as simple as that. So, what is the big deal?"

Now reaching into the same folder, I pulled out one of the photocopies that Julia Gomez had made of the same invoice, but it had been altered to show a much higher charge than the original. I put it side by side with the original invoice.

"How do you explain this, Mister Romero?" I asked not wanting to provide an explanation for him.

He sat up in his chair, squinted hard at the photocopy, and said, "I don't have a clue. They look the same to me except for the total. Maybe someone altered the photo. How the hell should I know? Invoices were taken care of by Ruben."

"Mister Romero," I continued, "what can you tell me about an account titled DBA EFR that we also found at Merchants Bank of the Southwest? Is this account yours? If so, what did you use it for?"

Squirming, Romero answered, "Yes, it is my account. I initially set it up as an additional account for the restaurant. DBA EFR stands for Doing Business As El Farolito Romero, but I never really used it much. So what?"

Not wanting to engage in debate, I placed the most recent bank statement for Green Chile Enterprises from Merchants Bank of the Southwest in front of him. Beside it, I placed the same month's bank statement from DBA EFR beside it. There had been a twenty-two-thousand-dollar withdrawal from the Green Chile Enterprises account and an electronic deposit for the same amount, on the same day, into the DBA EFR account. They were both highlighted in yellow.

"Take a look at the highlighted lines on each statement. Tell me what you see." I said probing.

Romero looked at the highlighted withdrawal from Green Chile Enterprises and the deposit into DBA EFR account. He thought for a minute, then he said, "Oh, yeah. I remember. Wyman was paying me back a loan I had given him. He told me to take it out of the Green Chile account. Yeah, that's it. He had been having some cash flow problems, so I helped him out. Like I said before, he had no business sense. He was a real moron."

"So," I began, wanting to wrap-up this part of the interview, "you acknowledge that these funds deposited by Randolph Wyman into the Green Chile Enterprises account were then withdrawn and redeposited into the DBA EFR account. Correct?"

"Yeah, that's right. It was to pay a loan. So what?" Romero challenged.

"And you also acknowledge that the two invoices you saw were the same invoices except that one had been altered with a different amount. Is that correct?" I asked wanting to begin tightening the noose.

"If there was any change, it had to be made by my cousin Ruben. I don't know anything about it." Romero replied.

Pushing, I said, "But you do acknowledge that these are the same invoices with one of them having been altered. Correct?"

"Yeah, that's right, they look like the same one." He conceded.

"Thank you." I said seeming appreciative for his support. "Let's take a short break."

The interview with Romero on the larceny charge had gone well but before he got too defensive or aggressive, I wanted to take a few minutes and consult with Miguel about presenting Romero with information we had about Julia's homicide.

65

My brief huddle with Miguel, Ed, and Dolores led us to believe that we had enough circumstantial evidence to put in front of Romero to hopefully push him toward a confession. I armed myself with a file folder full of the evidence we had accumulated, my laptop computer, and entered the arena of the interview room once more. Miguel remained behind the one-way mirror.

Romero and his attorney, Max Brooks, appeared to have been conferring.

Sitting down and laying my file folder and laptop on the table, I began, "Mister Romero, I have several items I would like you to help me understand."

Romero, with a scowl on his face, said "Whatever you show me, I want it on record that I am being set up. I have done nothing wrong."

Choosing to ignore his rebuke, I placed the threatening notes we had in possession on the table one at a time, side by side.

First, the threatening note that had been sent to Julia.

Next, the threatening note I had received tacked to the front door of my house.

Last, the note that had been tied to the brick and thrown through the window of the conference room at the Guadalupe restaurant.

"Mister Romero, do you know anything about these notes?" I asked.

"Not a clue," Romero responded.

"Do you notice any similarities?" I probed, wanting to get Romero engaged.

"Not really," he replied. "Just looks like writing on paper to me."

"Well, Mister Romero," I replied, "we have had the opportunity to research these notes from the kind of stock they are written on to an analysis of the handwriting. We have found some definite similarities that you may be interested in."

At that point, attorney Max Brooks stepped in to challenge. "Are we here to talk about notes and note paper? If you don't have anything more substantial than this, I suggest we terminate this interview and that you release my client. We do not have the time or the inclination to study someone's note taking. This is absurd."

Ignoring Brooks' complaint, I continued, "First, Mister Romero, these envelopes and note paper are all very high end, not ones you would find on the shelves of your local stationery store. They are the kind of stationery that prestigious law firms might use. In fact, the stationery in front of you was all custom ordered from Write Impressions. Let me show you something.

Rotating my computer screen so that Romero and Brooks could see it, I pushed the "play" arrow and the video of Michele Ronaldi purchasing the stationery came up. I could see Romero straining to see exactly what was happening.

Once the scene had played, Romero said, "So what? You are saying that Michele purchased some stationery, this stationery? Why don't you ask her about it instead of wasting my time?"

I then replied, "Actually, Mister Romero, Michele told us that she had picked up the stationery at your request. You should also know that we engaged a handwriting expert who has concluded that all of the notes were written by the same hand. Extensive comparisons of the handwriting on the notes to writing samples of a number of people, including yours, concluded that these were all written by you. In other words, all of these threatening notes were written by you."

Romero slumped back in his chair and was silent for a moment, calculating his next response.

Once again, his attorney stepped in, "Doctor Hunter, it is a real stretch from writing notes to murder. People write angry notes all the time. In fact, people in your line of work often recommend putting your feelings down on paper as a way of dealing with them. If this is all you have, I suggest we conclude this discussion."

"Well, counselor and Mister Romero, we have more to show you."

I now withdrew the photos of Roberto Montoya with a target on his back from my folder.

"Recognize these, Mister Romero? In searching the photos on your cell phone, we discovered these very photos. So, in addition to having written the threatening notes, you also implied that if I continued my investigation into Julia's murder, you might kill Roberto. Was this also part of dealing with your feelings?" I asked rhetorically and sarcastically.

"One more thing," I added, getting another document from my file folder. "Our pathologist determined that Julia's death was a result of tetrahydrozoline poisoning. Mister Romero, are you familiar with tetrahydrozoline?"

"How the hell should I know? I am not a poison expert," Romero replied defiantly.

I replied, "If you have ever used a nasal spray or eyedrops, you may by more familiar with this substance than you think. You see, it is a common ingredient in both, and it can be toxic if taken orally."

"Oh, I get it," Romero replied haughtily. "Julia killed herself with eyedrops. She used them like they were going out of style. We all joked about it.

Then, taking a deep breath, Romero said, "Okay, okay, so I wrote those notes. I felt like you were not the right person to be looking into Julia's murder. I was trying to get the *real* police involved so they could catch the killer. Instead, you stayed in control and now you have me here when you should be out looking for the man who really killed Julia."

"Very creative, Mister Romero," I challenged, "but we have a few more things to discuss with you. When searching your cabin in Pecos, our officers found several large bottles filled with a solution that our lab identified as having the tetrahydrozoline in it. As I have already stated, the only identified uses of tetrahydrozoline are for either nasal sprays or eyedrops. We asked ourselves why anyone would need such a large supply, and in bottles too large for normal use. But here is something even more interesting."

I then put the pièce de resistance on the table in front of him, the photocopy of the simple spreadsheet that Julia had pieced together.

"Apparently," I started, "Julia had come across many of the 'doctored' invoices that had been sent to Randolph Wyman. She created this simple spread sheet noting the differences between the doctored and the real invoices. Her spreadsheet shows the total amount of money that you took from Wyman.

"By our calculations, you stole well over two hundred thousand dollars from Wyman in the past year alone. We have been able to confirm this by looking at transfers of funds from the Green Chile Enterprises account into the DBA EFR account. We believe that Julia was going to use this information to either blackmail you or, more likely, come to the police with it. You found out and decided that your only option was to kill her. Is this about right?"

Both Romero and his attorney were stunned.

Max Brooks abruptly said, "Doctor Hunter, I need some time to confer with my client. Could we take a few minutes break?"

66

After about thirty minutes, Max Brooks stepped out of the interview room and asked us to return. At this point, Miguel joined us rather than remaining behind the one-way mirror. He was the actual police department representative.

There in front of us was a forlorn Fernando Romero, red-eyed and looking defeated.

Max Brooks began, "Chief Detective Montez and Doctor Hunter, my client and I have discussed the situation and recognize that Julia Gomez' murder was a tragic mistake. My client is willing to discuss the events of the night of Miss Gomez's death if you will consider a plea bargain."

Needless to say, this development was unexpected so early in the interview and it was one that could expedite the process. We knew that our case was circumstantial, but the evidence was strong. Romero had already admitted to having written the threatening notes; he had acknowledged that the DBA EFR account was one that he had established in order to steal from Wyman; and we had found the cache of tetrahydrozoline on his property. We had means, motive, and opportunity.

We also knew that jury trials only require one dissenting juror for a verdict to go sideways. Murder trials must have unanimous juries. Keeping in mind how proud Romero was and how conscious he was of his reputation, I thought we could use this to our advantage.

Miguel replied, "Mister Romero, I am sure that whatever happened between you and Julia was some kind of terrible mistake. I also know how much you, your family, and El Farolito mean to the community. Maybe we can keep this from getting out of hand."

Miguel excused himself and contacted the District Attorney's office. Miguel informed the prosecutor, Virginia Velasquez, that this was

Romero's first offense and that he was a member in good standing in the community. Based on that information, Miguel asked if the prosecutor would be willing to consider a plea deal in exchange for Romero telling exactly what happened.

Prosecutor Velasquez accepted, knowing that the evidence was circumstantial. She requested to meet with Mister Romero and his attorney. She invited Miguel and me to join her.

It was a short walk to Prosecutor Velasquez office. She invited us all to sit in her office and explained the terms of the plea deal to both Romero and his attorney. She then asked Romero to explain exactly what had happened.

Romero's recounting was really a story of woe. He described how he had "rescued" Julia from the Rolling Burrito food truck and given her the opportunity of a lifetime. He explained that Julia was a culinary genius whose dishes were wonderful and lauded by patrons and other chefs. He said he believed that she was a rising star who someday could even take over Michele's position.

In fact, as Romero explained, he and his family had worked to make Julia feel at home. They had invited her to events at their home and he had given her raises at work regularly. He was loyal to her and thought she was loyal in return.

He said that he became aware that Julia was having conversations with Randolph Wyman about a year ago. He learned, through Michele, that Wyman had offered Julia the head chef's position at Rojas. In fact, Romero believed that Julia was still in conversation with Wyman right up until his death. He said that he never confronted Julia on the issue for fear that a confrontation would cause her to leave prematurely.

Romero stated that the point of managing Wyman's vendors was not to steal his money, but to put him out business. He believed that only by putting Rojas and Wyman out of business would he be able to keep Julia with El Farolito. He lamented that the business failure of Rojas led to Wyman's suicide. He said, appearing to be sincere, that he never imagined that outcome. Nevertheless, Romero's behavior made him seem despicable in spite his working to appear sincere.

When asked about Julia's murder, Romero admitted that he had written the threatening note to her and placed it on one of the tables for a staff member to find and deliver. The "R" on the note represented how Julia had referred to him when they were together. He knew that, if the note got into the wrong hands, using "R" instead of his name would provide some anonymity.

He also admitted that he was the one who was at the Farmer's Market that night when Julia met with me. He mistakenly believed that Julia was going there to meet with Randolph Wyman. When it turned out not to be Wyman, he made a hasty departure. He said that he did not recognize me at the time, since we had not previously met.

It was only when Romero saw that I was involved that he became fearful and wrote the other two notes. He was adamant that he never intended to hurt Roberto Montoya but wanted to scare me away by threatening Maria's father. When that didn't work, he found out about Maria and I meeting at the Guadalupe and threw the rock through the window with yet another threatening note. He wanted me off the investigation.

In addition to her possible defection to Rojas, Romero said that Julia had become aware that he was stealing from Wyman, and she was going to go to Wyman with evidence. Romero recalled that he usually 'doctored' the invoices that went to Wyman in his restaurant office. He was careful to shut and lock the door before working on them. One day, Julia knocked on the door and said a patron was there to see him.

"In my haste," he said," I left the door open with the invoices on top of my desk. I believe that is when Julia saw them and used her phone to take photos of them. At the time, I think she was still considering working with Wyman. She showed me a photo of one of the 'doctored' invoices on her phone and told me she was going to tell Wyman I was stealing from him. You can understand that I couldn't just let that happen."

I asked him specifically about Julia's murder and the use of tetrahydrozoline.

A few weeks earlier, Romero's young son had put some eyedrops in their Labrador Retriever's dog food. The boy was angry at having to take the dog out for a walk and, on the spur of the moment, put several of his own eyedrops into the dog food. Almost immediately after ingesting the dog food, their Lab became sick and vomited. The Lab was ultimately okay, but not until after a trip to the veterinarian to flush all remnants out of the Lab's system. The boy admitted his crime and begged for forgiveness.

What happened to the dog gave Romero a similar idea. Because he believed his attempts to win Julia's loyalty with more money had failed, he concocted a different scheme. He thought that if he could "rescue" Julia from a serious illness, she might be so appreciative that she would forget any thoughts about leaving El Farolito. He reasoned that because Julia was known for her heavy use of eyedrops, his using them to induce illness would not arouse suspicion.

He acknowledged that he emptied several vials of eyedrops into the mezcal bottle. He knew that Julia would often close up the restaurant at night and then have a nightcap from her stash of mezcal before leaving for home. He said that she had two special bottles of mezcal in her locker that were not carried by the restaurant. He thought that if he put eyedrops into the opened bottle of mezcal, she would drink it and become ill just like his dog had.

The night that he put the drops into the mezcal, he made sure he would be present when Julia closed up, though hiding in the shadows. He thought that she would take a drink of the mezcal, become ill, and he would be there to rescue her. He stood by the side door and heard her get out the mezcal, what sounded like a cocktail glass, and some other items he could not recognize. He thought he heard her pour mezcal into two glasses but was not sure. It wasn't long before he heard a loud "thump" and believed she had fallen to the floor.

Romero recalled that he stepped inside from the doorway to find Julia lying on the floor, vomit by her body, and eyes wide open. He said he tried to rouse her and then heard someone coming in from the alley. He waited by the side door and knocked over a pan as he ran out.

"I never meant to kill Julia," Romero lamented. "I only wanted her to keep working for me and not tell Wyman about the invoices. I just thought that if she knew how much I cared for her by saving her, she would feel grateful, change her mind, and all would be forgiven."

At that point, Romero began to sob uncontrollably, saying over and over, "Oh God, oh God, what have I done? What have I done?"

EPILOGUE

It had been six months since Fernando Romero's sentencing and demise. He had been convicted of second-degree murder in the killing of Julia Gomez. He had also been convicted of second-degree felony larceny in the theft of funds from Randolph Wyman. The accolades that Romero so desperately wanted, and the positive notoriety he sought, had both cruelly evaded him. His obsession to become one of Santa Fe's elites was a tale of tragic proportions.

It occurred to me that whenever people "take a sideways glance" and compare themselves to others they envy, they usually take a journey that leads to hell. There will always be someone richer, more respected, better looking, and on, and on. Unfortunately, in his quest for fame and recognition, Romero failed to appreciate and value what he already had. There are many people in the world overrun with insecurities who often seek extreme measures to deal with their demons. In some cases, like some of the characters in this story, these measures can backfire with deadly consequences.

El Farolito had now been shuttered and was available to a new owner. Following Wyman's death, the Saint Julian hotel was able to purchase the property on which Rojas stood. They were now both part of the same enterprise and all under the same roof. For the first time in a very long time, the future of this restaurant space was bright.

A shattered and broken Wyman family journeyed to Santa Fe to claim Randolph's body. Their unopened letters and offers for help found in his house only added a heightened degree of sorrow to his death. When the family members made their way back to Boston, they vowed never to return to Santa Fe. Wanting some good to come out of Randolph's death, the family created the Randolph Wyman Foundation offering assistance to young people experiencing depression or other mental health issues.

William Dirschauser lost yet another job. George Mayfield, his fraternity colleague and the managing editor of the *Santa Fe New Mexican* terminated his contract. Mayfield had received several complaints from local restaurant owners regarding Dirschauser's horrific behavior toward their female chefs. Dirschauser left town immediately, hoping once again to stay one step ahead of the law.

It was late afternoon as I finished up paperwork in my office at the police department when I received a text from Maria asking me to join her at the Guadalupe restaurant. Always anxious to see her, especially after another taxing day, I sent her a thumbs-up and a heart emoji.

Upon arriving at the Guadalupe, I noticed a sign out in front of the entrance announcing a "Private Event." I was unaware that Maria was asking me to come to a social gathering. I immediately wondered if I was dressed appropriately.

I stepped through the entrance and there, staring at me, was a two-by-three-foot poster of a photograph of someone I immediately recognized. Under the photograph was the identifying name "Julia Gomez." I was initially dumbfounded and caught off guard. I felt my chest begin to heave and my eyes water up as I took in her beautiful features.

As I walked into the main dining room, there were large photographs on all the walls of dishes that Julia had made popular in Santa Fe. There were photos of her empanadas, precisely prepared tlayudas, carne asada dishes, and several of her signature dishes with her fusion mole and green chile. It was indeed a celebration of her time in Santa Fe.

There was already a small crowd with more people following me into the dining room. I found Maria and she told me that, in talking to former El Farolito and Rolling Burrito staff and patrons, they told her they wanted to have a final, and loving, sendoff for Julia. The Guadalupe kitchen had prepared Julia's dishes with food stands around the perimeter. Oaxacan cocktails with mezcal were also being served.

In traditional fashion, Maria clinked a spoon against her glass to get everyone's attention.

Maria began, "We come today to honor our friend and adopted Santa Fean, Julia Gomez. Julia's time here was not long, but her influence was huge. She changed our way of understanding how our local foods could be fused with those from other regions, or countries, to produce new and distinct flavors. Many of you told me that you wanted to have a proper farewell for Julia, to remember her both in and out of the restaurant. At this time, I would like any of you, as you wish, to tell us about your experience with Julia."

I was again astounded. One individual after another spoke of their relationship with Julia. They described her warmth and generosity, behaviors that the investigation had obscured. One woman described Julia lending her money in her time of trial. Another described Julia making a special casserole dish and bringing it to her ill mother. Yet another told of Julia coming to her home to teach her the finer points of making Oaxacan infused dishes. Even Michele Ronaldi, also about to depart from Santa Fe, added a personal story of how Julia had expanded her thinking about recipes and new dishes.

The testimonies went on for a long time, one surprising story after another. Julia was much more multifaceted than I had imagined. Just when the conversation began to recede, Maria clinked her glass yet again. Out from the side of the dining room came a lovely woman dressed in a traditional Mexican dress. Maria introduced her as Julia's very good friend from Oaxaca, Adelina Cruz.

In perfect English, Adelina provided a shortened version of Julia's background, what she had overcome, and what a wonderful friend she had been. It was a moving testament of someone whose difficulties in life had not made her bitter and cynical, but kind and generous. Adelina closed her description by raising her glass to her dear friend, Julia Gomez, and saying "salute mi amiga." We all followed Adelina's lead and, raising our glass, repeated, "salute mi amiga."

It was a wonderful sendoff and there wasn't a dry eye in the crowd.

READERS GUIDE

1. Why did Julia Gomez seek out Scott Hunter instead of the police? What would you have done in her situation?

2. Julia came to Santa Fe looking for a better life. Was that a mistake? What other choices could Julia have made?

3. In coming to the United States, Julia left her mother and siblings behind. How do you view that? Can you think of another option Julia may have had?

4. William Dirschauser regularly used his position with newspapers to exploit others. If your career depended on a positive review from him, how far would you have gone to stay in his good favor? Have you ever been the victim of unfair business or personal practices? If so, how did you handle it?

5. Would a woman in William Dirschauser's position be as likely to exploit her business contacts? Why or why not?

6. Randolph Wyman grew up with a powerful and successful father. Do you agree that it is hard to succeed in that environment as a son? Did his father do the right thing by cutting him off?

7. Michele Ronaldi was known for losing her temper when things did not go her way. Is this behavior effective for long-term success? How did this strategy serve her? Did it work against her? What other choices for her career ambitions did she have that she had not explored?

8. Fernando Romero desperately wanted to be respected and admired. Have you, or someone you know, compared yourself to those around you with regard to things like finances, status, power, relationships, etc.? How has that worked for you?

9. Is there anything Scott Hunter could have done differently in order to solve the case more quickly? What?

10. Scott Hunter worked this case with his partner Maria. How was her knowledge beneficial to the case?

11. Julia Gomez' culinary capabilities made a difference in the Santa Fe food scene. Do you think it is easier, or more difficult, for an immigrant to be successful? Why or why not?

12. If a friend is in serious trouble, like Julia was, and he or she asks you for help and does not want to go to the police, what would you do? Is there anything Julia should have done differently?

13. Miguel Montez, the Chief Detective, is on an anniversary vacation. Should he have interrupted his trip to return for the investigation? Do you know of anyone for whom being loyal to their work and their family obligations is a struggle? How do they manage the split loyalties? How would you?

14. Are there any unanswered questions about the case that you have and would like to have explored further? What and why?

8. [Gertrude Russell,] does every ... wanted to be respectful and ... that ... have you or someone you know contained yourself without murmur ... with regard to an unpaid ... [business] at ... never relationship ... it ... has that worked for you.

9. Is there anything Scott Foley could have ... done differently ... to ... solve the issue more quickly? What ...

10. Scott Foley worked this one well. He praises Matt. How are Joe, Roderick, Joe ... [benefited] to ... ses.

11. ... The Gómez country connection made a difference to the Santos family ... Do you think it ... and ... important ... their ... family ... be the result. Why, or why not?

12. It is tempting to ... down ... family. Like Joan who ... and her relatives. As you ... help and ... someone more ... quote the police who ... would you do? Is there ... to ... ... this problem ... realm, differently?

13. Miguel Alonso, the Chief Detective is ... certain ... ... Should ... have he ... up trip to ... exhibit the presentation. Do you know of anyone for whom being ... is their work ... and their family obligations are ... ? How do they ... coming the split? What ... would you ...

14. ... for any interview of ... above the ... ... you have, and I would like to have enjoyed Carmen Daz and Marta.

www.ingramcontent.com/pod-product-compliance
Lightning Source LLC
Chambersburg PA
CBHW011647010726
47495CB00011B/2949